Praise for John Baker

'One of Britain's most talented contemporary crime writers'
The Times

'Witty and confident with deftly sketched idiosyncratic characters who are established and built upon with deceptive ease. His writing is clear and intelligent and manages to convey mood without breaking the pace of the story'
Sherlock Holmes Magazine

'Assured and entertaining. Sam Turner is a wonderful creation' *Yorkshire Post*

'John Baker brings heart, invention and wit to the business of adapting the tough-guy novel to the realities of contemporary Britain. [He] stirs the traditional (detective's office trashed yet again) and the fashionable (alcoholism, bulimia, self-mutilation and paedophilia) together with a slapdash hand but the heady mix he produces certainly has an authentic tang to it. He has a fine eye for urban sleaze and an ear for the turn of contemporary speech' *Independent on Sunday*

'A tough, gritty read ... black comedy with a touch of surrealism' *Irish Times*

'With a few deft strokes Baker paints an intriguing and believable portrait of his hero ... Tightly written in an urgent and individual style. An engrossing read which grips from the first chapter' *Yorkshire Evening Press*

'Builds to a climax on York Minster that Hitchcock would have relished ... Thumbs up to Mr B. for avoiding the easy option of aping American writers to give us something braver and bolder' *Shots*

By the same author

Poet in the Gutter
Death Minus Zero
Walking with Ghosts

Born in Hull in 1942, and educated at the university there, John Baker has worked as a social worker, shipbroker, truck driver and milkman, and most recently in the computer industry. He has twice received a Yorkshire Arts Association Writers' Bursary. The other novels in the series featuring PI Sam Turner, *Poet in the Gutter*, *Death Minus Zero* and *Walking with Ghosts*, are also available as Indigo paperbacks. He is currently working on *Shooting in the Dark*, the fifth in the series. John Baker is married with five children and lives in York.

KING OF THE STREETS

John Baker

INDIGO

An Indigo paperback
First published in Great Britain by Victor Gollancz in 1998
This paperback edition published in 2000 by Indigo,
an imprint of Orion Books Ltd,
Orion House, 5 Upper St Martin's Lane,
London WC2H 9EA

A CIP catalogue record for this
book is available from the British Library.

ISBN: 0 575 40284 9

Typeset by SetSystems Ltd, Saffron Walden, Essex

Printed and bound in Great Britain by
Cox & Wyman Ltd, Reading, Berkshire

'There's no success like failure.'

Bob Dylan

The city and places in this novel owe as much to imagination as to physical reality. The characters and institutions are all fictitious, and any resemblance to real people, living or dead, is purely coincidental.

I would like to express my thanks to Anne Baker and Simon Stevens for their helpful criticism. It is also necessary to say that any offended sensibilities are the responsibility of the writer alone.

CHAPTER 1

At first glance she was a nice old lady, but when you got to give her another look you saw right away that she was weird. Something about her walk, perhaps? The way she nodded her head from side to side or kept glancing back at the passing cars? There was nothing immediately wrong about the way she was dressed. Cal could see colours on these new closed circuit screens, still hadn't quite got used to it; rust colour to her print skirt, maroon cardigan hanging from her shoulders, draped. Looking closer he could make out strong leather shoes, hair permed and reminiscent of the forties, stiff with setting lotion, tight little kiss curls framing the upper part of her face. No, he was remembering his grandmother. The screens did that to you sometimes, gave a fairly good outline and somehow forced your imagination to fill in the details.

When you watched them night after night you could pick out the characters who were going to put on a show. It was like they had to signal it somehow, not take the world entirely by surprise. Geoff, Cal's friend and colleague, would say, 'Here's one. God knows what he's gonna do, but he's gonna do something.' And Cal would walk over to wherever Geoff was standing and they would watch the screen together. And usually Geoff was right. Nine times out of ten the guy would break into a car, or start a fight, or he would look around, wait for a gap in the traffic, then hop over a wall to break into a house or shop.

There were several of those on every shift. The other

CCTV operators talked about it sometimes. And before he'd started this job, when he was still on surveillance in Northern Ireland, Cal would often spot a troublemaker on the street before the guy even knew he was going to cause trouble.

Different areas you got different characters, of course. What he could see on this screen, the one with the old lady who was gonna do something but hadn't got round to doing it yet, was the Bar end of Micklegate. Most of York's inner city was covered now, together with the inner ring road and the city's major arteries. Micklegate was a busy shopping area during the day, but at night the pimps brought out their protégées to prowl the bars and clubs, and the local (and not so local) kerb crawlers came out in droves. From time to time local residents would cause a fuss, and sometimes the street would erupt in violence. But usually the police turned a blind eye and pocketed some of the profits, and the smoke went up the chimney just like it had been doing since the world began. The cameras had only gone up here during the last months and some of the local councillors, like the average resident, couldn't understand that; they thought a notorious area like this should have had cameras installed before the residential districts and the outer ring road, but they were out of touch with modern policing methods and excluded from the complicated system of payoffs and bribes and corruption.

This time of the evening, though, was the dead zone. The late shops were putting up their shutters, and the clubs and bars were waiting for their staff to arrive. The day was closing down, and the night hadn't yet got under way. People who walked across Cal and Geoff's screens, like the old lady who nodded her head from side to side, they could be from the day or the night, it wasn't always possible to tell. Or they could be nothing to do with the area at all. They might be just passing through.

Cal and Geoff were also excluded from the payoffs and bribes and corruption. But they were not excluded from the real world, and were ever capable of turning it to their advantage. They understood free enterprise, what it meant and how to make it work. Both of them had grown into maturity during the eighties. They'd been educated, learned how to add up.

'What's she up to?' Geoff asked. He was leaning against the wall, an unlit cigarette dangling from his bottom lip.

'The old biddy?' replied Cal. 'I don't know. She stopped there a couple of minutes ago. Hasn't moved since. Maybe trying to turn a trick?'

Geoff snorted. He lit his lighter, but didn't light the cigarette. 'That's Angie's spot. If she's still there an hour from now we're gonna see a fight.'

'Here we go,' said Cal. 'She's on the move.' He watched as the old lady moved off the pavement on to the road, pulled up her skirt and squatted. A car stopped and honked its horn. Several pedestrians turned to watch the scene. The old lady gave the car driver a two-fingered salute. 'Jesus,' said Cal.

'She's taking a leak,' said Geoff.

'And then some,' said Cal. 'She's doing a full-scale crap in the middle of the road.'

'Shall I call Mr Plod?'

'You'd better. Somebody might decide to run her over.'

Geoff picked up the handset and spoke into it. 'Got an elderly female defecating in the middle of Micklegate,' he said. 'Just inside the Bar, holding up traffic.' He put the handset down and looked over at Cal. 'You know what Micklegate means?' he asked.

'There's nothing I can possibly say that'll stop you telling me?'

'Great Street,' said Geoff, who studied local history, mainly for the benefit of others. He knew the churches and ancient buildings, and sometime in the past had worked as a guide for visitors to the city. 'There was a Roman Temple of Mithras there,' he said. 'Just about where she's doing her business.'

Cal shook his head. 'I know you're trying to tell me something,' he said, 'but the inner meaning isn't getting through.'

'Women weren't allowed into the Mithraic religion,' Geoff explained. 'Not into any part of it. So what I reckon is, she's just getting her own back.'

'A little late, though, Geoff, don't you think? Like around two thousand years.'

'This is women for you,' said Geoff. 'They can hold a grudge for ever. Two thousand years, that's nothing to them. Five thousand years, ten thousand, it doesn't make no difference, if you've done them down one time, even if it was a mistake, one of these days they're gonna come back and crap on you.'

Cal stopped listening and watched the screen as a police car pulled up next to the old lady and a young constable got out. There was no sound system attached to the screens, but Cal imagined he could read the young constable's lips doing a parody of Mr Plod. He got the same two-fingered salute as the motorist before him, and went scuttling back to his radio to order up a roll of toilet paper and a WPC.

Eventually they bundled her into the squad car and took her off to the torture chamber, and a kind of aura descended over the street. Geoff unpacked his portable editing equipment and set it up on a spare table at the back of the control room. There were two quick money-spinners, and over the course of the last months Cal and Geoff had milked both of them for as much as they could get. The first was their compilations of porno clips, which essentially consisted of drunken couples, and the occasional foursome on speed, going for gold in shop doorways. They hadn't a clue they were being watched, thought the whole world was tucked up in bed, and they would go at each other like professional athletes. Cal had a contact who would pay up to a grand for one tape, cash in hand, no questions asked. And without a lot of sweat being involved Geoff could splice together a new tape every month. Four or five weeks later these tapes would turn up in the sex shops and the markets, sometimes with sound effects added, and fancy titles like *The Meat Eaters*.

The other quick money-spinner was to get a couple of good shots of a guy in a posh car doing the kerb-crawl routine, a shot of the car registration number and a close-up of the guy's face. Then another shot of the broad's ass as she disappeared into the passenger seat. It was a really strange thing, but if you took that video round to the guy's office the next day and waited ten minutes while he looked at it, he'd very probably come out and give you money. Nine times out of ten you wouldn't have to threaten to show it to his wife, no unpleasantnesses like that at all, he'd just reach for his wallet and raise his eyebrows, like you'd done a job *for* him instead of *on* him.

Money was coming easily these days. And it would continue to flow as long as they didn't get greedy. Cal and Geoff had been around and understood the pitfalls. Neither of them would put the operation in jeopardy for the sake of a quick profit. Anything that looked at all dodgy, they'd avoid.

While Cal looked idly at the screen a white Porsche Carrera Targa crawled along the street. It was still too early for crawlers, none of the girls was out yet. Could be the guy was desperate, playing at being the early bird, make sure he got a good worm. Or he didn't know the routine of the street. Or, and this was more likely than the other possibilities, the car was from out of town and the driver was lost. Beautiful vehicle, though, not the kind of car you'd easily miss, sprayed white or cream and tended with real love and affection. Shortly after it had gone through the Bar and disappeared from view a small figure ran across Micklegate, moving fast, from a doorway near Scruffy Murphy's to Bar Lane on the other side. Cal couldn't make out if it was a child or a small adult. He didn't do anything about it, just made a mental note to watch out for any movement around the entrance to Bar Lane. Something might be brewing, though it didn't feel like it at all. Since the old lady had taken her crap the street had gone to sleep.

'Jesus,' said Geoff from his table at the back of the room. 'I know her. Used to.'

'Who's that?' asked Cal, getting to his feet and walking over to Geoff's screen. There was a frozen image of a woman's face and a cock. The cock seemed to be trying to get into the woman's head via her ear, and the woman didn't appear to be too keen on the idea. 'So?'

'So I used to know her,' Geoff said. 'When I was in the force. Must be ten years back, she lived in Fulford. She was a fucking virgin, wouldn't let me get anywhere near her. I tried for weeks, spent a teenage fortune on her. Got nowhere. I'd take her to the pictures, and it'd be raining and she'd be wearing one of those plastic macs, buttoned up to the neck, and a plastic scarf, rain hood, whatever they're called. And she'd keep it all on in the pictures. In the back row. I'd be trying to undo this wet plastic coat, get one button loose and my hand inside, groping round her chest. Underneath she'd have a cardigan, all buttoned up, then a blouse, and underneath that something else, a vest, I suppose, or a T-shirt. And then the bra.

'I'd have my hand in up to the wrist and still not manage to make contact with any skin. I'd come out howling. You know, inside myself I'd be so frustrated I'd be howling. And then I'd walk her home, all the way from town to Fulford, and she'd invite me in, and we'd have a cup of tea with her mother and her father. Then she'd come out with me and I'd go on the outside of the gate and she'd still be inside the gate, with the gate closed, and I'd have another last try. It was impossible. Worst days of my life.

'And now look at her, she's got a cock growing out of her ear.'

'What's she called?' asked Cal.

'Joan,' said Geoff, as he released the freeze frame. The girl's head turned quickly towards the offending cock, her mouth opened and she caught it swiftly between her teeth. For a reason he would never understand, Geoff had an image of the choir stalls in the Methodist Chapel of his boyhood. He raised his eyes to Cal. 'People change, don't they?' he said.

Cal smiled, nodded at the picture on the monitor. 'She might be thinking about you,' he said.

The white Carrera was back, and not crawling this time. It slewed to a halt in the middle of Micklegate and both doors flew open.

'Nice car,' Geoff said. 'Pity about the driver.'

'And his friend,' added Cal. The two occupants of the car were on the road, and moving quickly across it in the direction of Bar Lane on the other side. They were like TV

Gladiators. They didn't have the gear, but they each had the build, enormous shoulders and barrel chests. The first one, the driver, was blond, short but well developed, and fit. He moved like a cat, and took in the whole street at a glance, aware of everything that was happening. He wore a pair of World Gym training bottoms with white loafers and a Gorilla Wear T-shirt. The other one looked dumb; he was taller and dark-haired with a permanent smile on his face. He didn't move so easily, there seemed to be something wrong with his right leg, and Cal had the impression of someone who moved half his muscles across the road, then went back for the other half. He wore a Gorilla Wear shirt with short sleeves and a hat to match, and his striped baggy bottoms finished about four inches above his trainers.

'We're talking athletes here,' Geoff said. 'Shall I call in The Man?' He reached for the phone.

Geoff had a really sick way of laughing, something he did with the back of his throat. He did it now, and Cal glanced over at him to see what it looked like. Couldn't tell though, because he had to snap his head back to the screen in case he missed anything. The two hulks reached the other side of the road, and the tall dark one came alive and shot off down the narrow lane. The short blond one ran back to the car and began manœuvring it towards the lane.

Cal switched cameras so he could follow the tall dark one. He'd already outrun the range of the second camera, and Cal switched to a third to catch up with the guy. He was halfway along Toft Green, chasing a much smaller figure and rapidly gaining on it.

There was something wrong with the hulk's right leg. It appeared to be permanently bent at the knee, so that he only ever came down on the toe of that foot. The spastic leg was shorter than the other one and this gave the impression that he was forever about to topple head over heels. But he didn't fall, he moved surprisingly fast, and though his gait was somehow comical, there was a grim determination about him that made you forget about laughing.

When he drew level with the smaller figure, who Cal now recognized as the boy who had crossed Micklegate earlier, the hulk reached out and pushed. The kid sprawled forward on his face. He was moving as fast as his legs would carry him, and the force of the fall could have broken his neck. It opened his face and ripped his shirt off his shoulders. The hulk's momentum had taken him a few metres past the kid, and he walked back as the smaller figure was trying to raise himself from the ground. The hulk stamped him, only once but hard, on the lower back. The kid's neck snapped back and Cal and Geoff clearly saw the youngster's mouth come open in a scream of pain.

'Jesus,' said Geoff.

The white Carrera arrived then, and the tall, dark hulk, still with that stupid smile on his face, picked up the kid. He lifted the boy with no apparent effort, and half carried, half dragged him to the Carrera. He opened the door quickly and seemed to fold the body of the kid in two before throwing it into the back. Then he climbed in himself and closed the door.

Cal still had the presence of mind to zoom the camera in on the car's registration number. It had designer plates, and for a moment before it accelerated away the rear plate filled the monitor screen. It read: FRANC O.

The two operators looked at their screens for several seconds after the car had disappeared from view. Then Geoff said, 'Should I call the police, Cal?'

Cal shook his head slowly from side to side. 'I get the feeling this is going to make us very rich,' he said.

Geoff looked puzzled. 'I don't see how.'

Cal pushed his chair back and stood. 'I don't know how either,' he said. 'Just an instinct. Better cut it out of the tape.'

CHAPTER 2

Going to see Janet with butterflies in your stomach. Geordie had heard the expression before. Celia said it when the postman came, but he'd heard it before that, maybe right back in the time he was in the children's home. It was one thing to hear people say they had butterflies in their stomach, another thing altogether to actually have them in your own stomach. They didn't just flutter about in there, they affected your whole body, so everything was jumping around, like at a rave.

Geordie stopped at a shop window and adjusted his look. Pulled the hem of his shirt down at the back so it lined up with the hem at the front. Straightened the line between his left trouser leg and the top of his left trainer. Finally took off his Kangol cashmere and placed it back on his head like it had been born there. He nodded at his reflection and the reflection gave Geordie the nod.

When he got to Janet's flat it would be all right. It wasn't as if she didn't like him. She had seemed to like him. Only actually going up to the door and knocking on it, waiting for her to answer, that wasn't how he'd planned it. How he had planned it was to get her on the telephone, so she wouldn't be able to see his eyes, put on like a real laid-back voice and have his stereo playing in the background. That way he'd have been able to feel it out, hear if she sounded pleased or not, before he actually asked her if she wanted to do something with him. See a movie. Go to a pizza joint. Or just sit around and play some sounds together.

But plans don't always work out. Geordie's plan hadn't worked out right from the beginning, because Janet didn't have a telephone. When that fact had eventually taken root in his brain, Geordie decided to write her a letter. And after two days he had produced a letter and even bought one of those envelopes from the post office that already have the stamp on. Trouble with letters was, you post them and wait for ever to get a reply. If you don't get a reply you never really know for sure if the letter was delivered at the other end. The other thing you don't know, is you don't know what Janet looks like when she reads it, if she's smiling and pleased about getting it, or if she doesn't remember who you are, and maybe even thinks it's a letter delivered to the wrong address. And – and this is what finally clinched it and made him tear the letter up – there was no real way of knowing if all the words in the letter were spelt right. Well, apart from spending another two days with a dictionary, checking them all out.

So now it was Plan C, arriving at the door to her flat with no telephone conversation already in the bag, no letter sent and answered, no actual invitation. Like, what might probably happen is she's got a boyfriend, and they're in there together, really wanting to be alone. And Geordie's out on the step knocking on the door. Janet and her boyfriend, who's probably eighteen foot tall, and maybe twenty-five, twenty-six years old, a guy who shaves *every* day, they're having a quiet night together because they haven't seen each other for about a month. The last thing they want is some creepy kid to come knocking at the door.

So it's rat-a-tat-tat, and Janet looks at her boyfriend, and he looks back at her with a question mark on his face, and she says, 'I don't know. I'm not expecting anyone.' And the boyfriend gets a jealous leer over his face and pours a can of spinach down his throat. He goes to the door and lifts Geordie off his feet with one hand, breaks him in pieces and throws the pieces away.

Geordie briefly considers Plan D, which involves waiting outside her flat in the freezing cold until Janet comes out, and then accidentally bumping into her. Like he was just passing.

But he doesn't want to do it like that. And not because it's freezing cold, the wind sharp enough to cut your face to ribbons. He wants to be up front, like Sam. He wants to do it like he thinks Sam would do it. And he wants to be able to tell the story afterwards, after it's actually worked. Like other people do, tell stories. He wants to be able to tell Sam, and Celia, and Marie. He wants to be able to tell everyone he knows how he got it together. How he thought about Janet for weeks and weeks, and then how he thought he might meet up with her again accidentally, and how that didn't happen. And how he forgot about her, or thought he forgot about her, and then he'd wake up in the morning, or maybe he'd be on a job, surveillance, or something like that, really concentrating, and she'd just pop up in his head. And he hadn't forgotten about her at all. And how she came into his dreams. Well, maybe he wouldn't tell everybody everything. He'd tell Sam about the dreams, one day. One day. But it would be a straight-up story he'd have to tell. Nothing about skulking around her flat waiting for her to come out. In the story Geordie would tell he'd stride up to the door like a man. And if that was gonna be the story, it would have to be the reality too.

Geordie couldn't tell a lie convincingly. Sometimes you

had to do it, but whenever he did it he got found out immediately. He'd tell the lie, and Sam, or Celia, or whoever it was he'd told the lie to, they'd look at him and shake their head. They just knew. It must be something in his voice, in the tones he used. Whatever it was, it meant he had to tell the truth most of the time, otherwise people wouldn't take him seriously.

It was a handicap on the job, not being able to lie convincingly. When you were a private eye you had to tell the occasional porkie. Like Sam had these different calling cards in his wallet, saying he was an insurance investigator, or a builder's salesman, or a telephone engineer. All kinds of things, he had about ten or twenty different cards. And he'd pull one out and hand it to somebody and they'd take it and look at him and there wouldn't be a hint of a question in their eyes. That was Sam. If Geordie was faced with the same person, and he handed them the same card, they'd immediately tell him to get lost. Sam said it was to do with confidence, that it would get better as he got older. But Geordie wasn't convinced. Sure, Sam was usually right, and Geordie hoped he was right about this, and that eventually he'd be able to tell a good straight lie. But he didn't really believe it. Maybe he had a genetic defect, like what you get if your mother smokes before you're born.

When she came to the door there was too much to take in all at once, and Geordie felt himself reeling backwards. Not physically, he didn't actually move at all, but metaphorically – as Celia would have put it in one of Geordie's English lessons – metaphorically he was lifted up off his feet and placed down again on the other side of the road.

First of all there was the door opening and Janet appearing there. Like the barrier that kept her in and him out was suddenly gone. He was face to face, looking right at her with his mouth open. There was all that. Then there was the smell of cats, which Geordie wasn't used to, because Sam didn't have a cat, and Geordie only had Barney, who was a dog, and came with a completely different smell. Then there was the music, must've been coming from a tape deck or CD player, and it was the voice of one of The Beatles, Geordie recognized it because Sam played it sometimes. And that got another part of his brain engaged. The part that wasn't dealing with the reeling backwards and the metaphors and the smell of cats, and the amazing fact that this was Janet standing in front of him with a kind of recognition spreading over her face. The guy – the Beatles guy – was singing 'Do You Want to Dance', and he was at that bit that goes *Do Ya, Do Ya, Do Ya, Do Ya*, over and over again, like the thing might be stuck, except you know it isn't and he's actually building it up to a kind of climax.

And then he was there, at the climax, and Geordie was metaphorically transferred back from across the street to Janet's doorstep, and the smell of cats was just a kind of catty smell, nothing he couldn't cope with. And Janet had said something to him that he hadn't heard, and now she was shifting from one foot to the other and looking at him like he might have come out without all his faculties. So he had to say, 'Is that John McCartney? The one singing?' And as soon as he said it he realized that it was the wrong name, he knew the guy's real name, but he couldn't remember what it was. It was on the tip of his tongue. The one from Liverpool. Really famous.

Janet tossed her head, and Geordie knew he'd blown it. 'John Lennon,' she said. 'McCartney was called Paul.'

'Yeah. I mean John Lennon. Not McCartney.' He looked her straight in the eye. 'Slip of the tongue.'

The twinkle was back in Janet's eye. Maybe he hadn't blown it after all. 'We were going to have a biscuit,' she said. 'Orchid's been learning to dance.' Geordie didn't know how to respond to any of the things she'd said. He looked at her and tried to think of something profound. The whistle of a kettle came from a room behind Janet. 'I was going to make a drink,' she said. 'If you've got time.'

'Yes,' he said, as profoundly as possible for such a short word. 'Oh. Time? Yes, tea, or coffee. Yes. Please.' He followed her into the interior mystery of her flat. And she drew him through into the room where the sounds of the singer and the whistle of the kettle and the cats were all located.

Really strong, sweet smell of cats. If Barney was in here he'd just howl. There was a black cat on the arm of a sofa, and a black and white one threading its way between Janet's legs. A gas fire made the room very warm. Geordie was sweating within seconds, wondering if he should take his coat off or just stand there and drip.

'There's some hooks over there,' Janet said. 'Back of the door.'

'Oh, yes,' said Geordie. 'Hooks?'

'For your coat,' Janet said, busying herself with the kettle and a couple of brightly patterned mugs. Geordie didn't reply. He slipped his coat off and hung it on one of the hooks, over one of Janet's woollen jackets. So his coat enfolded her coat, which was nice to think about. Kind of symbolic.

He sat on the sofa, at the other end, away from the black cat. 'That's Orchid,' said Janet. 'Say hello, Orchid. This is Geordie, who saved your life. The other one's Venus.'

'Hello,' said Geordie self-consciously. Neither of the cats acknowledged him. Orchid – the black one on the arm of the sofa – looked up at the wall above the fireplace, where Janet had hung a large poster of John Lennon. The cat looked at the poster for several seconds, then glanced over at Geordie for a moment, as if to make a comparison. Without giving away a thing it then slipped off the sofa and left the room.

Janet handed Geordie a mug of coffee and sat down on the sofa next to him. She half-turned towards him and gave him the smile which, if nothing else happened, would keep him happy for several months to come. And then she said, 'Well? You haven't said why you're here. Is there something I can do?'

Geordie had practised this bit. He knew exactly how to say it. He took a sip of the hot coffee and put the mug down at his feet. 'I was thinking about that time when the psycho put your cat in the river.'

'Orchid,' she said. 'She's never really got over it. I've never been able to get her into a cat carrier since. It affected her mind.'

'I'm not surprised,' said Geordie. 'She nearly drowned.'

'She would have done if it hadn't been for you,' Janet told him. 'Me too. We might have drowned together.'

'I dunno about that,' Geordie said. 'But since then I've been thinking about you. Sometimes. Know what I mean? Like, I'll be walking along the street, and I don't know what I'm thinking about, and then I see I'm thinking about you.'

'Yeah.' Janet gave him another brilliant smile. 'I sometimes think about all that. I remember you looked really funny walking along the street. Well, the two of us, really, both dripping wet, and you said we were "wetter'n a frog's drawers".'

Geordie smiled at the memory. 'And there's this problem,' he said. 'Like if you're a professional, like me and Sam being investigators, then you're not supposed to get emotionally involved with the clients. 'Cause that's not professional. It's bad for the job. Only, well, you're not – I mean, even at the time, you weren't the client. You just somehow got involved in it all through the psycho.'

'Trust me to pick the wrong guy,' Janet said. Venus suddenly leapt on to her lap and she began stroking the cat with both hands. 'I don't know how many times that's happened. You see a guy in the street and he's really sexy and handsome, and then as soon as you get to know him you find he's just a pile of shit.'

'You're not, like, into men, then?'

'Not if I can help it,' she said. 'I fall from time to time. But when I'm on top of myself I give them as wide a berth as possible. When it's just me and the cats, and I've got my neighbours upstairs, Trudie and Margaret, that's enough for me. As soon as men get involved everything goes to the wall. They always want everything their own way.'

'Oh,' said Geordie, unable to keep the disappointment out of his voice. 'Shit.'

'Something wrong?'

'I remember when we got back here,' he said, 'after we'd got the cat out of the beck. You went up to get a bath, and when you came down you had a white blouse on, and white jeans, and white trainers, and you had a little white handbag, leather, with a long strap, and we went out again and walked into town.' He looked over at her, and she looked up from Venus, and Geordie locked on to her eyes. 'You looked great,' he said. 'I remember walking tall 'cause you was there next to me. People thinking you was with me.'

Janet shook her head. 'But I was,' she said. 'We were together.'

'No, you don't get it,' Geordie said. 'I mean *really* together. People might have thought we were really together, like lovers.'

'Lovers!' Janet's voice went through another octave and

Venus left her lap and the room in one movement. She giggled. 'Oh, my God,' she said. Then she giggled again.

'You think it's a joke?'

'No,' she said, reaching out and stroking the back of his hand. She laughed again, tried to stifle it, but didn't entirely manage. 'It's not a joke. It's just a surprise. That's why it's funny. I'm not laughing at you. I like you. I think you're funny.'

'I'm really glad I came,' Geordie said to Venus who had reappeared in the doorway.

Janet turned Geordie's hand over and took it between both of hers. 'Listen,' she said, 'I didn't mean it like that. I thought you were funny right from the start. When you said that about us being wetter'n a frog's drawers, I thought it then. I thought you were nice, and funny, and somehow cosy. I've had it with good-looking sexy guys, like I said. You don't know where you are with them. When I was really young I wouldn't have given someone like you a second look, but I'm more mature now.'

'You've escaped the penal colony of adolescence,' Geordie told her.

'The what?'

'I read it in a book.'

'When you came today I didn't know what you'd come for,' Janet said, laughing. 'I couldn't work it out. But you came to ask me out, didn't you? On a date?'

'Yeah,' said Geordie. 'Didn't I say?'

She squeezed his hand. 'I accept,' she said. 'I'd like to go out with you. I bet it'll be great fun.'

Geordie looked at her face again, returned her smile. 'Shall we do it now?' he said. 'I mean we could go to a movie, or have a drink.' He patted his pocket, make sure his wallet was there. 'I've got money,' he said. 'Could stretch to a pizza if you're hungry.'

CHAPTER 3

Jeanie Scott had an eleven-year-old daughter called Karen, an estranged ex-husband called Cal – the more estranged he was the better Jeanie liked it – a new boyfriend recently arrived from over the water in Ireland. She also had another husband who was no longer of this world, except as dust. She had scattered that dust from the window of a train somewhere between Glasgow and York sixteen years earlier.

She saw her life in compartments, and although she was the main player in all those separate compartments, the only one she really recognized was the one she was playing now. The girl, the child at home in Glasgow, was a distant memory. Her life with her first husband was at the same time a promise and a betrayal. It could have taken her into magical realms, but ended in death. The time with Cal, her second husband, was a mistake, except for the birth of her daughter. And her present life contained an Irish lover.

Another first, that. Michael, the Irish boyfriend. There'd been several Englishmen since she'd finally got rid of Cal, one German (one-night stand with Wolfram), and an absolutely huge Canadian.

She smiled to herself, thinking about Michael last night. If all else failed they could always land jobs as contortionists. An Irishman who knew the Kama Sutra, now there was a combination.

Eleven-year-old Karen upstairs in her room was playing Eternal's 'Good Thing', kindly sharing it with her mother and everyone else in the street. There was absolutely no point in shouting up the stairs, no human voice could get through that racket. The child had inherited the sensitivity of her father.

Jeanie climbed the stairs and opened Karen's bedroom door. Karen hit the volume button and mouthed 'I'm sorry', opening her eyes wide to prove she hadn't done it on purpose, just simply forgotten again.

Jeanie walked back down the stairs and found Cal in the kitchen. He'd always done that. Walked in without knocking, like he owned the place, which he certainly did not, or like he lived there, which he was never going to do again.

'Hi,' he said. With a smile.

Jeanie had forgotten he was expected. Saturday morning, time for his visit with Karen. Karen had obviously forgotten as well, lost in her bubbly music. 'How are you?' she asked. No point in saying anything about him walking into the house without an invite. Anything Jeanie had ever said to him he'd ignored. Well, he'd smiled and said he'd change, towards the end he'd even got down on his knees and begged, but he hadn't changed. It was like he was forged out of iron. There were no parts of him that had any flexibility. That's what made him so reliable. He had always been reliable. Impossible, but reliable. Like God.

'I'm frozen,' he said. 'The wind's really bitter.' Jeanie looked at his face. His nose was red and his cheeks and chin were pinched. 'Is she ready?'

Jeanie shook her head. 'Playing records,' she said. 'I'll tell her, but she's not even dressed yet. D'you want a cuppa?'

Cal said he'd have coffee and proceeded to fill the kettle himself, just like it was his kitchen. Jeanie sighed and walked upstairs to tell Karen he was here.

When she returned to the kitchen the kettle was singing and Cal had taken two cups and saucers from the cupboard. He was returning to the table with milk from the fridge. 'What's new?' he asked.

He took a real interest in Jeanie's love life, more, she

thought, than he had when they had lived together. Perhaps he got off on it, hearing her talk about her boyfriends? Jeanie didn't mind. If that's all it took she was happy to oblige. 'Michael,' she told him. 'From Belfast. The body of a god, and he seems to know more about women's bodies than I do.'

'Really,' said Cal. 'Did he find the G-spot?'

Jeanie nodded. 'G-and-H-I-J, and K, and L, and M.'

'Christ,' said Cal. 'It does exist, then? I thought it was just a rumour.' He spooned powdered coffee into both cups and poured boiling water from the kettle. 'Did *you* know where it was?'

Jeanie shook her head. 'Only vaguely. Until last night. I know where it is now.'

'You'd better draw me a diagram,' said Cal. 'In case I ever need it. If I had to find it myself I'd start off mid-afternoon, go right through the night and still be late for work the next day.'

Jeanie laughed and shook her head. Cal would never spend that much time on sex.

What Cal had found when he was married to Jeanie was that she was boring. Especially after Karen was born. At that time all the other women in the world had seemed really interesting and inviting. Then, after Jeanie had kicked him out, and after the divorce, when he was living alone, Jeanie had begun to seem like a very attractive proposition, and all the other women in the world seemed like they wouldn't be worth the effort.

So he'd hit on a plan. He wouldn't be pushy, but he'd go see Karen at least once a week, sometimes twice. And during those visits he'd be the kind of soft guy that he thought Jeanie liked. He'd make the drinks and clear away the cups and saucers when they'd finished. And he'd talk sex to Jeanie. And show an interest in what she was doing, who she was seeing. And at some point, sooner or later – he'd know when the time was right – she'd realize what a good thing she was missing and ask him to move back in.

And there was one extra clause in Cal's plan. If none of that worked, with the help of the video tape in his pocket, he would probably end up having so much money that Jeanie would be begging him to come home. Just like he had begged her not to throw him out.

In Karen's room, while Karen was in the bathroom taking the obligatory thirty minutes to get herself ready, Cal lifted the cover off a small box chair and tucked the video tape inside. Then he made sure the cover was securely back in place.

Cal's partner, Geoff, had checked the registration of the Carrera, and found that the owner was Franco Tampon, a heavy operator, suspected at one time or another of every crime in the book.

'My vote is, we leave him alone,' Geoff had said. 'Throw the tape away and forget the whole thing.'

'But what I think,' Cal had countered, 'is that the reason he's never been prosecuted is because he's rich enough to buy himself off. Look, Geoff, we've got video evidence of a kid being abducted. That's got to be worth money. And we know the guy's got plenty of that. His car's worth more than my house.'

'I don't know, Cal. I don't like it.'

The beginning of Geoff's capitulation. He wanted someone to take over, show him all the advantages, smooth away all the possible wrinkles. Cal of the silver tongue had always been capable of that.

Especially with Geoff. Though there was a part of Geoff Cal had never seen. When Geoff had been in the police force, during the Miners' Strike, Geoff had suddenly packed it all in. He was part of a special duty, ordered to break up a picket line. And he just handed the sergeant his helmet and walked away. Went home and had some Weetabix. That's how he came out of the force. Finished the Weetabix, put his warrant card in an envelope, popped it in the post and never went back.

Cal shook his head. Never could read people. They always had a way of surprising you. But if they played Franco Tampon right they'd both be rich. He'd be able to get on the phone to the guy: 'Hey, Franco, send me a new Merc.'

And Franco at the other end of the line: 'Mercy.'

But the copy of the tape hidden here in Karen's room was good insurance. Franco Tampon was heavy duty. His boys wouldn't think twice about doing over Cal's room and Geoff's house. Anything to get their hands on the evidence. But they'd never think of looking for it in Jeanie's house.

He came down the stairs two at a time, whistling that 'Making Whoopee' song that Jeanie's father used to sing. Karen came down after him, one at a time, like a little lady. And she couldn't whistle to save her life.

Cal opened the door for her, and then, with a wave to Jeanie, he ushered his daughter to his car at the kerb.

He seems lighter, Jeanie thought to herself. Like somehow, in the time he was here, he took a load off.

CHAPTER 4

Whenever he was talking about it later Sam would say the whole thing started when he met the woman from Scottish

Widows. But it wasn't like that at all. The whole thing started much earlier in the day. Sam and the woman from Scottish Widows came later.

But it's strange how your mind changes events round like that. If your memory had its way, all the events of your life would be rearranged. Sam had married when he was young, and his wife, Donna, had presented him with a daughter called Bronte. When Bronte was two years old both she and Donna were mowed down by a hit-and-run driver and Sam drank himself into oblivion. When he looked back on his life now it seemed to Sam that he had always been an alcoholic, that his wife and daughter had been a blessed interlude in a continuous drunk.

He cut off the train of thought. It was true that he was an alcoholic, but he was dry, had been dry for eleven months, one week, four days and seven hours. And before that, that lapse, the time before that he had been dry for nearly ten months. This time he'd cracked it, a day at a time. That was the way, one day at a time. Today he hadn't had a drink, hadn't even thought about having a drink, and he wasn't going to have a drink, not at lunch, not during the afternoon and not throughout the course of the evening.

Tomorrow? Well, who's making plans? Let's live today to its full. Tomorrow we'll deal with when it gets here. But Sam didn't think he'd drink tomorrow. Apart from ruining your life, booze ruined your looks. The only way to remain a Gene Hackman look-alike was to stay away from the juice.

'What's happened to you?' Sam asked Geordie. 'You walk around for months on end with a baseball cap on your head, usually the wrong way round, so when you're going you look as though you're coming. Then all of a sudden the cap disappears and you start combing your hair. What is that stuff? Brylcreem?'

'Brylcreem?' said Geordie. 'This is planet Earth, Sam. Jesus, get real, will you! The end of the century's coming round. I listen to you, it's like nineteen forty or something. Brylcreem? I might use a touch of gel from time to time, 'cause my hair's sometimes got more bounce than sense.'

'OK,' Sam said. 'What about the hat, Air Jordan, or whatever it was, Boston fuckin' Braves, I can't remember?'

'What is this?' said Geordie. 'It wasn't Boston Braves, that was a T-shirt; it was Air Jordan in homage to . . .'

'. . . Michael Jordan, I know that,' said Sam. 'I just asked what happened to it.'

'It's upstairs,' Geordie said. 'It's having a rest. And I'm having a rest from it. It's like a trial separation, we're seeing if we can live without each other.'

Sam laughed. 'I see. Janet doesn't like it.'

'You're fuckin' unbearable sometimes,' Geordie told him.

Sam walked to the shelf and took down a plate. He tapped himself on the head with it. 'You're right,' he said. 'I'm sorry. You want, I'll smash the plate over my head.'

'I'd rather have a pay rise,' said Geordie.

Sam put the plate down. 'You using emotional blackmail to screw money out of me?'

'Looks like it,' said Geordie. 'Did it work?'

'Only on this occasion,' said Sam. 'It won't work again. All future pay rises will have to be tied to increased productivity.'

They were in Sam's flat, which consisted of the ground floor of the house. Geordie's flat took up the first floor, but Geordie spent most of his time in Sam's room. The only other occupant of the building was Barney, Geordie's dog of no particular breed. Barney slept in Geordie's room most of the time, but sometimes in Sam's, where he anyway spent most of his waking life.

It was morning. Outside the wind was howling. Rain was not so much coming down as being hurled in horizontal sheets against the windows and doors. Officially darkness was over, but they had the lights on.

Geordie had put *The Basement Tapes* on, and the man was singing 'Tears of Rage'. They'd finished eating and were part way through the washing up when Geordie said, 'Janet told me a joke. But I didn't get it.'

Sam didn't turn to face him, he finished drying a plate and put it away in the cupboard. 'Did you laugh?' he asked.

'Yeah,' Geordie said. 'I laughed in the right place. We both laughed. Had a good laugh, together.'

Sam glanced back at him, a smile on his face. 'Come on, then. Let's hear it.'

Geordie frowned, making sure he'd got the thing straight in his head, then he said, 'If women ruled the world there'd be no wars; just intense negotiations every twenty-eight days.' He paused, then made a laughing sound, 'Ha ha,' and shrugged his shoulders.

Sam turned and put the drying cloth down. He put his arm around Geordie's shoulder and walked with him to the table.

'You gonna explain it?' Geordie asked.

'Yeah,' Sam said. He sat opposite Geordie and collected his thoughts.

'What's it about?' Geordie asked, impatient to get to it.

'If women ruled the world there'd be no wars; just intense negotiations every twenty-eight days?'

'Yeah,' said Geordie. 'I know the joke. I know how it goes. It was me just told it to you.'

'But you don't know why it's funny?'

Geordie rubbed at an imaginary spot on a glass tumbler. 'Not hilarious, no,' he said.

'But you know about menstruation?'

'Oh, yeah, like that period thing?'

'You know what it is? What actually happens?'

'Yeah, bleeding, innit? They have to wear them things, you know, like on the telly, absorbent things.' He thought for a few moments. 'Towels, innit?'

Sam paused over the sink. He wanted to ask Geordie to quit saying 'innit' after every sentence, but told himself to stick to the point. 'What I'm trying to establish here,' he said, 'is if you know what is actually happening during a woman's period.'

'I've jus' told you,' said Geordie. 'It's bleeding.'

'OK,' said Sam. 'Go on.'

'Well, it must come from the stomach or somewhere,' Geordie guessed. 'The womb, it's to do with getting pregnant.'

'You *don't* know, do you? That's OK, nothing wrong with that. But for your age group it's probably essential information. What happens is that female mammals produce eggs.'

'Hang on,' said Geordie. 'Female mammals?'

'Women,' Sam said. 'Women produce eggs once a month. If the egg is fertilized, then she becomes pregnant and the egg eventually becomes a baby. But if the egg is not fertilized . . .'

'Like by screwing?' said Geordie.

'Yeah, like by screwing,' Sam agreed. 'If the egg isn't fertilized it's rejected by the body. It disintegrates and is excreted via the vagina. That's what you call bleeding. It's not really bleeding, but it looks like that.'

'So the towel is just to clean it up?'

'Yeah, kind of. Does all that make sense?'

'Yeah,' said Geordie, still unsure. 'But it doesn't explain the joke.'

'Around the time they have the period,' Sam continued, 'some women get pre-menstrual tension, PMT.'

'Yeah, I've heard that. PMT. What was the other thing?'

'Pre-menstrual tension. PMT is the same, just a shortened version.'

'That's when they get antsy, innit?' Geordie said.

'You know all this, don't you?' said Sam.

'Yeah, I know all this. Sam, what I don't know is why the fuckin' joke is meant to be funny. I can hear what you're saying, but it's not making it any clearer.'

'OK, try it this way. Because women have babies, people think they're more nurturing than men. It might not be the case. There're lots of women these days wouldn't agree with that. Men as well, they don't see why women should be labelled one way, and men another. But traditionally women have been regarded as more nurturing. So people think that men are more violent, more warlike, and women are gentler.'

'The gentler sex,' said Geordie.

'Yeah, but you shouldn't say that any more. That women are the gentler sex. They get upset if you say that.'

'But it's all right to think it?' Geordie asked.

'No, you shouldn't think it either,' said Sam. 'Except for the purposes of the joke. "If women ruled the world, there'd be no wars." That's the first part of the joke, OK. You understand the first part?'

'Almost,' said Geordie. 'It's not politically correct, but traditionally if women ruled the world there'd be no wars.'

'Yeah,' said Sam. 'But there'd be "intense negotiations every twenty-eight days". Because of the PMT. You understand?'

'No,' said Geordie, 'what's twenty-eight days got to do with it?'

'That's a month,' Sam said. 'Twenty-eight days is a month. That's when they get antsy, so there wouldn't be any wars, but everybody would get a row once a month.'

'Oh,' Geordie said.

'You understand it?'

'Yeah,' said Geordie. 'It's not even funny.'

'No,' said Sam. 'It's not particularly funny.'

'And it's not even true. According to you, if women ruled the world, there'd probably be just as many wars as always.'

'I dunno,' Sam said. 'What do I know?'

'Nothing,' said Geordie. 'Absolutely nothing, innit?'

Sam pushed his chair back and stood. 'Why'd you have to say "innit" after every sentence? It's not even a word.'

'Christ,' said Geordie. 'He's getting antsy. Must be the time of the month!'

Celia was already in the office when Sam arrived. She was sixty-nine years old and had recently taken to Eastern European jewellery in a big way. This morning she was sporting a huge silver ring which obliterated most of her hand. 'Good morning, Sam,' she said. 'I've opened the post. It's on your desk.'

'Anything interesting?'

'Not really. A couple of cheques.' She walked to the window and looked out over St Helen's Square. 'It's brightening up a little. Didn't think you were coming.'

'Sorry,' Sam said, poking through the mail on his desk. 'Got held up with Geordie. Had to explain menstruation to him.'

'Oh, my goodness,' said Celia, who never failed to be amazed at Sam's frankness. 'How on earth did you explain that? I could never explain it satisfactorily even to myself.'

'It wasn't a philosophical discussion, Celia. Just the bare facts.'

'Even so,' she said. 'Sometimes I think it would be nice to be young again. But when I think about things like that I'm quite happy with what I've got.'

'Yeah,' said Sam. 'The past always looks better than it was; it's only pleasant because it isn't here. Anyway, you're not old, Celia. Bet I'll be a hell of a lot older'n you when I'm your age.'

Celia turned from the window and gave him one of the wrinkliest smiles in the universe. 'Oh, and Marie rang,' she said. 'She's not feeling well enough to get in again.'

'Geordie's day off,' said Sam. 'So that leaves you and me. And next to nothing in the post. Maybe we should close down for the day.'

Celia shrugged. 'You go off if you've got something to do. I want to reorganize the accounts. But I can easily hold the fort for a day.'

'I'm worried about Marie,' Sam said. 'What is it, do you think? Some kind of bug?'

'Deeper than that, Sam. What we used to call a soul illness. She's got a lot of spirit, though. I'm sure she'll pull through.'

Sam sighed and straightened up the mail, so it was in roughly the same shape as when he arrived. 'Think I'll call round and see her,' he said.

He left the office behind and walked past the post office in Lendal, over the road to the Museum Gardens. He colonized a bench and sat quietly, watching as a squirrel came over the grass towards him. They were so inured to the hordes of tourists who tramped this way that they had little fear of humankind. This one hopped over the path and joined Sam on the bench. 'I've got nothing for you,' Sam told it, and the squirrel cocked its head to one side and watched the man's hands, as if to say, 'Me neither.' They only had each other.

Marie Dickens was the widow of Sam's ex-partner, Gus, who had been killed on the job some months earlier. After Gus's death, Marie had given up her job as a nurse, and joined Sam Turner Investigations. She had thrown herself into the job with a lot of energy and will, but over the past weeks she had been withdrawn and uncommunicative. For the last ten days or so she had been pleading illness. Sam didn't believe it. He believed something was wrong, but it wasn't a bug.

Sam got up from the bench and the squirrel shot up a tree. He walked to the rear of the Gardens and along the river to Marie's house.

He knocked and walked in. She was sitting by the window, devouring a bag of salted nuts. The wrappers from a couple of bars of Nestlé chocolate were on the table in front of her. Gus used to say that no bar of chocolate was safe when Marie was in town.

She was a big woman, in her early thirties now, with real flesh stacked up on her hips and behind. The description of her bosom as 'generous' was not really ample. She smiled and placed the bag of nuts on the table in front of her. 'Hi, Sam.'

'Heard you called in,' he said. 'Not been feeling too good?'

'It's passing,' she said. 'I'll be OK tomorrow.'

Sam walked to the table and pulled out a chair. He sat over from her. 'You sure?' he asked. 'Nothing I can do?'

Marie shook her head. 'Women's problems,' she said

with a smile. She reached over and took his hand. 'It's sweet of you to come, Sam. But I'm nearly over it now. I'll be OK tomorrow.'

Sam couldn't think what kind of women's problems she could be referring to, but he let it pass. They lapsed into silence together. A bag of nuts between them.

'I saw a duck being gang-banged down by the river,' he said.

Marie opened her eyes wide. 'Goodness, what did you do?'

'I didn't do anything.'

'What happened?'

'There was this duck, by the verge. Small. And there were several drakes, six or seven of them. They took her in turns. When one had finished another took over. Just held her down. Whenever she tried to get away they'd get her by the neck. In the end she gave up and took it.'

'And you didn't do anything?'

Sam shook his head. 'What could I do?'

'Jesus, you could have stopped them!'

'I was paralysed,' he said. 'My first thought was to stop them. Chase the drakes away and wait until the duck was safely in the water. But then I thought, hell, they're ducks. I mean, this is nature, this is what ducks do, for Christsakes. It's not right to interfere.'

Marie shook her head. 'Only a man could say that,' she said.

'I kept swinging back and forth. First I thought I should interfere, then I thought I shouldn't. Then, in the end, I didn't know what I should do.'

'So you didn't do anything?'

'I watched them,' he said. 'I watched them, and her, and it. When they'd had enough they just waddled off and left her there. Eventually she got to her feet and headed back to the river.'

'You should've stopped them,' said Marie.

'Maybe. It didn't seem right, though. Like the whole concept of interfering in other cultures, always thinking we know best. You know what I mean? The great white western way. Like it's our duty to teach the rest of the world how to live. How many cultures have been undermined and withered away because of that attitude?'

'Sam, we're talking ducks here, not culture. You see a duck suffering, any animal suffering, and you do something about it.'

'Yeah, I know,' he said. 'I admit I was confused out there. I couldn't work out if it was suffering or if it was natural. If it would solve anything by me interfering, or if it would make it worse.'

'A woman would have stopped it,' Marie said. 'Any woman would have stopped it. You don't stand and watch somebody get raped, any*thing* get raped.'

'I don't know if an animal can get raped,' Sam said. 'Or if they get raped all the time. I mean, they can hardly give their consent, can they?'

'I can hardly believe you're saying these things, Sam. They come on heat, they give off some kind of scent, or they give other signals. When it's OK, when they're ready, then they have their own ways of making the invitation. If they don't do that, if they're not on heat, then it's wrong. It's like rape.'

'Yeah. Except I'm not a duck, Marie. If I was a drake then maybe I'd get the signal, know when to do it and when not to do it. Hell, those drakes this morning, they might have all thought they got the signal. The duck, she might have given off too strong a signal, woke up all the drakes in the neighbourhood. Christ, there's no way of knowing what was happening. For all I know the drakes were turned on by a factory chimney, an exhaust emission.'

Marie sat and looked at him. 'I can see you find it interesting,' she said. 'That's the trouble, though, Sam. That's why I can't agree with you. I can't ever find rape interesting. It's never interesting, it's always wrong. Wherever, whenever you come across it, it's simply wrong.' There was something final in her voice. Like that was the last word.

Sam thought she might be tired. 'OK,' he said. 'Next time I'll scatter them, throw a bucket of water over them.'

She walked to the door with him. As they passed the kitchen he noticed a full round of Brie cheese near the kettle. He kissed Marie on the cheek and told her to rest. She touched his cheek with her lips and said again that she would be better tomorrow. Back in the office.

As he walked past the spot where the gang-banging of the duck had taken place, Sam suddenly wondered what Marie was doing with a whole Brie cheese in her kitchen. The only time people bought full rounds of Brie was when they were having a party. But Marie wasn't having a party. If she was having a party, she would have invited Sam. She would have invited Geordie and Celia. She was ill. People who are ill don't have full rounds of Brie in the house.

Sam walked through the Museum Gardens still thinking about it. Then he turned round and walked back again. He wasn't a man to interfere in the gang-banging of a duck, but when it came to friends, he couldn't leave it alone. He lengthened his stride along the river and made his way back to Marie's house.

He knocked and walked in, fully expecting to find Marie sitting by the window. But she wasn't there. He walked through to the kitchen and examined the round of Brie. Lifted it and weighed it in the palm of his hand. Several pounds of full-fat cheese. 'Marie,' he shouted. There was no reply.

He walked to the foot of the stairs and shouted again. 'Marie. Marie, it's Sam. Back again.' But there was no reply. She wasn't in the house. She was ill. She couldn't come to work. She had several pounds of full-fat Brie in the kitchen. And she'd gone out. Sam Turner was a detective. This kind of situation got bells ringing in his head. He was hooked now, and he wouldn't be satisfied until he'd got to the bottom of it.

He sat by the window for twenty minutes, then moved over to the couch. She goes out and leaves the door unlocked. You'd think she'd only slipped out for a minute or two. But no, she's gone out to do something. Something that takes time. Sam wasn't going to move until she returned. There was something wrong about the situation. It wasn't a lot. But it didn't fit. And he'd started worrying at it, like a tongue at a broken tooth.

It might have been a few minutes later, or it might have been an hour or more. Sam had dozed off and slipped down on the couch. Too many late nights. He was awoken by the door opening and closing. Footsteps padding down the hall to the bathroom. Marie's footsteps. Unmistakably Marie's footsteps. Who else would walk into the house like that and go straight to the bathroom? It was a real advantage in the business he was in, having this deductive kind of mind.

She obviously hadn't seen him when she came in. He staggered to his feet and walked slowly over to the bathroom door. Marie had not closed it behind her. She stood over the washbasin, and she had pulled her arm out of the sleeve of her blouse. Sam began to turn away, finding himself in a position that could be embarrassing to both of them. Marie didn't look round, and obviously was not aware that he was there.

As he turned away, Sam stopped and let his glance return to Marie and what she was doing. He couldn't believe his eyes. But he watched her take an apple corer and dig the sharp end of it into her upper arm. She twisted it, just like you would if you wanted to get the core out of an apple, and a stream of blood ran down her arm and into the washbasin. Then she removed the apple corer and stuck it in again, a fresh spot, just above the first injury. She did it with no trepidation whatsoever. She stabbed away at the white flesh with real aggression. The drakes by the river earlier in the day had not relished their task half as much as Marie was now doing.

Whatever was going on here, Sam didn't know if it was natural or not. But he didn't hesitate. He took two steps forward and removed the apple corer from her hand. She looked round at him then, and great tears oozed their way from her eyes and streamed down her face. Sam put his arms round her and held her while great heaving sobs shuddered their way up from the depths of her.

CHAPTER 5

'Uh uhn,' Gog said.

Ben was immediately awake. A thin shaft of early-morning light slipped through the gap in the blue curtains and sliced the room in two. Gog's bed on one side, Ben's on the other. 'Aghhhhh,' whispered Gog. Then again with a softer, breathier tone. 'Aghhhhh. Ugh. Gog.'

'Yeah,' said Ben. 'Morning already?' He strained his ears, listening for the sound which met him every morning of his life: the slow rustle of bedclothes from the other side of the room as Gog explored his abdomen and thighs before taking on his already erect prick. 'You at it already, Gog?' he asked.

Gog did a laugh. Should've been an actor, like Steve Reeves or Arnold Schwarzenegger. Could've played monsters. He'd have made a fortune. 'Ohhhhhh,' he grunted. 'Nahhhhhhh.'

Ben peeled the sheet away from his face and watched Gog turning from side to side on his bed. He had kicked the blankets down to the end of the bed now, and was cupping his balls in one hand while he massaged away in long sensuous strokes with the other. His head was arched backward and his jaw set forward. He took in and expelled long breaths through his nose. His eyes were closed. It was his pre-training warm-up.

Ben felt good, surprisingly, because he'd dreamed of Roid Rage, the madness that comes from the abuse of steroids. Ben and Gog, of course, did not abuse steroids, theirs were prescribed by a doctor, a legitimate doctor who had been trained and who knew what he was doing. But there were people who came into The Monster Gym who did abuse steroids. And there had been cases of Roid Rage down there, and there would be again. The main pushers knew that Ben and Gog were against steroid abuse, and they were careful not to get caught. But there were lots of users. More people were using than weren't using. They didn't buy the gear in The Monster Gym itself, Ben was strict about that. They bought it outside, in the alley.

Gog was up on his knees now, stroking his prick with both hands, alternately, long strokes beginning at the scrotum and travelling the whole length of the thing, finishing at his lower chest. His fingers took on a kind of grace during this operation. He seemed to have the hands of a dancer. The room was getting lighter every minute and Gog's huge bull head and ripped neck were awesome in silhouette as he bounced up and down on the bed. He looked over at Ben and grinned, made an animal sound in the back of his throat, pursed his lips at an imaginary female.

Imaginary females were the only ones Gog had ever had. He'd been with Titus and Vince, the progeny of a stolen moment between a prize-winning whippet bitch and an equally celebrated collie, but neither of those were female.

And they didn't have the dogs now. When the last one, Titus, had died they hadn't replaced him. Too much trouble. You had to train them, take them for walks last thing at night, first thing in the morning. Worse than having kids about the place. The Monster Gym was alarmed anyway, and if anyone ever did break in Gog and Ben would make as much of a mess of them as any dog.

Gog was moaning softly now. Still on his bed, he had got up on to his feet, completely naked. He was striking a pose, forcing his abs into relief, the huge delts on his shoulders glistening with sweat. His hand strokes were quickening, his breath now coming in short gasps. His head moved backward and forward in a rhythm that kept pace with the moaning song. Ben glanced down at his brother's spastic leg, but quickly filtered it out. Positivity, that was the thing. Don't be led astray by the one thing that was not quite right.

Ben pushed back his own sheets and got up on to his bed. 'OK,' he said, laughing. 'OK, Gog, let's do it.' Ben had no time for the slow preparation, the build-up, he went straight for the climax. The two of them together, rushing for the finish, spurting their loads on to the sheets and down to the carpet beyond. They finished together, groaning in unison, greeting the world and the day with total physical comprehension. The room was awash with sweat and musk.

Gog jumped down from the bed and opened the curtains wide. He felt down by the side of his bed and plucked his T-shirt from the floor. He pulled it over his head. The slogan on his chest read, STEROIDS – THE BREAKFAST OF CHAMPIONS.

Ben walked over to a chest of drawers and put on a clean T-shirt with the legend, IF YOU'RE NOT A MONSTER – MOVE ASIDE. Shorts and trainers followed, and then downstairs to a breakfast of skimmed milk and carrots. And seven different coloured capsules.

Half an hour later they were in The Monster Gym warming up for their first session of the day, the best session of the day, the one they always did together before the customers arrived.

Gog warmed up with ten reps of a Swan Lift, while Ben did ten minutes with the rope. Then they each bench-pressed 250 lbs., lowering the barbells to the nipple area, inhaling as the bar came down, exhaling as it went up. 'Imagine you're blowing it up,' said Ben. And Gog made his laugh come again.

They'd started working the Schwarzenegger Split: chest, biceps and forearms on day one, legs, triceps and lower back on day two, and today they were on upper back, shoulders and abdominals. But first Gog wanted to do half a dozen sets of the Donkey Calf Raise, because he thought his lower legs needed extra work. Ben didn't agree with the diagnosis. Gog's lower legs were one of his best features. Well, his left lower leg was. And it didn't seem to matter what they did with his right leg, it never got any better. Never would. But Ben knew that if Gog got an idea in his head there was no point arguing about it. Gog leant forward with his upper body and head on the bench, feet on the floor. Then Ben sat on his lower back while Gog raised himself high on to his toes and back again. He did fifty reps, with only a few seconds' rest. Six sets in all.

Ben didn't believe it, but what they'd been told was that their mother had syphilis when Gog was born. That was the explanation for his leg. Congenital syphilis. There was no cure for it. You couldn't ever make it right.

They began their abs exercises with Hanging Knee Raises from the horizontal bar, fifty reps each for four sets. Then a series of Bent Knee Sit-ups on a bench, thirty reps, five sets. By the end of it Ben felt elated. He felt different, good, not tired at all, his bowels were working better, his body felt tighter. It was like this all the time now, even when something failed he wasn't disappointed because other things were always working well to compensate. He looked over at Gog and could see that Gog was the same, very pleased, a smile on his face, feeling good. There was a visible hardness to his biceps, delts and quads. 'This is good stuff,' he said breathlessly. 'The best.'

When they measured up, after practising some poses in the mirror, Ben found he had put an inch on one of his arms, half an inch on the other.

Later in the day Gog went to lie down with a headache. Ben took a banana upstairs for him, but Gog was sleeping. That wasn't right. Getting headaches all the time. That wasn't supposed to happen. They would have to talk to Doc Squires about that.

The Monster Gym was a short walk from Acomb Green. The building had gone through a period of neglect, but had originally been a flourishing gym. According to legend, the Wharton boys had trained there, under one of those old-time managers from the Eastern bloc. Manny something or other; they all seemed to be called Manny something or other. Ben didn't give a shit. If you look behind all those sentimental legends you find the Manny guy from the Eastern bloc is just a front. The real manager, the man who nobody ever hears of, but who can spot the champ in the undeveloped boy, he's a Brit. Like Ben. Ben was a Brit, as was his brother Gog. All the way through, like that writing in a stick of rock.

But that was the past, when it was a gym. The place was derelict for a while, then some budding entrepreneur had used it to store other people's furniture. Franco Tampon had bought it for a song and brought in some muscle from Bradford to clean it up. Now Ben and Gog who were also muscle, but intelligent muscle, had both of their names on the lease and were entrepreneurs themselves, the proprietors of The Monster Gym, open seven days a week for enthusiasts of hard-core body building. Ben and Gog weren't at the gym seven days a week themselves, except in the early mornings. They had plenty of work of another kind from Franco. Franco called the work he gave them 'odd jobs'. But it was more than that.

'You're good lads,' Franco told them. 'Three new customers since last time.' He ran his forefinger down the column of figures. The accounts. Checking the receipts and expenses. He always did that since they'd got into trouble with the bank manager. He'd lent them money then, rescued them from the clutches of the bankers. All bankers were part of an international conspiracy. Everybody *knew* they were. But most people ignored the truth.

Ben wasn't worried about Franco checking the figures, though. Not any more. He'd been over those figures three times. They added up. Franco looked at him again, a broad smile on his face. 'And you look professional, too,' he said. Ben and Gog were dressed identically in plain white T-shirts and black polyester jogging pants with Nike Air Cross trainers. Ben was blond and the smaller of the pair, with shoulders like a bull and biceps straining at the cotton sleeves of his T-shirt. Gog, his brother, was taller by a head, and always had a smile on his face. He was dark and swarthy and sometimes suffered from depressions. But he smiled through everything. Like Ben, he had developed his upper torso to the limit.

Ben and Gog had been deprived children. Their mother had run off with a Chinaman shortly after Gog was born. No one knew where. Ben and Gog both thought it must be to China, since no one had seen her since. It was odd that she'd run off with a Chinaman. Very odd. No one else's mother had run off with a Chinaman. No one in York, anyway. In fact, in York, hardly anyone had ever met a Chinaman. There were those Chinamen who ran Chinese restaurants and takeaways, but they didn't count. They just talked funny. Seemed like the only real Chinaman who ever came to York came for the sole reason of running off with their mother.

Ben and Gog didn't think that this had anything to do with the fact that they both, independently of each other, without conferring in any way, hated Chinamen. They had talked about it for the first time two years previously after trashing a Chinese restaurant and putting two Chinese waiters in the local hospital, one of them separated from several of his fingers and the other divorced from two of his teeth and one of his eyes. They had not premeditated this act. It had been spontaneous. Something to do with the cerebral cortex. Which is how they got off and had the charges against them dropped.

It was bad luck that their mother had run off with a

Chinaman. That's all you could really say about it. Other people's mothers had run off with street cleaners, butchers and, on one memorable occasion, a TV personality. Actually a producer's assistant, not someone who had a face. And other people's fathers had run off with schoolgirls, grandmothers, single-parent teenagers, nurses, shop assistants, housewives and fucking fruit cakes.

So there was plenty of choice for people who were going to run off. But a frigging Chinaman was the last thing anyone would have expected.

Ben watched the smile on Gog's face. That was another thing. They could read each other's minds. Someone else watching that smile on Gog's face might think he was pleased with the praise that Franco Tampon was coming out with. But Ben knew that the smile on Gog's face had nothing at all to do with Franco Tampon. Gog wasn't even listening to Franco Tampon, he was thinking about trashing that Chinese restaurant. He always smiled like that when he thought about trashing the Chinese restaurant. It had been one of the high spots of his life. His mystical experience.

That's what he called it. Ben, being rather more intelligent than Gog, realized that it wasn't a real mystical experience at all. It was simply a substitute for the lack of bonding with a mother person when Gog was a small infant. But Gog wouldn't understand that, so Ben didn't burden him with it. He let him go on thinking it was a mystical experience. It wasn't the truth, but it didn't do any harm.

'Is Doc Squires coming tonight?' Ben asked.

Franco consulted his watch. 'Yes, should be here any minute now. Why is that, Ben, are you anxious to be off?'

'No,' Ben said, defensively. He wasn't wanting to be off. It hurt him that Franco thought he wanted to be off. As if he wasn't committed or something. A dilly-fucking-tanty, or whatever they called them.

Franco was smiling to himself, avoiding Ben's eyes. 'Thought you might have a date or something, Ben. Got yourself a girl. Am I wrong?'

But Ben didn't take the bait. Franco was like that sometimes, making jokes. Ben and Gog stayed away from girls. You couldn't afford to get involved like that when you were in training. It wasn't just the direct energy loss, in fact that was something you could replace easily enough by eating a couple of raw steaks. It was something else about women that really drained you. To someone in training, serious training, like Ben and Gog's, a woman was like a vampire.

'I was looking forward to seeing Doc Squires for a number of reasons,' Ben said. 'First, me and Gog have nearly run out of those blue tablets. The capsules. And Doc Squires said we could double up on the dose from this month. And second, Gog's been having more headaches than usual, and I wanted to talk to the doctor about that. Maybe get something that really helps.'

'Is that true, Gog?' said Franco Tampon. 'The headaches getting worse?'

Gog put a brave smile on his face.

'He doesn't complain,' said Ben. 'He never complains. But I know when he's under the weather. I can tell these things. We've got telepathy.'

Franco shook his head. 'I thought the headaches were getting better,' he said. 'Doc told me they were getting better when you started on the steroids.'

'They did at first,' Ben said. 'And they help as soon as we take them. But after a while the headaches come back. And they come back worse than they were before.'

Gog made a sound in his throat, which could have been agreement or dissent. Ben glanced at Franco to see if he had interpreted it correctly, but Franco didn't know what to make of it. 'Gog thinks the doctor will be able to fix him up,' said Ben.

'I hope so,' said Franco. 'I want you two to be efficient. I don't want anything to go wrong. You're my best men. When I give you a job I want to know that everything will be all right. I want to go home and sleep.'

'Doc Squires has got everything under control,' Ben said. 'He knows what he's doing.'

Franco made a church and steeple with his two hands, opened it up and looked inside at all the people. 'Bosnia?' he said.

Ben smiled. 'Great isn't it,' he said. Gog flapped his arms and made that sound at the back of his throat. Ben continued, 'Wish it was here,' he said. 'Ethnic cleansing.'

'Yes,' said Franco. 'God knows we need it.'

'Nignogs,' said Ben. 'Fucking nignogs.'

Gog said something that had two syllables.

'Yeah,' said Ben. 'Chinese nignogs.'

'It'll come,' said Franco. 'It's remarkable, don't you think, that the masses seem to know instinctively what is right in these situations? The leaders are bankrupt, of course, decadent, but the indigenous masses know what to do. It's as if they feel it like a physical pain when their blood is being diluted. They become an endangered species, the last of their kind, and when that happens they stand up and fight.'

Ben counted out the tablets that Doc Squires had given them. He transferred them to the jars marked BEN and GOG, so they could start on them first thing in the morning. When he went upstairs Gog was already sleeping. Peacefully. On his back, his arms and hands thrown back on the pillow like a baby.

Everything was going to be all right. Doc Squires had increased the doses, and he'd prescribed a new tablet for Gog, to undermine the headaches. It wouldn't happen straight away. They'd have to be patient. But eventually Gog would get better. The headaches would disappear.

Ben stripped off his clothes and got into bed. He switched off the light and peered up through the gloom to the ceiling. Franco Tampon was useful, but Ben didn't like him. First off, he wasn't a Brit. With a name like that? Do me a favour. Frank, maybe. If the guy was called something regular like Frank Taylor, you'd know where you stood. But Franco Tampon, fucking Italian name. Fucking grease-ball. How they got into the country in the first place, that was what Ben didn't understand. The government kept saying they were taking measures to ensure that illegal immigrants couldn't get into the country. But they did. They flooded in. All the time, like there was no one really stopping them.

A government that was serious would build a wall or something. The ancient Chinese had done it, built a wall. Probably copied it off Hadrian. And look at York. Those guys back in the Dark Ages had built a wall that was still standing today. With a moat round it, drawbridges. All the way round the city. Anybody wanted to get in they had to present themselves at the gate. If they were illegal immigrants, Chinamen or Italians, they got a dollop of boiling oil thrown over them. At least that. Something to make them think.

Franco, secondly, was full of all this stuff about international Jewish conspiracies, about ethnic cleansing. He'd bring it up, he'd talk about it from time to time, but it was like something he'd read in a book. You looked at Franco and you knew straight off that he wasn't serious. He was puny. He didn't do any work on himself. He was rich and he had various scams going in the town, and in other towns, Manchester, Bradford, Nottingham. Things he managed for other guys, bigger guys. He had contacts, big contacts. Could get things done. He had cars, as well. Great cars like that Carrera they'd borrowed the other day. But he wasn't a monster like Ben and Gog. He was letting himself go to fat. In a proper world, a world where men could be proud of themselves, guys like Franco would be fixed. Ben and Gog had talked about that. They would have guys like Franco fixed, like you fix a tomcat. You cut off those bad genes, like with thoroughbred horses. In the end you'd have a race of giants.

And not just physical. Ben didn't mean physical, muscles. He meant intellectually and morally as well. And that was something guys like Franco would never get their heads round. You might be able to start him on a programme, get him lifting weights, building himself up physically. But you wouldn't be able to stop him messing with little boys and girls. You'd never be able to stop him doing that. The guy was a fucking toilet.

CHAPTER 6

'Oh, fuck. I've forgotten the word.'

Geordie had played the best game of football he'd ever played in his life. Then he got a lift home, to the end of the street, and walked, covered in mud, to the house. He couldn't remember the word. The word that described it. But Sam would know what it was.

Sam Turner, the boss. He was also Geordie's family, in a way, though the two of them were not related. Sam had quite literally picked Geordie out of the gutter one night and helped him get somewhere to live. He had washed him, given him a job, got Celia to educate Geordie in the English language. What else had Sam done? More like it was easier to list the things he hadn't done, because there weren't any. When you thought about it he'd done more for Geordie than anyone, ever, in his whole life. And Geordie did think about it, sometimes wondered how he could ever pay the guy back. Sam, Geordie sometimes thought, was short for the original good *Sam*aritan, except he wasn't an Arab, he was a private detective.

Geordie walked into the flat and sat on the edge of Sam's table. Sam was playing a tape of the 'Skin to Skin' duet between Harry Belafonte and Jennifer Warnes. He'd been playing it constantly for the last few days. Sam was in love with Jennifer Warnes. He didn't know it, and if Geordie pointed it out Sam would deny it. But he was in love with her all the same. He looked up and widened his eyes when Geordie sat on his table.

'What's wrong?' he asked.

'Why should something be wrong?'

'You're covered in mud,' Sam said. 'If you come in and sit on the table where we eat our breakfast when you're covered in mud, something's gotta be wrong. Besides, you look like you always look when something's wrong. So what is it?'

'I can't remember a word.'

'An emergency, eh?' Sam said. 'Move your ass off my table and start at the beginning. I'm all ears.'

Geordie moved away from the table and sat on a hard chair. Barney, his dog, came over and sniffed at the mud on his legs. 'Aw, Sam, I played brilliant!' he said. 'Everybody said I played brilliant. But that's not the word. Oh, what's the word?'

'Geordie, think. Describe it. What was the game like?'

'Christ. I got the ball just after half-time. They'd nearly scored, so it was somewhere near our goal mouth. I started running with it. I realized I was on my own, but it felt right. I took it past four of their players, you know, selling dummies, dribbling it round them or through their legs. Nobody could stop me. It was like I was charmed. I left them standing. When I got over the halfway line, their backs put up a solid wall, so I sent it out to the left wing.

'I was in the goal mouth. The ball came back in from the left wing, almost down by the corner flag. I saw I could get there. It was impossible to get there. It was like I was drowning. I could see the surface, at least I knew the surface had to be there, but I didn't know if I could get there before my lungs filled up. That must be what it feels like, when you're drowning. Anyway, I went for it. I was way past the goal mouth, Sam. Even if I got to the ball, there was no way I was gonna score. Maybe the best I could do was get close to the right goal post. It was never gonna go in. The goalie had it covered, anyway, except for the top corner. And I was breathing really hard, my legs had gone. I'd just come the whole length of the pitch.

'I struggled upwards. I couldn't get that high. But I got there, Sam. The ball came towards me, arcing over the others clustered round the goal mouth. I knew it was coming to me, but I had to get my head still higher. I'd already passed the height of my leap, and I had to wriggle, flap my legs like a fish's tail, force my head higher still to connect with the ball. I arched my back, then came forward with my head, and the ball came down and made the connection. I hit it, Sam. I connected with the middle of my forehead, and it spun off like a bullet into the net. The goalie saw it at the last moment, but he didn't have time to think it. It was in the back of the net.

'I looked down. I had, like, you know, about a hundred miles to travel. There was no way of getting down safe, and I just collapsed into a heap of arms and legs. I saw the ball had gone in, and then nothing, I turned into a heap on the pitch. And there was the clapping. Everybody was clapping and cheering, even guys on the other team, and they all came over and patted me on the back, tried to kiss me, and one of them said, 'Geordie, you played a . . . you played a . . . a . . .'

'A blinder,' said Sam.

'Yeahhhhhhhhhhhhhhh!' Geordie leapt in the air. 'A *blinder*, man. I played a fucking *blinder*!'

There it was again, that word, blinder. He played a blinder. He played a blinder. 'What does it mean? Blinder. I mean, I know it means a good game, but why do they call it that?'

Sam shook his head. 'Maybe it means you blinded yourself. You'd been blind because you couldn't see that it was possible.'

'It wasn't possible,' Geordie said. 'That's why it felt so good.'

'And it means you've blinded everybody else to the everyday world. You've come through the shit, you've achieved something perfect. You've made the world open its eyes and see. You've made the world realize something that it will never be able to forget.'

Geordie laughed. 'Hang on, Sam. I was only playing in the Railway Cup. And I don't even work on the railway.'

'I was there,' Sam said. 'Wouldn't have missed it for the world. I saw it. I clapped as well, Geordie, clapped and cheered with the rest of them. You played a blinder. Reminded me of George Best when that ball went in.'

Geordie was strutting round the kitchen, really pleased with himself. 'George Best,' he said. And he stopped, then, and looked back at Sam. 'George Best,' he said. 'Christ, Sam, he's old enough to be my grandfather.'

'Wasn't always, though, Geordie. When I was in Didsbury we used to go to Old Trafford on a Saturday to see him play. He was like a prince.'

'Oh-oh,' said Geordie, 'story coming on. 'Bout way back in the nineteen sixties. Eric Cantona, now he was a real player. Lives in the modern world. Better than all those old guys.'

'People from Liverpool were always saying they had the Beatles, and Adrian Henri, and Gerry and the Pacemakers, all those guys. Later they had Willie Russell, and Bleasdale. You know what I mean? Bragging about all the talent came from Liverpool. And we'd say, "We've got George Best." And then we'd stand back and see how they'd try to cap it. But Best was the best. There was no way you could cap it.

'Except occasionally you'd get one of the real clever idiots who would say, "George Best, he's not from Manchester, he's Irish, he only *plays* for Manchester." '

'And what would you say to that?'

Sam smiled. Thinking back. 'We'd say, "Yeah, and *we* can go see him every week." '

'You gonna have a party or what?' Geordie said, backing out of Sam's fridge with a full round of Brie.

'Ah,' said Sam. 'You can eat as much of that as you like.'

Geordie gave him the eyeball. Sam looked back. 'You don't have to tell me why all this cheese is in your fridge,' Geordie said. ' 'T'aint none of my business. Jus' because I'm curious, and Barney here, who's a little dog who hardly ever asks for much, jus' because he's curious, that shouldn't make you feel under pressure to let us in on it. I mean if you don't want us to know – me and Barney – like, what it was that moved you to buy such a Brobdingnagian chunk of full-fat cheese when you spend a considerable amount of time worrying about your blood pressure. And me and Barney spend jus' about the same amount of time *listening* to you worrying about your blood pressure – then we wouldn't – in fact we don't – expect you to let us in on it if for some reason it's, like, a secret.'

'OK,' said Sam. 'Thanks, Geordie, Barney, nice of you to be so understanding.'

Back in his own room Geordie put on the tape of John Lennon songs that Janet had given him. He played 'Mother' again, then rewound the tape and played it again. Geordie's mother had run off with the landlord when Geordie was still a boy. After that Geordie was taken into care, eventually running away and carving out a life for himself on the streets.

After Sam had got him off the streets and life had begun to get better, Geordie had stopped thinking about his mother. Hadn't thought about her for a long time, except in dreams when it wasn't possible to choose if you thought about her or not. Because you were asleep and you didn't have any control over her. She just walked about inside your head. But then Celia and Sam and other people he knew said that he *should* think about her, that if he suppressed thoughts and emotions about her he'd get ill. Geordie didn't understand *why* he'd get ill by not thinking about his mother.

For a while now he'd thought about her once a day. Not for long, just a minute or two, sometimes less than that. Some days he only managed a second or two, and there were some particularly busy days when he didn't even manage a second. But he thought about her more than she thought about him. You could guarantee that. Geordie would've betted money on it, that she never thought about him.

And he couldn't understand it, that she was his mother and she never thought about him. If he ever had children of his own, say if Janet and him had a child, Geordie would think about that child every minute of every day for the rest of his life. He couldn't see how there would be room for any other thoughts, except thoughts of that child, to get inside his head. Maybe there'd be the odd chink of room for the odd thought about Janet or Sam or Celia or Marie or Barney. But mainly he'd think about the kid.

So maybe his mother *did* think about him. Maybe she thought about him all the time. For all anybody knew she'd finished with the landlord guy and gone back to the house they used to live in and found Geordie had gone. And now she spent all her time searching for Geordie. Tramping the highways.

Barney came over and nuzzled Geordie's hand. 'OK,' he told the dog. 'Jus' having a fantasy, innit?' When John Lennon got to the end of 'Mother', Geordie let the tape roll on.

'You know something, Barney?' he said. 'This Janet I've been telling you about. She's got two cats.' Barney sat back and cocked his head to one side, like 'cats' was a very interesting word, which, of course, it was.

'And I don't want anything to go wrong between me and Janet. So you and me are gonna have a few little chats. Janet is very keen on her cats, which are called Venus and Orchid. Well, fuck, Barney, that's the kind of names that cats have. Dogs are called more down-to-earth names, but cats are more uppity. You have to accept that.

'The thing is, if you were to take against these cats, or even if you were to take against just one of them, Orchid, say, and give it a hard time, then that would cause problems between me and Janet, and I'd be really pissed off at you.

'So what we're gonna do is, when we go out and we see a cat, instead of you leaping up and down and barking your head off, and then chasing after it like cowboys and indians, what you're gonna do is, you're gonna say, "Hello, little cat, pleased to meet you," or something like that. And get yourself used to the idea that one day, if me and Janet decide to live together, you might have two cats in the same house as you, like brothers and sisters. OK?'

Barney had put more and more weight on his front legs until they had slid away from him. His head had dropped forward on to his legs, and all that was now visible of his face was one eye. That eye returned Geordie's stare for a moment or two. Then Barney let it fall closed, probably imagining there was no Heaven.

On his way out of the flat Sam stopped him. 'Did you say Brobdingnagian?'

'What you talking about?'

'Earlier,' Sam said, 'when we were talking about the cheese. Did you say Brobdingnagian?'

'Yeah.'

'Do you know what it means?'

''Course I know what it means. You think I use words I don't even know what they mean? Do *you* know what it means?'

'The way you said it, it means big,' Sam said.

Geordie looked up at Sam and smiled. 'It means gigantic,' he said. 'Celia gave me *Gulliver's Travels*, and there's this place in there, called Brobdingnag. Land of the Giants.'

'And you remembered that?'

'Yeah.' Geordie opened the door and stepped outside.

He looked back at Sam, still smiling. 'The people in Brobdingnag, they all have full rounds of Brie in their fridges, and when anybody asks them where they got it they just play dumb.'

'Walk slow. I can't walk as fast as you.'

Geordie slowed down. 'I'm not walking fast. I'm just walking normal.'

When he'd first got to her flat he'd given Janet a third of a round of Brie. 'Sam had it in his fridge, and he can't eat it,' he explained.

'Venus'll eat some, and I love it,' she said. 'But Orchid won't touch it.' She grabbed her coat and suggested they walk into town.

Geordie didn't really mind what they did, so long as he could spend the evening with her. Have her all to himself. He didn't have to go to work until tomorrow, which meant he could follow Janet around all evening, talk to her, listen to her, look into her hazel eyes and let her lead him through her wacky life.

Geordie had played her a tape of a Presley song, 'Too Much', because he didn't understand what it meant.

'It means, like she's pretending to sigh,' Janet said.

'Why would she do that?'

'To turn him on, encourage him.'

Geordie thought about that. 'That's ridiculous,' he said. 'Wouldn't work with me. If I was with somebody and they were *pretending* to sigh, it'd put me right off.'

Janet laughed. 'I've done it with you,' she said. 'And it doesn't.'

'Doesn't what?'

'Doesn't put you off. Quite the opposite, gets you going a treat.'

'Why'd you do that?' he asked. 'I dunno if I like that,

pretending. Like you have to pretend 'cause I can't make you do it naturally.'

Janet laughed. 'Male ego,' she said.

'How's that?'

'Male ego. That's what you've got. You think the world goes round the sun just to keep you happy.'

'Round the sun?' Geordie said, real confusion spreading over his face.

'Yes, you ought to take it as a compliment. I'm pretending for your benefit. I don't have to sigh at all. I could be totally unresponsive. You wouldn't like that, would you?'

Geordie thought about that longer than he'd thought about the last one. 'Yeah,' he said eventually, a hint of a sigh in his voice.

'Yeah, what?' asked Janet. 'What does *yeah* mean?'

'Means it's a really good song,' Geordie said. 'Perceptive, innit?'

They walked alongside the beck into town, then followed the inside of the wall, ending up in a high-tech pub with terminals and speakers over every table. The joint was called Fischingers, and sold Budweiser for three times the price you could buy it anywhere else in York. And it didn't even taste better. You paid that much for it, Geordie told Janet, it made you feel like you couldn't enjoy the rest of the evening.

Then he worried about it. 'You don't think I'm tight, do you?'

'No.' Janet smiled. They had to shout to make themselves heard above the loudspeakers. 'You've just been ripped off. Wouldn't be normal if you didn't feel mad about it.'

That's true, Geordie thought. The trouble with it was that he *knew* Janet would see right through it, and even be able to explain it. That was because she wasn't only beautiful, but she was bright as well. Quick in the brains department. She would never have thought he was tight. She *expected* he would be pissed off over the price of the drinks.

Geordie was getting brighter himself. He was still having English lessons with Celia, learning poems and writing essays about them, and if you lived and worked with Sam you had to be fairly quick or he'd ride all over you. But, compared with Janet, it was obvious that she was quicker and brighter than him.

What Geordie worried about was that she would get bored by him. That she'd look around for somebody as quick as she was. If she waited, then with all the work he was doing on himself, Geordie would probably get as bright as her, and then they'd be equals. But if she couldn't wait, he'd lose her, and that'd be a real drag, because he'd only just got her. Geordie hoped it wouldn't work out like that. He hoped she'd see that he was catching up, and that if she had the patience to wait for him, it would be worth her while. He still went on thinking and pondering about things for hours after she'd said her last word on the subject.

'All this sighing you've been doing,' he said. 'I know you've explained it, but I'm still not sure I like it.' He had liked it, Janet sighing when he took her in his arms, when he kissed her. But that was when he thought she couldn't help it. Now he knew she was doing it for his benefit he felt pissed off.

Janet knitted her brows together and took his hand over the table. 'Geordie, I like you. I like you more than I've liked other boyfriends. A lot more. I shouldn't have told you about the sighing.'

'I'm glad you told me, Janet. Even if it hurts a bit, even if it gets me pissed off, I still want you to say it.'

'I sigh because you like sighers, Geordie. It's as simple as that. I like being with you.'

'I like you, too. I like you just as you are. You seem like you're almost perfect to me.'

Janet smiled at him, then looked down at the table. 'Yeah, and you seem like almost perfect to me as well.'

When they left Fischingers Geordie hesitated outside a lingerie shop.

Janet pointed to a pair of crotchless scarlet knickers. 'Margaret's got a pair of those,' she said. 'Christ, look at the price. No wonder she's always broke.'

'I like that, though,' said Geordie, indicating an underskirt in blue lace.

'What, for me?'

'Yeah, you'd look nice in it.'

Janet took his hand and walked him away from the window. 'It's overrated, Geordie. If lingerie was so wonderful, men would be wearing it.'

Sam was already in bed when Geordie got home. Either that, or he was out somewhere. But it felt like he was in bed.

Geordie couldn't remember exactly what happened later. But he'd gone out with Barney, and he'd not bothered to put a lead on him because it was so late. Barney had done a crap and then gone sniffing on up the road while Geordie collected the crap in a plastic bag. Sam and Celia had said it was best to collect it because if you didn't the little kids in the neighbourhood would get brain damage. And Sam and Celia both collected the crap themselves when they took Barney for a walk.

Then a car came round the corner with a load of louts in it. They were hanging out of the windows, and shouting at Geordie, but the guy who was driving the car was picking up speed. Out of the corner of his eye Geordie saw Barney run on to the road. And that was a strange thing to happen, because Barney had been trained not to do that.

Then everything happened quickly. Geordie watched it, knowing exactly how it was going to be. But he was powerless to stop it. The car was tearing along the road. Barney was running across the road. There was a point where they would meet. The only way to avoid that was if the car or Barney stopped.

Geordie shouted, but it didn't make any difference. Barney ran straight into the side of the speeding car. He bounced off it and screamed. Later Geordie thought that Barney must have squealed, because that's what animals did, they didn't scream. But at the time it sounded to him like Barney really screamed. Like a human.

The car didn't stop. And neither did Barney. With a series of screams he belted off along the road, the way they had come. Running along the middle of the road. Geordie called after him, but Barney wasn't at all receptive. He just kept going, and in a few seconds he was out of sight.

Geordie ran home and found Barney by the front door. The dog was shaking and whimpering, and his nose was smashed and bleeding, but he wasn't dead.

CHAPTER 7

Mama was making ice cream and Doc was laying down lines of cocaine on the bread board. Franco watched Doc add the food colouring to the lines of coke. Red, yellow, blue, bright primary colours for the little darlings.

They were in the big kitchen on the ground floor, but

Franco had left the doors open so they could hear the Three Tenors playing on the stereo.

Doc mixed the colours into the white powder and sucked up each line with an antique dispenser that Mama had found in a junk shop. Then he laid the colours on top of each other in a leaded glass bowl and stood back to get a better look.

'Do you think they'll go for that?' he asked.

Mama looked up from her own creation and smiled. 'Yes,' she said. 'They won't be able to resist it. Looks like a rainbow.'

Doc looked across the table at Franco, engaging his eyes, looking for confirmation, approval.

'Yeah,' said Franco, speaking through tight lips, the word coming out like a hiss. Doc was an artist. He knew they would all like his coloured coke, it always went down big when they had a party. But you had to tell him. He had to hear it.

Mama put her ice cream into a round baking tin and referred back to Delia Smith's *Complete Illustrated Cookery Course*. It was a new recipe, one she hadn't tried before, but Delia reckoned it was an unbeatable party dish, and in that department Mama was prepared to call her the boss.

'You want a hand?' Doc asked Mama.

'Yes, you can help me with the acid,' she said.

Doc went to the fridge and brought back a small container of acid and an eye dropper. He filled the eye dropper and asked, 'How many?'

'Ten,' she told him. She switched on the electric whisk and moved the thick white mixture around in the bowl.

'Now?' asked Doc, raising his voice above the sound of the whisk.

Mama nodded and they counted aloud together as Doc squeezed the ten drops into the ice cream.

Franco went downstairs, left them to it, his mother and his brother playing at getting ready for the party.

He stood in the bathroom and looked at the black tiled walls and floor, noticed how they reflected the light. He sniffed at the air and caught a whiff of the new Coty soap Mama had bought. There was something else there as well. Dettol? He listened to the silence and saw his own reflection in the mirror.

There were no sudden and violent movements, no cries for mercy, no blood spattered on the walls. The air was clean. The smell of death had vanished.

Franco walked through to his cellar study and rang Mr Julian's number. He counted the rings. Mr Julian usually picked up on the eighth ring, but this time it didn't get past four. And the voice was wrong.

'Mr Julian?' he said into the mouthpiece.

'Who is this?'

Franco recognized the voice. It was the old man's son. He was coming of age, would eventually take over the organization. He was difficult. His inexperience was almost tangible, like a rash of acne.

'It's Franco,' he said. 'I want to speak to your father.'

'Not available, Franco. Anything I can help you with? Father's away. I'm in charge.'

Franco said he'd ring back later, at the weekend when the old man got back. He hung up the phone. He'd sort it out himself. The young Mr Julian was only a kid. Franco wasn't going to leave it to a kid. This was man's work.

Mama answered the door and smiled at him. 'Benjamin,' she said. 'He's waiting for you.'

Ben would've hated Mama even if she called him Ben instead of Benjamin. He returned her smile and followed her downstairs to Franco's study. She ushered him inside and closed the door. Franco was sitting in his leather chair, and as usual the room was in near darkness, lit only by a dimmed spotlight on Franco's table. Ben tried to make out the expression on Franco's face, but all of his features were hidden in the gloom. All that was available was a black silhouette, and the hissing sound of Franco's breath.

Franco didn't speak. He touched a key on a handset and a TV monitor came to life in a corner of the room.

Ben turned towards it and watched pictures of himself and Gog and young Andrew. He watched Gog chasing young Andrew and stomping him, and he watched Gog fold the kid up and throw him in the back of the car. And then he watched the car drive away as the camera fixed itself on the custom number plate: FRANC O.

The screen went black and Franco switched it off. Ben didn't know what to say, but after a minute or so he thought he'd better say something.

'That was us,' he tried. 'Me and Gog, when we was getting the kid.'

Franco sighed. 'That was you being filmed when you picked up the kid,' he said. 'And you were doing it in my car.'

'I can explain that,' Ben said. 'Mama wanted to use the other car. She said we should take yours.' He pointed at the now blank television screen. 'How come you've got pictures of it? Was somebody following us?'

Franco didn't have to say anything to make you feel bad. He didn't sigh exactly, he expelled air through his tight lips, made a whistling sound, but not like music. And you knew immediately, when you heard that sound, that you weren't worth shit. That you were the lowest form of life.

Then he explained it. How the video tape had arrived. He showed Ben the blackmail note asking for five grand. And he said he wanted whoever was behind it stopped.

'The most important thing,' he said, and he used that same whistling sound all the time, so you'd know you had to listen good, 'the most important thing is to find the original of the tape. Once you've got that you can waste the guy who did it. But I've got to have the tape. Do you understand?'

'Do you understand, Gog?' Ben asked his brother. 'What we should've done was bury the kid on the moors, same as the others.'

Gog raised his eyes to his brother and nodded his head. Then he looked down again, shuffled his feet.

'You couldn't help it,' Ben continued. 'It's no good blaming yourself. Oh, sure, if you hadn't been sick we'd have gone up to the moors like usual. But you were sick, so we couldn't make the trip. Some people would've done it differently, maybe. Like some people might've stashed the kid's body under the floorboards in the gym until you was feeling better. Then we could've got it out from under the floorboards and took it up to the moors. Now you think about it, that would've been better than dumping it in the river. But it's easy to say that after the fact, with fucking hindsight. At the time you had the sweats and your head was splitting open and you couldn't see right so I thought the best thing was to dump the body and get you home to bed. And you would've done the same for me if it was the other way round and it was me that got sick. Except I don't, ever get sick, that is.'

Gog put his hand on Ben's head, but Ben shook it off. 'Gog, I'm not looking for gratitude here. What I'm trying to say is, Franco's pissed off because somebody got a photograph of his car and the kid being loaded into it. But Franco still thinks the body is safely buried up on the moors. So how much more pissed is he gonna be when he finds out the kid's body is floating about in the river?'

Gog made a sound like an explosion.

'Yeah,' said Ben. 'Precisely. He's gonna hit the roof. Except Franco doesn't hit the roof, he makes other people hit the roof. And in this case it's you and me who're gonna have the dynamite stuffed into the orifices at the top of our legs, round the back there, you know what I mean, so we get a real good lift.'

'Ugh, Gog,' said Gog.

Ben shook his head. 'I don't know what we're gonna do,' he said. 'Either we sort it out somehow, or we think of a really good excuse when Franco catches up with the news.'

CHAPTER 8

Sam and Geordie left home shortly after nine-thirty. The rain was still holding off, and St Helen's Square was bright and busy. The smell of coffee coming from Betty's got Sam by the throat and almost pulled him inside. But he followed Geordie, who was carrying his dog, up the stairs to the office.

The vet had said there was nothing he could do about Barney's nose. It was badly damaged, and was going to be sensitive for a time. Perhaps his sense of smell would be impaired, a major disadvantage for a dog. If that happened Geordie might think of having him put to sleep? Geordie shook his head, picked up his dog and walked out of the vet's surgery. Sam followed. It wasn't the vet's fault. Sam was preoccupied with the image of his own wife and daughter, taken from him by a mad driver who didn't stop. A hit-and-run driver. Probably a drunk.

Celia met them as soon as they entered the office. 'Sorry, Sam,' she said. 'There's a lady to see you.' She motioned behind her, to her own office. 'Mrs Bridge. She doesn't have an appointment, but I think you should see her.'

Sam made a face of resignation. 'Give me a couple of minutes,' he said, taking his coat off and hanging it on a peg behind the door. Geordie got Barney into his basket and sat at the desk with Sam. Celia brought Mrs Bridge over to them and sat her down in the clients' chair.

She was a small woman, black, with large doleful eyes. Early thirties, Sam guessed. She wore soft flat shoes, and her tights had gone into holes. She had a round smiling face. She wasn't smiling, but her face seemed to give that impression. There was something else about her bearing which undermined the effect of the smile. A great earnestness which travelled over the distance between her and Sam, and kept Sam from smiling himself, even superficially.

'You'll have to tell me what the problem is, Mrs Bridge. I don't know if I can help until I've heard your story.'

'It's my boy, Mr Turner,' she said. 'Somebody's killed him.' Her voice was surprising. There was a high-pitched quality to it that Sam guessed was not usually there. The woman was in a state of shock. She continued, 'Andrew was thirteen last month.' She looked over at Geordie momentarily, then back to Sam. 'He was supposed to have a friend over here, in York. We live in Leeds, you see, in Chapeltown. Some boy from school, but I think it was a lie. Anyway, he was coming over here twice, three times a week at first. Then he disappeared altogether.

'We went to the police in Leeds, but they didn't seem as if they wanted to help. He was only a child, but still they didn't take it seriously. After he'd been gone for six weeks, yesterday . . .' She faltered, brought her right hand up to her hairline and rubbed it lightly. 'No, it was the day before yesterday, although it seems a long time ago. Such a long time. Tuesday. I got a telephone call from him, four o' clock in the afternoon. "Mother," he said, just like that, "Mother, come and get me." He told me he was in Micklegate, just near the Bar, and he'd wait there for me. He didn't have enough money for the phone, and we were cut off.

'I got a taxi and came straight over to York. The driver knew where Micklegate was, and we went straight there. He let me out at the Bar, and I stood there for an hour. I walked round the area for another two hours after that. But there was no sign of Andrew. I went to the police in York, but they were even less helpful than Leeds. They discriminate against the colour of our skin. I'm sorry if you don't agree with that, Mr Turner, but it is the truth, nevertheless. In the end I went back home on the train.'

Mrs Bridge stopped speaking. She covered her face with her hands and hung her head for perhaps a minute. Then she felt in the pocket of her coat and brought out a handkerchief to wipe the tears away from her face.

Geordie got up from the desk and walked quietly over to Celia's room. He returned a moment later with Celia in tow. Celia put her arms round the woman and offered to make her a cup of tea. Mrs Bridge said she would love a cup of tea. 'You'll have to bear with me,' she said to them all. 'I've been up all night. And I've seen the body of my boy.' Then she hung her head again and let her arms dangle loosely by her sides.

Celia disappeared to make the tea, and after another minute or two Mrs Bridge had composed herself enough to continue with her story.

'A policeman came to the house last night,' she said. 'A policeman and a woman, and they told me they'd found a body in York and they thought it might be Andrew. They brought me over to York and showed me my boy.

'They'd found him in the river, in some kind of lock in the middle of the town. What the water had done to him, I could hardly recognize him myself. But it is him.

'I've been in the police station all night long. Now they want to know everything about him. If they'd wanted to know half of that before, maybe Andrew would still be alive.'

Sam leant forward on his desk and took advantage of the woman's pause. 'Were the police sure he was murdered?' he asked. 'Was there anything to indicate that?'

The woman looked at him silently for some time, before she said, 'Mr Turner, when they fished my boy out of the river he didn't have his penis.'

'I'll do what I can,' Sam told her. 'I can't promise anything. The police are the ones best placed in a case like this.'

'I don't trust them,' she said. 'If they'd listened to me in the first place, Andrew would still be alive.'

'Still,' Sam said, 'they have the resources.' He held eye contact with Mrs Bridge, and she showed him a brave face. 'What we can do is ask around. Try to find out where he's been during the last weeks. What he's been doing. If we can get that far, there's at least a chance we'll discover what happened to him. But don't hold your breath. We might get nowhere.'

He walked down the stairs with her, to the door on to St Helen's Square. The weather had stopped being bloody and turned bloody vicious. Sam opened the door and they stepped back while a torrent of rain poured into the building.

'You can wait a while if you like,' he said. 'Celia'll make another drink.'

She shook her head and reached for his hand. 'I'll wait to hear from you,' she said. And she stepped out into the downpour. Sam stood and watched for a moment until she turned the corner.

Then there was just the rain. It was as if God was throwing builder's skips of water directly at the building.

CHAPTER 9

Gog had done good. After they'd blown away the CCTV operators they didn't have a lot of time. Ben had gone to the address of the one called Geoff, and Gog had gone to the other one's house. The one called Cal.

A video tape, that's what they were looking for.

Gog had gone in through the front door. He could have gone in the back, through a window. That would have meant breaking the window and then finding something to climb on – lots of messing around. And Ben had said they didn't have much time. The front door was a piece of piss, even rattled before he opened it. Gog gave it two kicks with his good foot and it caved in. There was another flat next door, but nobody came out of there to investigate. So Gog had the whole building to himself.

He didn't find any video tapes though.

The guy had a television, but that box they have under the television, the thing with a slot for the video tapes – he didn't have one of those. He had a stereo system, with tons of those old records, like Ben used to have, called albums, before they got CDs. Gog used to like those album things. Liked them better than CDs because you could look at the pictures on them without screwing your eyes up. But Ben had never let him take the records out of the sleeves, in case he scratched them. Whereas, when Ben'd got the CDs he let Gog do what he liked with them. That was because Gog didn't want to do anything with the CDs, they were too small to be interesting.

There was a load of girlie magazines. The ones with double pages in the centre you could fold out and they had mucky women on. Women you could do anything you liked with, like animals. But Gog preferred animals.

He spent some time with the magazines but never forgot what he was there for. Remembered that he didn't have all the time in the world.

Under the sink was a collection of plastic carriers. Gog found the telephone on a sideboard, and spent some time going through the drawers in the sideboard looking for an address book, but couldn't find one. He looked on the mantelpiece and even through some more drawers he found in the kitchen. But the address book wasn't there. It would have been easy to panic and break something, but Gog didn't do that. He kept looking.

When he found the address book he laughed out loud, because it was under the telephone. Gog thought that was funny. Because that's where he'd started, with the telephone. He'd known all along that it would be somewhere near the telephone, that's why he'd found the telephone first, before starting to look for the address book. But what he'd done, he hadn't looked closely enough at the telephone. The guy had put the address book so close to the telephone that Gog had missed it.

Gog put the address book in the plastic carrier and thought about it some more. If he ever wanted to hide something he'd put it right next to where it should be. That way it made it really hard to find it.

Only thing was, with what Gog wanted to hide he couldn't think what to put it next to or under. He patted his pocket, his handkerchief pocket. Because that's where the kid's prick and balls were. Wrapped up in Gog's hanky. In Gog's pocket. He'd looked for somewhere safer to put them at home, but couldn't think of anywhere that Ben wouldn't find them. Perhaps he should put them under the telephone. Or even better, he smiled to himself, he could get a screwdriver and open up the telephone when Ben wasn't at home, and then he could put the kid's prick and balls inside the telephone and screw it back up again. That way nobody would find them ever.

If the guy whose flat this was, who they'd just blown away, the one called Cal – if he'd put his address book *inside* the telephone with a screwdriver, Gog would never have found it. Not in a hundred years. Or even longer. Except if he hadn't found it he might have got really mad and smashed the place up and thrown the telephone at the wall, and broken it, and then the address book would have fallen out, and he would have found it. And that wouldn't have taken a hundred years. Nothing like it. So was it safe to put the kid's prick and balls inside the telephone?

Yes, because Ben didn't even know about the kid's prick and balls being in existence. And Ben never got mad and threw things around, except maybe in Chinese restaurants. So he wouldn't be throwing his own telephone around, in his own house, what he paid for every month and complained about the bill. He'd never do that. 'Cause if he did do that, who'd have to find the readies to buy a new phone? Ben would. Ben would think about things like that. At the end of the day he'd decide not to throw the phone at the wall. It'd be crazy to do that.

But what if, when he picked the phone up to throw it at the wall, before he got round to deciding not to throw the phone at the wall – what if when he pulled the phone back to throw it, he heard the kid's prick and balls rattling around inside? Then he'd get a screwdriver out and open up the phone and the kid's prick and balls'd fall out, and he'd've found them.

So how d'you stop that happening? Easy-fucking-peasy. You get a piece of Blu-tack and you stick the kid's prick and balls to the bottom of the inside of the phone with it. That way when Ben picks the phone up to throw it he doesn't get a rattle, and the thought of getting a screwdriver never enters his head. Brilliant. And in any case Ben hardly ever used the phone these days, since he'd got the mobile.

Bloody brilliant. People would look at Gog when he walked down the street, and they would never know how brilliant he was. They'd probably think he was just a body builder. All brawn and no brain. That was because they couldn't see all this stuff going on inside his brain box.

Gog did it again and felt the warm spunk spill on to his belly and roll down his thighs on to the sheets. Ben still wasn't back from his search of the other guy's house. The one called Geoff. Gog didn't move. He was lying in an ocean of semen, in his own bed. He had done good. He hadn't found the video tape, but he'd done everything else good.

He hadn't been seen breaking into the flat, he hadn't been seen leaving it. He'd found the guy's address book and brought it home with him. He'd had a brainwave about where to hide the kid's prick and balls, and he'd come home and found a screwdriver and some Blu-tack and done the business.

And those weren't even the best things that he'd done today.

He'd done some wanking. But he could do that any day.

No, the best thing he'd done was with Ben when they'd blown those two tossers away. Gog just loved it the way they got that look on their faces, between when you fingered the trigger and they actually died. Like their eyes and their eyebrows and their mouths and their whole faces turned into a question mark. And the question was always the same, what Ben called Gogspeak. Like they'd be saying, *Uh, uhn, agh, fuck, God, oh no*. Something like that. Gogspeak, 'cause that's the way it sounded when Gog spoke. It didn't sound like that to Gog, but it sounded like that to other people, and that's what freaked them out. Freaked them out more than the size of him, all his muscles.

Gogspeak. It was a new word. Ben had invented it. And it was a word like Christian or Freudian, 'cause it had the guy's name in it, and there was another one called after the guy who'd invented electricity. Gog couldn't remember what he was called. And there was loads of drugs that had the names of the guys who'd invented them. Like steroids was probably invented by a guy called Stero. Must've been foreign.

So, anyway, Gogspeak probably meant that Gog would be famous one day. Once the word got around a bit, and then someone would come along and put it in the dictionary.

They'd gone in as Robert De Niro and Joe Pesci. Ben had been De Niro, as usual, and Gog had been Pesci. Neither De Niro nor Pesci were really developed enough. They weren't real monsters, they were little guys. But they were true gangstas.

There had been a time when Gog had real trouble with being Pesci. Right up until the time Pesci was in the video where he smashed people up with the telephone. That made Gog laugh. That look Pesci got in his eyes when he was mad at somebody, and then he'd have the phone in his hand and he'd just lay into the guy, slap him across the head with it. Then when the guy was down he'd kick him, carry on kicking until the guy was asleep. Brilliant. Ben had bought the video in the end, so Gog could watch it and have a good laugh when Pesci got started on people.

Anyway, they'd gone into the control room and knocked the two guys around. Ben made them both kneel on the floor and put their hands behind their heads. The one called Cal had shit his pants, and Ben had said that would be the last time he ever shit in his pants if he didn't hand over the video tape.

The guy had stuttered and started crying, so Ben shot him in the head.

The other one, the one called Geoff, caught some of Cal's blood as it came out of his head. Most of it went on the wall, but a slick of it laid itself along the side of Geoff's face, and some of it went on the collar of his shirt. So then he started gagging, and ended up being sick on the floor, and Ben said if he did that any more he'd rub the guy's nose in it.

'Gimme the tape,' Ben said.

The guy looked up at him. He looked over at Gog, and he had a kind of pleading look on his face, like he didn't believe this was real. 'I don't have it,' he said.

'If I ask you again,' Ben said, 'I'll fucking kill you.' He sounded like De Niro. He could do the voice really good. The whole thing was like being on a video. Like they were the mob. Made guys. From the five families.

'It's not here,' Geoff said. 'Cal took it home with him. Must be in his flat.'

Ben did a De Niro nod over to Gog. Geoff didn't even see it happen. So Gog took a step forward and grabbed Geoff by the hair, yanking his head back. Then he stuck the barrel of the gun in Geoff's mouth, broke some of the front teeth getting it in. Shoved it in as far as it would go.

Ben came close to the guy's face and said, 'You sure you don't wanna change your statement, sir?'

Geoff said something. And when he said it Ben and Gog looked at each other, and both of them laughed, because it was pure Gogspeak. They didn't say anything else. Gog shot the guy dead. His ass was grass.

They had a quick look round the control room, made sure the tape wasn't there. But they knew that Cal and Geoff wouldn't have told them any lies. Then they split, and Ben went over to Geoff's place to do a search, while Gog did the search at Cal's flat.

And that was the best thing Gog had done today, but there was still something else he'd done that was nearly as good. And even Ben didn't know about that yet. But he would as soon as he got home.

Shouldn't have moved. Once you moved the warm wet sheets turned to cold wet sheets. Then you had to get out of bed and go in the shower. After that you had to take the sheets off the bed and take them to the washing bag and put them in there. Then you had to get clean sheets from the cupboard and make the bed up like you hadn't been in there. But you had to do all that anyway, before Ben got home.

In the shower Gog looked at his prick. It was definitely getting smaller. If it carried on getting smaller he'd tell Ben about it. And Ben would arrange for Doc Squires to have a look at it, give Gog something to make it grow big again.

The kid's prick and balls were getting smaller as well. Gog had noticed it when he Blu-tacked them inside the telephone. Not that they had ever been big. But they were definitely shrivelling up quickly. Why he'd taken them was because he didn't want to waste them. They were testicles, and anabolic steroids were made out of testicles. Ben had explained all that to him one night. How in history they'd taken testicles from prisoners and injected them into other prisoners. And that's why the steroids made your muscles grow.

When Gog cut the prick and balls off the dead kid, he'd thought that somehow he'd be able to inject them into himself. But he hadn't thought about how you would inject a prick and balls into yourself. There must be some way you chopped them up and turned them into liquid. Also you had to get them into a syringe, and it had to be so fine that they'd go through that thin needle at the end of the syringe. The bit that you stuck in your arm.

Gog didn't know how to do that. That's why he'd Blu-tacked the prick and balls inside the telephone, so they would be safe until he'd found out how to inject them. He thought maybe he could ask Doc Squires. Go to the house where the doctor lived with Franco and Franco's mother. Except the problem with that would be getting past Mama without telling her what he wanted. Because Mama was a dragon, and she talked posh, and she looked at you like school teachers used to look at you when you were still in short trousers. Gog didn't know how he'd get past her, but once he'd managed it, it would be simple with the doctor. No need to give anything away, he could tell the doctor he was asking for a friend. Like he had this friend who didn't want to get a testicle into a syringe, but this friend wondered how people who did want to get a testicle into a syringe would actually go about it.

Yeah, that would do the trick. Gog would have to keep a straight face when he asked Doc Squires, but he could do that. Just like Joe Pesci.

*

'Did you find the tape?' Ben asked as soon as he came through the door.

Gog smiled and shook his head.

'The bastards,' said Ben. He pulled his sweatshirt off and threw it on the floor. 'They hid it somewhere else. What about an address book?'

'Ugh,' said Gog, and he held it up so Ben could see he'd done good.

'It was the first one, the one called Cal,' Ben said. 'I'd bet my life on it. The bastard covered his back. Now we have to find out what he did with the tape.'

Gog told Ben he'd done good.

'Yeah, you got the address book,' said Ben. 'That's good, Gog. We wouldn't be able to manage without that.'

But Gog shook his head and took Ben by the hand. The address book was only one way he'd done good. He wanted to show Ben the real way he'd done good. Much better than the address book.

He took Ben upstairs to their bedroom and sat him down on the side of his bed. Then Gog opened the drawer where they kept their shirts and took out the cardboard box he'd put in there when he came home from the search.

'What is it, Gog?' Ben said. 'What've you got there?'

Gog shook his head and waved his finger. Patience, Ben. You have to be patient. Their father had always said that: 'Patience is its own reward.'

Gog sat opposite Ben on his own bed and placed the cardboard box on his knee. He opened the lid and took out a bag. He took a knife from the bedside table and sliced open the bag. Then he passed it over to Ben.

Ben took the bag and looked at it, looked back at Gog and then brought it slowly to his nose. He sniffed at it. There was a smell there, so it wasn't Semtex. A certain recognition came into his eyes. He shook some of the contents of the bag into his open palm. White. Crystalline. He looked over at the box on Gog's knee and saw that there were a lot more bags of the same.

'Was this at the flat?' he asked. 'The guy's flat?'

Gog nodded. He told Ben he'd done good. He didn't ask Ben if he'd done good. He told him. Gog knew he'd done good.

'It's no good by itself,' Ben said. 'Was there anything else? Any kit with it?'

Gog looked down into the cardboard box again, and shook his head slowly from side to side. But he was playing with Ben now. He put his hand inside the box again and came up with several small electronic devices. He opened his hand to let Ben see.

'Wonderful,' said Ben. 'Detonators. Anything else?'

Gog passed the box over to his brother. There was everything in there that anyone would ever need. Cords. Blasting caps. Even a quantity of charcoal powder. Looked like the guy, Cal, whatever his name was, had worked in bomb disposal at some time. Either that or he was a part-time terrorist.

Ben sniffed again at the bag that Gog had handed him. 'The real thing,' he smiled. 'Ammonium nitrate. This's what they used in the Oklahoma City bomb. Robert De Niro would make a big bang with this stuff.'

CHAPTER 10

Jeanie wondered if she'd come to the right office when she saw the old lady. The old girl could still walk, but she was a real antique. Jeanie had psyched herself up to meet a broad out of an old movie. Something with peroxide hair and high stiletto heels, stockings with seams at the back. Well, she was right about the stockings with the seams at the back, but they weren't exactly wrapped around the kind of legs she'd envisioned. The old lady looked like she might have been a school ma'am in the nineteenth century, and then discovered lipstick and jewellery in the twentieth. Now she was trying to marry both parts of her life together. All in all she represented Jeanie's worst nightmare.

The old lady came forward and extended her hand. She raised a pair of bushy white eyebrows. 'Hello,' she said, and she used the kind of educated voice that was originally designed to keep the workers in their place. 'I'm Celia Allison, Mr Turner's secretary. Can I help you?'

'Jeanie Scott. I don't have an appointment. I just came on spec.' Jeanie tried to ignore Celia's accent, told herself she shouldn't be intimidated. But she could hear the Scots accent in her own voice, and that was something that only happened when she was nervous.

'He's not here at the moment,' Celia said. And there was a twinkle in her eye. Maybe she wasn't as formidable as her accent suggested. Some people couldn't help how they looked, how they sounded. 'I expect he'll be in soon, within the next ten minutes or so. I'm sure he'll see you, if you don't mind waiting.' She pointed to a chair. 'I was going to make some coffee. Can I tempt you?'

'Please,' croaked Jeanie, realizing that her throat had dried up. She sat in the chair and looked round the office while Celia set about rattling cups and saucers.

It must be Sam Turner's desk she was sitting in front of. Old weathered oak with three or four spots where someone had taken a knife to it and gouged out chunks of wood. A solid desk. He had a swivel chair under the window, and the window itself had been stencilled so that the name of the business showed itself to the square outside. It said:

SAM TURNER – INVESTIGATIONS, or it would if you were reading it from outside. From where she was sitting Jeanie only had a mirror image of it.

Celia brought the coffee over and placed it on the desk. Next to it was a small plate with tiny triangular sandwiches with the crusts cut off, rather like Jeanie used to get at birthday parties when she was a girl back in Glasgow. 'Brie,' Celia explained. 'We have rather a lot of it at the moment. I thought you might be feeling hungry.' She walked back to the other side of the office and then returned with her own coffee and sat down next to Jeanie.

'I never ask clients about their problems,' she said. 'Usually it's personal. But I play a little game with people. Well, with myself really.' She took a tiny sip from her cup. 'When I meet someone new I try to guess what they do for a living. You, for instance, I get the feeling that you work with children, small children. Something to do with a kindergarten, perhaps?'

'I'm a nurse,' Jeanie told her.

Celia looked disappointed. Then brightened. 'A children's nurse?'

Jeanie shook her head. 'General. I work privately. For an agency. Old people, mainly. Invalids.'

'Oh dear,' said Celia. 'Dead wrong, then?' She took another sip from her cup. 'It's a good job I'm not the detective.' She raised those white eyebrows again. Twinkled her eyes. 'Help yourself to the Brie, dear.'

Jeanie felt a pang of guilt. 'But I've got a daughter,' she said. 'Karen. She's eleven. Maybe that's what you felt?'

'Could be,' Celia said enigmatically. 'I'd have thought younger than that. But maybe Karen's what I picked up.'

There were footsteps on the stairs, and both women turned towards the door.

Jeanie's first impression of Sam Turner when he came

through the door was that he was a hunk. But she had to start revising that impression almost immediately. There was something hunky about him. But there were also a few flaws.

He took everything in at a glance, and Celia was on her feet and introducing them. 'Sam Turner, Jeanie Scott. Jeanie's a nurse,' she added, as though that might be important. Then she walked away, through a door that must have led to an adjoining office, and left Jeanie with the detective.

He walked round his desk and sat in the swivel chair, motioned to Jeanie to sit down again in the chair on her side of the desk. 'I see Celia's been feeding you,' he said, looking at the triangular sandwiches. His voice, the timbre of his voice, went straight to a place somewhere below her belt.

Jeanie's eyes flicked to the sandwiches and back to Sam Turner's face. She tried to date him, thought quickly he was over fifty, then revised it and thought he was maybe in his late forties. He smiled at her hesitation. Was the smile about her hesitation? Or was it the smile guys gave you when they wanted you to know they liked what they saw?

Jeanie breathed in through her nose, made her back rigid, and said, 'I used to be married to Cal Pointer, one of the camera operators who was killed yesterday.'

The smile on the detective's face evaporated. 'I'm sorry,' he said. 'I read about it in this morning's paper. You say you *used* to be married to him.'

Jeanie nodded. 'That's not why I'm here,' she said. 'Not directly, anyway. My house was broken into last night. I took Karen to her grandmother's after we heard about Cal. I didn't want to be by myself. We stayed there the night, and when I got back this morning, someone'd been in the house.'

'You think the two things are connected?'

'Yes,' Jeanie said. 'I wouldn't have thought that, but there was nothing taken. It was like someone had been looking for something. But I haven't found anything missing. I can only think they were looking for something of Cal's. But I don't have anything of his. We haven't lived together for years.'

'You've informed the police? What did they say?'

'They told us about Cal. About the shooting. And then I told them about the break-in this morning, and they came round. But when they saw the place – it was a real mess – they didn't think it was anything to do with the shooting. They said it looked like kids had done it. They looked for fingerprints, white powder all over the place. But they were convinced it was a coincidence.'

'And you're not convinced?'

'I'm worried they'll come back. Whoever did it. If it was the same people who killed Cal and Geoff . . .' Her voice tailed off. 'I mean, what'll happen if I'm in the house on my own, or just me and Karen?'

'There are a couple of things you could consider,' Sam Turner said. 'We can put round-the-clock surveillance on the house, which might put your mind at rest, but would cost you a small fortune. Or you could consider moving in with Karen's grandmother – is that your mother, or Cal's?'

'Cal's mother,' said Jeanie. 'I couldn't move in with her. I mean, it was all right for one night, but . . .'

'But?' Sam prompted.

Jeanie looked over the desk at him. 'Am I being hysterical?'

The detective shrugged. 'I don't know you,' he said. 'You might be overreacting. But that's not surprising in the circumstances.'

Jeanie felt a smile playing around her lips. She let it

come. 'I actually feel better for talking,' she said. 'I was really tense before I got here, but talking to you, and Celia – I don't know, the sandwiches and everything – it doesn't seem too bad now.'

'I've been thinking of changing the sign on the window,' Sam said. 'Cross out detective and put in psychotherapist.'

Jeanie shook her head. 'I still need a detective,' she said. 'Your round-the-clock surveillance sounds excessive, but could you see if there's a connection between the break-in and Cal getting killed? The police have already given up on that, but I'd like to be sure.'

He asked her to sign a form saying she agreed to his terms, and Jeanie signed without reading it. He spent a few minutes telling her what she'd agreed to, what she'd signed her name to, but by the time she got outside and stood in St Helen's Square she'd forgotten it all.

She hadn't stayed at Cal's mother's house last night. So why had she told him she did? Because she'd left Karen at Cal's mother's and gone over to stay the night with Michael Caffrey, her Irish boyfriend. Jeanie shook her head. She hadn't told the detective about Michael because she'd wanted the detective to think she was alone. Not involved with a man. She was hoping that she and the detective would get together.

But why? Michael Caffrey was all she really needed, all she really wanted. True, Sam Turner looked like an interesting man, and in other circumstances – and were he to ask – Jeanie couldn't imagine herself saying no. But these weren't different circumstances, and Sam Turner hadn't asked her. The only thing he'd asked her was to sign his form. And she'd done that.

She wondered if Sam was married. Well, most of them were, weren't they? Michael, her Irish boyfriend, wasn't, he was single. But this Sam Turner, he'd definitely been married. He was branded. If he was still married now, she couldn't say with absolute certainty. If he was, that would be the end of it. Some of Jeanie's friends thought if a woman couldn't keep her man satisfied then she deserved to lose him. But Jeanie didn't think like that. You didn't take another woman's man. Even if he was half dead. Sam Turner didn't look like he was half dead. He looked very much alive. But maybe it wasn't to be. Perhaps nothing would happen.

Still, there'd been some magnetism there. In his voice, in his eyes. The way he'd been with her. She could make do with that. The little things in life, that was what was important.

She was like the woman from Scottish Widows. Mother-of-pearl drops at her ears, slightly hollow cheeks, but wide eyes and full lips. Sam extended his hand to the nurse when she left. 'I'll be in touch,' he said. 'Soon as I've had time to look around.' Her hand was warm. She had long thin fingers. She turned and shook hands with Celia.

Jeanie Scott smiled, two separate smiles, one for Celia and then another one for Sam. Sam would have bet money on the smile bestowed on him being warmer and slightly longer than the smile given to Celia. The difference between the two smiles was more connected to quality than to quantity. You had to be a connoisseur, but given that, you'd have spotted the difference, no trouble.

Sam found himself hanging on her every word, internalizing her accent, and more than once during their interview he had to stop himself emulating it. Each time he spoke there was a danger of his words coming out in a parody of a Glasgow accent. He smiled instead, with his mouth open, made a kind of strangled sound. She's a real handsome lassie, he thought. She wasn't yet forty, although this was the year it could happen. A good sign, because Sam didn't have the energy for someone who couldn't remember the Beatles. He'd tried it from time to time, and always ended the evening with a rictus smile.

Marie took the wheel of the Volvo, saying it was better if she drove. She didn't elaborate but Sam knew what she meant. That if she drove she'd eat less. She produced a large bag of dry-roasted peanuts which she ripped open and placed on her knee. 'I'm on a diet,' she said. She drove out of town.

'It was kind of a shock seeing you like that,' he said. 'With the apple corer.'

Marie shook her head. 'For me too, Sam. It's the first time I've been caught.'

He left it a few moments, trying to find the right space, the right way to formulate the questions. 'How long?' he asked.

'I used to cut myself before I met Gus,' she said. 'But while we lived together I didn't do it at all. I thought I'd never do it again, that it was something connected to being young. I never spoke to Gus about it, or to anybody. It was a kind of secret shame, something I'd had to go through when I was young. I wasn't even tempted when Gus was alive, didn't think about it at all. But then it started up again after he got killed. A couple of months after the funeral was the first time.'

'How often?'

'The cutting? When you caught me, that was the first time for about nine weeks. But the bulimia started before that, and that happens more often. I get so disgusted with myself over bingeing and throwing up, then I start the cutting. That night, I'd bought the Brie, oh, and a lot of other stuff you didn't find, chocolate, supermarket cakes. I hadn't actually eaten any of it. I'd been holding out, and somehow I thought if I cut myself I wouldn't start to eat. I've been seeing a therapist. She thinks we're getting it under control.' She reached into the bag for another handful of dry roast, which she fed into her mouth in three goes. She chewed for a moment. 'I've always been a good eater, though,' she said.

Sam made a sound like a laugh. 'D'you think you're getting it under control?'

She nodded. 'Yes, I do. I want it to stop, Sam. It makes me feel like shit, that I do that to myself. I'll be sitting at home, maybe watching the box, not really worrying about anything, or thinking about anything, and I'll start pulling those little hairs on the back of my arms, pulling them out. And it'll just progress from there. I know it's crazy while I'm doing it. I hate myself.'

'But you can't stop doing it? Can't you say to yourself, look, this makes me feel like shit, and I'm not going to do it any more?'

'I *can* say that,' she said. 'I *do* say that. But then suddenly I'm doing it, and I don't know why.'

Sam understood that. He didn't understand it as a man, as a rational human being, as a responsible member of society. He understood it as an alcoholic. He told her so. 'I understand that. I have some kind of feeling for what you're going through.'

She glanced across at him. 'I thought you would. Sometimes I've thought of coming to you. Of pouring it all out. I've fantasized about that. But I could never do it when it came to the point. It had to be a secret.'

'How does the therapist help?' Sam asked. 'Is it all right to ask these questions? If I'm out of line just say so.'

'We've been working on childhood abuse,' she said. 'On the relationships I had with my parents when I was young.

My father interfered with me, and my mother didn't keep me safe.'

Sam let a stream of air leave his lungs. The word she used, 'interfered', disturbed him. It was one of those diplomatic words, designed to screen one from the real horror of its meaning. He didn't know if it was meant to screen him or her. Probably both. There was a period of silence and he didn't know how to fill it. 'I'm sorry, Marie,' he said eventually.

She had an ironic smile around her mouth. 'I don't want "sorry", Sam,' she said. 'I want to understand it, to grow beyond it.'

'I didn't mean . . .'

'I know what you meant. It's all right. If you get the wrong words, that's fine. I know you're not judging me. It feels OK. I'm glad you know about it.'

There was a sense of frailness, now, about Marie. He'd noticed it ever since that night. She was a physically large woman, and she used that physicality to ward off the world, hiding behind the bulk of her body. But there was something fractured about her, a fractured nobility. She was struggling to overcome whatever her father's 'interference' had done to her. Desperately trying to shake off the shackles of the past.

She glanced over at him, and as if he'd asked her to, she pulled into the side of the road and reached out for him. Sam responded, wrapping his arms around her huge frame, waiting for the shudder that would tell him she had let something go. But it never came. After a while she released him and sat upright in the driving seat. 'Thanks,' she said. 'I needed that.' She dabbed at her eye, but there was no tear, just a froth of emotion. 'A girl needs friends from time to time. I'm glad you're one of them.' She felt in her pocket and came out with a bar of chocolate. She broke it in half and offered some to Sam.

'No thanks,' he said. 'Thought you were dieting?'

Through the chocolate she said, 'I diet on anything I can lay my hands on.'

She started up the Volvo and pulled out into the road again. After a while he asked, 'What about work?'

'Do you need me?'

'It seems to be getting busy at the moment.' He told her about the boy the police had fished out of the river, and about Jeanie Scott.

'Andrew Bridge,' she said. 'The boy. He isn't the first one.'

'To be found in the river? No. He's the third over the last two years. The third boy, that is. There was a young girl, as well.'

'Beaten to death?'

'Some, yes. But he'd also been stabbed in the head. A knife pushed into his left ear and right on through his head.'

'I didn't realize,' she said. 'I'd read about the killings in the paper, but I didn't imagine we'd be involved with them.'

'Seems like everything comes at once.'

'I need to be needed,' she said. 'If it's busy, I think I should be there. Do you need me?'

'Do cows eat grass? If you change your mind, if it gets too heavy for you, I'll understand,' he said. 'But it feels good to know you'll be around.'

Marie pulled up outside Sam's house and they sat together in the front of the car. 'You can keep the car, if you like,' Sam said.

'What about you? Getting to work in the morning?'

'We can walk,' he said. 'Or Geordie can walk, and I'll take the bike.' He patted his stomach. 'Need the exercise.'

'I'll keep it, then.'

Sam felt around under the passenger seat and came up with a newspaper. 'Haven't read the stars yet,' he said.

'Go on then,' said Marie, 'put us out of our misery. What does it say?' She flicked on the overhead light.

'Listen to this,' he said. 'It says, "This is not just the best part of the week for you. It is as if all the positive aspects of your chart have come into their own at the same time, and what lies immediately ahead is possibly the best time of your life." '

'Is that me?' asked Marie, chewing up another mouthful of chocolate.

'No, that's me,' said Sam. 'I haven't got to you yet. What do you think it means?'

'The best time of your life? Must have something to do with Jeanie Scott, the merry widow.'

'You sound as if you know her.'

'I do, slightly,' Marie said. 'She used to work at the District when I was there. Her husband fell off something. That's her first husband. Can't remember what it was now, maybe a train. What does it say for Virgo?'

Sam mused with a smile on his face. He folded the newspaper and held it to his chest. 'The best time of my life,' he said. 'Hell, Marie, I really didn't expect that to come hobbling along today. I expected to live out these pre-Alzheimer years in quiet and solitude.' He looked out of the car window and tried to recall the vision of Jeanie Scott walking away across St Helen's Square. 'Is she, er, does she have a boyfriend?' he asked. 'Anything like that?'

'Several since she got rid of her husband,' said Marie. 'They don't seem to last very long. Last thing I heard she was seeing an Irishman. Still is, as far as I know. What does it say for Virgo?'

'Doesn't sound very serious, then,' Sam said. 'It's not as if she's engaged or anything, or contemplating moving in with someone.'

'Tread a little carefully, Sam. The word is she breaks hearts.'

He turned and looked over at Marie. 'Hell, I was only wondering,' he said. 'Not going to do anything about it. Just exercising my powers of fantasy.'

'Can we cut to the chase here, Sam?' said Marie. 'I've got to get to bed sometime tonight. Tell me what it says in my stars. Am I gonna lose any weight?'

'Jeanie Scott speaking,' she said. Sam couldn't remember if he'd heard the real woman from Scottish Widows speak, but if she did speak, she'd speak just like that.

'Sam Turner,' he said into the mouthpiece. 'Remember me?'

'Yes,' said Jeanie Scott. 'The detective. How can I help you?'

'What I've got,' he said, 'is a couple of tickets to see Sweet Willy Johnson, and I wondered if you'd like to come along.'

'Sounds like a singer,' said Jeanie. 'But not one I've heard of. What is it, blues?'

'Yeah,' said Sam. 'Are you tempted?' He pushed the receiver closer to his ear, eager to catch every nuance in her voice. Trying to imagine her face while he listened to her.

'I'm tempted,' she said. 'But I'd have to arrange the time off. When is it?'

'Tomorrow,' he told her. 'Is that too soon? Only, if it's

too soon, maybe we could do something else, another night.'

'Hold on,' she said. 'This's no way to chat up a woman, Mr Turner. Didn't your mother tell you not to appear too keen? At least at first. You can frighten them away like that.'

'I'm not that keen,' Sam said. 'I've been putting this phone call off all day.'

'Don't I know it,' she said. 'I thought you'd never get round to it.' The line went quiet for a moment, then she said, 'You like the blues?'

'I need them from time to time.'

'You *need* them. What, like food?' There was a twinkle of humour in every word she spoke. Even when it wasn't funny, she pumped it for anything that might be lurking below the surface.

'Yeah,' Sam said. 'I don't get them often, but when their time comes round I get them real bad.'

'The blues?'

'The blues,' he told her. 'Them real, low down, my woman done left me, and it don't matter how long the sun bin shining, mean old private eye blues. How 'bout you?'

'I get them: I'll scream if I empty another bedpan blues. I've got them now.' She laughed. 'You think if I come out with you you'll leave those blues behind?'

He did a long low sigh through the wires. 'No. I'm the original man of constant sorrow. I spread gloom around.'

'You talked me into it a minute ago, now you're talking me out of it. Say you'll pick me up.'

'Where do you live?'

'Highway 51 goes right past my door.'

Sam reached for the wall above the telephone, make sure he wasn't dreaming all this. 'You ever think of getting married again?' he asked.

She laughed. 'There's no advantage in marriage. Not for a woman. Before he marries you a man will lie awake all night thinking about something you've said; after the wedding he'll fall asleep before you've finished saying it.'

'I'm not like that,' Sam said. 'I'm the kind of guy, sticks rigidly to the traditional western custom of one wife and hardly any mistresses.'

'Sounds as though we've got a lot to work out.'

'Something to look forward to,' he said. 'I'm not gonna say anything else in case you start to evaporate. Sweet Willy sounds like he might do us both a power of good. If I don't hear from you I'll pick you up around seven-thirty.' He listened to the click come down the line as she replaced the receiver, then he did the same. He walked over to his tape deck and looked at the tapes on the shelf. But he didn't see any of them. It was spring and the world was full of beautiful women.

CHAPTER 11

Janet was beginning to get a life. She'd always known that she would. That one day it would start coming together. That it was feasible. No, that wasn't true. She'd always hoped it would come together, but there had been times, time after time in fact, when she'd despaired of it ever happening. Within the recent past, even, before Geordie had saved her from him, she had been in fear of her life from Norman, her last boyfriend.

But that was all behind her now.

She was beginning to get a life.

She had two cats and two pot plants in the kitchen and two neighbours upstairs, and she had Geordie as well.

Geordie also had two pot plants in his room, but they weren't like Janet's. Janet's pot plants were chatty and perky. Geordie's looked like no one had talked to them ever.

She'd been nutty for a good long time now. For nearly as long as she could remember. But when she was with Geordie she didn't feel as nutty as the other times. All women were nutty. They had to be. It was the only way they could survive in the world. When they were born they had to put up with mothers and fathers, and if they were really unlucky they had to contend with brothers as well. And as children, as well as later on, they had to cope with ridicule, religion, overwork, sexism, sadism, romance, child bearing and, finally, decayed and decaying plumbing, madness and death. She smiled to herself. Sometimes she sounded more like Trudie than Trudie.

Janet had her own flat in a shared house with two other women, Trudie and Margaret, called themselves working girls, and they both had wonderful stories, an endless supply of them. Margaret was tall and a smoker, which Janet thought was funny in itself, because smoking was supposed to stunt your growth. When they talked about it together they'd laugh and imagine how much taller Margaret'd be if she didn't smoke. Probably ten foot tall, stalking the pavements of York, gobbling up punters like a preying mantis.

Trudie was small and dumpy with bleached hair and dark roots, and together they unaccountably appealed to a class of punter who didn't frequent the pubs and clubs of York. They were passed around by word of mouth, being prepared to service any fantasy or perversion that didn't involve themselves being mutilated or having to suffer extreme pain. This, of course, meant that they were frequently in danger of being mutilated or having to suffer extreme pain which, ironically, they had escaped at the last count. But they were still young. 'We're entrepreneurs,' Margaret would say. 'The customer's always right.'

'You're not an entrepreneur,' Trudie would tell her. 'You're a public utility, darling.'

In the past Janet had turned the odd trick, usually when Trudie or Margaret had double booked. She didn't mind, the money was always useful, but she didn't want to depend on it. She wanted a husband and a family. She wanted what she called normality. She didn't want mutilation.

Normality.

Maybe Geordie would give her that?

But one of Janet's problems was that she couldn't seem wholly to make up her mind about anything. She felt she'd like to commit to Geordie, but she didn't do it. Inside her head she was looking around for other possibilities.

She knew she didn't have other possibilities, except maybe winning the lottery. And even if she won the lottery there would still be the question about Geordie. Because he was by far the best thing that had ever happened to her. He wasn't perfect. He wasn't even what she had hoped for. But he was good. He was great. If she lost him she might never meet someone as great as him again. She would go back to the interminable chorus of interchangeable young men.

It was true what Trudie said: 'Janet, if you find someone like that, someone who makes you feel good, makes you laugh, and doesn't want to punch you around, stick to him like glue. If he was mine he'd never get away. I'd hang on to him with both knees.'

Geordie was nice but he wasn't rich. Janet had always thought someone would come along who was rich. The only ones who'd come along like that were rich and weird. The rich bit was attractive. But she didn't want anything to do with weird. Norman, her last boyfriend, had been weird. Very weird. Out of his skull weird.

But Geordie wasn't like that at all. He was neither rich nor weird. He was funny. The only thing against Geordie was that he didn't have any real confidence. So he wasn't like a real man should be. Janet wanted a man to be like Geordie, gentle like Geordie, easy to talk to like Geordie. But she wanted him to be tougher, to know things and have answers. Geordie only had questions.

That was because he'd been in all those children's homes, and then he'd been homeless, and he hadn't been to school much, and his mother had abandoned him. All those reasons added up to why he was like he was. But they also gave him something else as well. A different kind of resilience. They didn't stop him being a man, a real man. Not entirely. Perhaps, if she had patience, Geordie would start to have answers as well as questions. Someone had once said to Janet, she couldn't remember who it was, that the best kind of human being was one who was still growing.

Well, Geordie was still growing. No one would deny that.

He'd said, 'I've got a C in English. GCSE. I did lessons with Celia and took the exam. I'd've got a B if it wasn't for my spelling.'

'That's what I got,' Janet told him. 'B in English. But I got an A in Maths. And I got B in Geography, and five Cs.' She just rushed into it. She hadn't meant to brag. But while she was telling him his face was crumbling away.

'Eight,' he said. 'You got eight GCSEs?'

'Yes. What did you get?'

'Just the one,' he said. 'I didn't take any at school. I ran away before the exams. But I wouldn't've got eight. I don't think I'd've got any.'

'Oh, you would, Geordie. Everybody does.'

He kicked his heels. 'Anyway, I nearly got a B in English. And next year I'm doing A level. You got any of those?'

'No,' Janet told him. 'I never went on. I wanted to leave home, get away from my mum.'

'Well, I'm going on,' said Geordie. 'It's different when you do A level. You have to read books and write essays. I can do that. And I'm better at spelling now.'

There was something else as well. Something else about Geordie. Whenever she thought about him she started to feel warm. Like now. She'd been thinking about Trudie and Margaret, about Norman and Sam Turner, Geordie's boss, all these people and acquaintances who cluttered up her life. She could think of lots of other people too, people in her past and in her present. And what they added up to were more or less interesting or boring people. But Geordie was different. He made her feel warm. When she thought about him she wanted to curl up beside him, or walk over some hills with him, or dance with him. Maybe she just wanted to do nothing at all with him. Whatever she might do with him it didn't make any difference. The thought of him alone warmed her up. She liked his hair, the way it grew, his eyes, the shape of them, the colour. She liked the sound of his voice and the silly way he walked.

The last thing that drew her to him, that made him more exciting than other men she'd known, was that he could think. Janet had met many people who thought they were thinking when they were only rearranging their prejudices. But Geordie wasn't like that. He wasn't like that at all.

He'd never be rich. Janet couldn't tell the future, she wasn't a fortune teller or anything like that. She wasn't a prophet. If her life depended on it she couldn't tell you with any kind of certainty what tomorrow would bring. But one thing was obvious.

Geordie would never be rich.

A lost day followed for Sam. One of those days when the telephone doesn't ring, or if it does ring you don't pick it up, or maybe you pick it up and ten minutes later you can't remember who rang. One of those days. A pale spring day in the north. If you were looking and there was nothing in the way you'd be able to see for miles. But you don't even think about it because you're looking inwards, or you're looking back, and every now and then you allow yourself to look forward. Not too far, though. Just as far as tonight when you call round for the woman from Scottish Widows.

A day that stretched onwards for ever, seemed to have no notion at all of ever folding itself away.

And yet a busy day for all that. He organized Marie to talk to everyone in the Brownie Dyke area, where young Andrew Bridge had been fished out of the river. Geordie concentrated on the Micklegate area. What they needed was just one person who had seen something. It was true that the local police had covered the same ground before them, but past experience showed that it wasn't always the first on the scene who came up with the right answer. Often people remembered something later, when their subconscious had had time to work on the question.

Through Marie's contacts at the hospital, Sam learned that the post mortem on young Andrew Bridge had turned up traces of cocaine, burn marks inside his nose. There was also a residue of anabolic steroids. He had not been a long-term user, but it looked as though he'd had access to plenty of drugs in the weeks before his death. What was even more surprising was that Andrew had been dead for some time before he was castrated. There had been no bleeding around the site of the amputation. After his death, Andrew had been left on his back and the blood had drained into the area of his back and the backs of his legs. If he had been castrated when he was still alive there would have been profuse bleeding from the wound. But there was none. When Andrew's genitalia were removed he had already been dead for some time.

The first suspicions of the police were that the killing was related to some kind of cult practice, maybe even witchcraft. These suspicions had been dependent on the assumption that Andrew was stripped of his sexuality while he was still alive.

Now they didn't know what to think. But Sam smiled to himself at the thought, because when had the police ever known what to think? Most of the time they didn't even know *how* to.

For today Sam left the Andrew Bridge inquiries to Marie and Geordie. He worked the area around Jeanie Scott's house, talked to her neighbours. Talked, in fact, to everyone in the street. Trying to build up a picture of the day her house was broken into, and anything that happened in the neighbourhood that day that was out of the ordinary.

After work he rode home on the bike and ate four thick slices of Brie with crispbread and something out of a can. Finished the Brie off. Made a pot of coffee and sat at the window, looking out at the garden, sipping the coffee and thinking back to the last cigarette. Eighteen months ago now. It had taken him eighteen years to quit. His blood pressure was down and he'd saved himself a small fortune. Spent almost all of it on getting the bike together and fixing up the flat. He felt good too, and it was better than dying.

By six he was out of the shower, dressed and sitting in the Volvo ready to go. He put the key in the ignition and turned it. The engine roared its assent, ready to go. Sam switched it off, withdrew the key and got out of the car. He had a ten-minute ride at the most to get to Jeanie's house. If he set off now he'd arrive an hour and twenty minutes early. She wouldn't even have finished work yet.

He walked round the car three times, then went back into his flat and read the last four chapters of *Dixie City Jam*. When he'd finished, put the book on the table, his watch said it was twenty-five minutes past seven. Sometimes the world works just right. He was gonna be five minutes late, maybe ten. No point in appearing too keen on a first date.

She was standing by the kerb waiting for him, wearing a double-breasted suit in light blue cotton, short skirt and long jacket. Bare legs. Her hair was loose, and she wore no make-up. Her face was shiny, scrubbed, like a nurse's should be. You looked at her and you had to wonder if she'd just thrown it all on and walked out of the door, or if she'd been at it for three hours in the bathroom. Another woman might know. But a fucked-up private eye with the hots didn't have a clue.

Sweet Willy was playing at The Whip, an old pub with a large back room out by the race course. The entrance and the walls of the back room were covered with posters for alternative comedy acts, women's events, gay rights, drumming and various therapeutic practitioners with upwards of three weeks' training under their belts. Geordie and Janet had saved them a couple of seats, which was no mean feat as lots of punters were already sitting on the floor. The heating thermostat had given up the ghost, and the boiler was gobbling gas. The room was packed with people, everyone slick with sweat. They were alternative comedians, feminist activists, acupuncturists, masseurs, gays and drummers. Correction: those types were all there, but in addition there was one female bottleneck guitarist, one country singer with a Texan twang learned in Wakefield and three bluesmen. If he'd come alone Sam could have picked them out, put them all into their various categories. But he wasn't alone, he was with the woman from Scottish Widows, and like everyone else in the room he was working up a real sweat.

'Whew,' he said. 'It's hot enough to grow orchids.'

'I'll get them,' she said, making for the bar. 'Beer?'

Sam touched her shoulder, and she turned her head. 'Coke,' he said.

She raised her eyebrows, not saying it, but implying something like, 'Coke? A big boy like you?'

Sam cocked his head to one side and told her: 'I'm an alcoholic.'

She smiled at him and continued her journey to the bar. The noise level was still rising. He realized she hadn't heard what he'd said. He thought she said something like, 'If that's what you want.'

She returned to the table and placed a Coke in front of him. Hers was a pint of foaming Tetley. Would have been easy to push her over and take it off her. Pick it up from the table and down it in one, then wipe his mouth with the back of his hand and go over to the bar for a chaser. Something with a bite.

She caught his eye and held it for a moment. 'Did you say "alcoholic"?'

He nodded, maintaining the eye contact, careful not to blink.

She looked directly at his face for several seconds. Then she shook her head. 'I've registered it,' she said. 'It's too loud in here to think. Can I just know it, and you know you've told me, and maybe come back to it later? When we're somewhere quiet?'

'Yeah. However you want to play it.'

She reached for his hand and held it in her lap. Sam kept looking down at them, her hand and his on the light blue cotton of her skirt. Two hands from different worlds. Beauty and the geek.

People were shedding clothes and pouring liquid from the bar into themselves to replace the liquid that was oozing out through their pores. Girls' and women's faces were sliding away. Sam glanced at Jeanie from time to time, and her face got a little more shiny as the evening progressed. But she kept her cool look. Janet was dripping, using a cardboard coaster as a fan. The room was more like a sauna than a concert hall. People were spilled all over the floor by halfway through Sweet Willy's set, and the girl who collects the glasses was wearing a diaphanous black lace blouse which just covered her short shorts. She picked her way through the jammed bodies of the audience like a rare dark flamingo on her long legs. Sweet Willy was nearly as sweet as the Scottish Widow. In fact, towards the end of the first set he surged ahead, though only for a moment at a time. On the other hand he was more than twice her age, hairless, with that grey tinge to his blackness that advancing years bring. His face was perfectly round and his bottleneck was perfectly designed to scour the lower reaches of your soul.

Jeanie went for a pee during the interval, and Sam saw her reading the posters by the door. 'Fairly radical place you've brought me to,' she said, returning to his side.

Sam looked at the faces around them and chuckled. 'Yeah, a radical is someone with both feet firmly planted in the air.'

There was magic everywhere in The Whip. The basics of acoustic and emotion combined with the failure of technology, and the striving of art and appreciation gave rise to a surging moment which prolonged itself in a series of ever dying breaths. Sweet Willy Johnson was into 'Goodnight Irene', serenading the lady with a passion that belied his age, and on the floor a young boozer with thick jowls was singing along with him. The drunk sang louder than Willy, but old Johnson just kept on pumping it out. He sucked in that steamy atmosphere and breathed it out into the heart of his audience. He'd been in hotter places than that. And after this life was over, no doubt about it, he was going somewhere hotter still.

CHAPTER 12

When the children arrived they let them loose in the big room in the cellar. Mama had hung balloons on a string up near the ceiling and the table was set with help-yourself goodies and finger foods.

Fancy-dress costumes were hanging on a rail near the entrance, and the speakers were blaring out a mixture of Boyzone and Technohead.

Doc was the only adult present for the first hour. He was dressed in his wizard outfit with the pointed hat and the long black cloak, and he dispensed multi-coloured lines of coke for a kiss and a feel. Doc always did the warm-up routine. He was good at it and he enjoyed himself. The kids were relaxed and floating by the time Mama and Franco joined the party.

Mama appeared first, in the guise of a jolly gym instructress. She wore a white peaked cap, a white T-shirt with no bra and shorts, which, had they been any shorter, would have disappeared.

She organized the games. Postman's Knock first, then, after a portion of acid-laced ice cream, a Bonniest Bottom Contest which was won by Doc. Mama sampled the ice cream herself and got a disapproving glance from Doc, but, 'What the fuck,' she said. 'It's not every day you get to go to a party.'

There were six kids, all, allegedly, between nine and eleven, though a couple of them were obviously older. They had been bussed to the party by the Deputy Head of the children's home, an old and respected institution on the outskirts of the city. The Deputy Head had worked with children for almost fifteen years before discovering what it was that attracted him to the profession.

The two eldest children, a boy and a girl, were obviously attracted to each other, and Doc didn't pay them much attention. There was a small girl called Juniper, with her thin hair in a long plait. She had huge eyes in a pale moon of a face and the look of a hunted animal. She kept herself apart from the others, pressed up against the wall, and the others ignored her.

Doc was particularly taken by a boy called David, who was loud and blond and precocious, a ten-year-old who snorted up a line of coke like a seasoned doper.

After the Bonniest Bottom Contest, Mama got herself settled on the sofa between two brothers, Richard and Paul. Their heads came up to the level of her breasts, and Mama told them they were custom made for what she had in mind.

Upstairs in the living room Franco dialled Mr Julian's number and listened to the line. On the fourth ring the young Mr Julian's voice said, 'Yes.'

'Franco,' said Franco. 'I need to speak to your father.'

'Sorry,' said the voice of the young Mr Julian, and there

was a hint of amusement in the voice. 'He's still not available. Are you sure I can't help?'

Franco put the phone down and looked at it for some time.

He picked it up again and got Ben on his mobile. 'Give me an update,' he said.

'We think the one called Cal left the tape at his wife's house. We had a look there but couldn't find it. Then she went to see a private eye, and we think he might have it now.'

'Offer him money,' said Franco. 'Pay what you have to, but get the tape. Who is this guy?'

'Called Sam Turner, he's got an office . . .'

'I know where his office is,' said Franco. Then he was silent.

After a moment Ben said, 'Hello?'

'I'm thinking. It's no good offering him money. What I hear, the guy makes a virtue out of poverty. Have a good look in his office. If you don't find the tape, make a mess, then threaten his mother or his wife. Everything I hear about this guy, he's difficult to crack. You have to get under his guard.'

'I don't think he's married,' said Ben. 'Might have a mother, though. There's an old biddy works in his office.'

Franco's voice became a hiss. 'Watch him. See who he's close to. I want to know who he's swapping spit with. Who he dreams about.'

'OK,' said Ben. 'We'll get on it right away.'

Franco put down the phone and took his knife out of the drawer. That was the business taken care of, now it was time to relax.

Go to a party.

*

When Franco entered, the room fell silent. He walked across the floor wearing an old RAF greatcoat, open at the front. He was naked beneath it. He dimmed the lights and turned down the volume on the CD player. He looked at Mama on the couch, her left hand on Paul's thigh, her right hand clenching Richard's penis.

Doc was on his back on the floor, the blond David sitting astride him. David was wearing trousers, but his upper body was naked. Doc was groaning softly to himself, his eyes closed.

The two eldest children were locked in an embrace which would not be broken without the aid of secateurs.

Franco turned to Juniper with her wide eyes and he went over and peeled her away from the wall. He lifted her off her feet and put her inside his enormous coat, next to his skin. She whimpered, but he held her tightly, and she was still.

He took her into the bathroom and closed the door. Set into the tiles were two brass towel rings, about a metre apart, and Franco put her hands through the rings and tied them there with a couple of red silk scarves. Juniper didn't resist. She watched him doing it to her.

He removed his greatcoat and he wasn't completely naked underneath it. He wore a black plastic jock-strap. Around his waist was a belt with a ten-inch filleting knife in a leather sheath.

He caught a glimpse of himself in the mirror, and when he turned to face the child there was a cynical smile around his lips. 'You're gonna be OK with me,' he said. 'I used to be an orphan.'

CHAPTER 13

The third time he looked at the clock it was still only three thirty-eight. Pitch black. The Scottish Widow had been on his mind all night. He wasn't going to sleep. Might as well get out and walk the pavements. Why not? He'd walked the same pavements a million times before. Maybe Barney'd fancy a walk through the night.

Barney gave him the old one-eye from his basket, but didn't move until Sam had opened the door and given him the nod. The dog looked sad since he'd smashed his nose, but he stood and shook himself in one movement and trotted out into the cold dark morning. Sam pulled the door closed behind him and set off at a brisk pace along the street. He thought of telling Barney to behave himself on the road, but reckoned the dog had learned its lesson. Barney's nose seemed to be twice as wet as usual since his accident, and it was very sensitive. But the dog didn't seem too traumatized by his experience.

Sam had slept briefly. What woke him was the old dream. In the dream he'd had a drink and it was OK. He hadn't known it was a dream. Hadn't picked up on the clues. He'd been having a drink with Jeanie. Scotch and dry ginger with a moon-shaped chunk of ice in the glass. Heavy leaded glass. He didn't put it straight down his throat, he drank it sociably, finished it about the same time she finished hers. He remembered swilling the remains around the bottom of the glass, letting the liquor linger for a moment on his palate, keeping the ice out of his mouth with his teeth. Using his teeth as a barrier. And looking over the divide between the woman and himself, getting ready to ask her if she wanted another. Then suddenly having the realization: You can drink normally like everybody else in the world.

But just as quickly waking up and realizing that it wasn't true. He was still an alcoholic. Would always be an alcoholic. If he stayed dry for the rest of his life, on his deathbed he would still be an alcoholic. Because there wasn't a cure.

People tell you there are no absolutes. Nothing is final. Relativity rules, OK? But it isn't true. And it ain't no use to sit and wonder why.

Or to pound the night streets of York and wonder why.

But it was always there, so you had to wonder why occasionally. It had been there in The Whip last night. She'd been there, the Scottish Widow, which would have been enough for most men. And he'd been there, Sweet Willy, giving it as much as any man could ever give. The broken thermostat and the place overheating had been too much for some people. All in all the evening should have been enough to make you forget. And in the middle of all that, Sam had found himself watching the people and wondering. Because when you're an alcoholic and you're drinking, and you're in a pub and pissed out of your mind, you think that everybody else is pissed as well. That's how it seems to a drunk. That everybody in the whole world – and the pub *is* the whole world – everybody else is pissed as well. At least as pissed as you are. Or worse. Or catching you up pretty quick. So when you're sober and in a place where people are drinking, say a dance hall, or in somewhere like The Whip last night, you look around from time to time to see who's staggering around. And you rarely see anyone; last night there was only one – and you think: That's strange, I always thought everybody got pissed here.

He walked past the cenotaph and up the short rise to

the Castle Mills Bridge. The lock at Brownie Dyke was quiet and still in the moonlight. Sam leant on the blue iron railings and gazed at the murky waters, the pool of tears beneath his feet. The area, which bristled with traffic during the daytime, was now silent but for the slow trickle of water escaping the lock gates. There was an accumulation of debris to the left of the gates, dead leaves and branches mixed together with Walkers crisp packets and discarded chocolate wrappers. The streetlights picked out a couple of red life-buoys hanging on the wall, each with a blue nylon lifeline attached. Neither of them had been enough to save the young life of Andrew Bridge.

'*. . . When they fished my boy out of the river he didn't have his penis.*' Sam shook his head, recalling the words of Mrs Bridge. Who'd do that to a kid? Who'd be mad enough, sick enough, to do that? Sam couldn't imagine. At least the kid was dead before he was castrated.

And he had an epiphany right there on Brownie Dyke, even checked his watch – four fifty-six – so he'd know later when it happened. He'd meet the guy who did it, come face to face with him. It was in the future, but it was written there. All Sam had to do was stumble towards it. Four fifty-six a.m., Brownie Dyke, a premonition of the inevitable.

Long ago Sam had been a father. The father of a small girl, Bronte, who had ended as the victim of a hit-and-run driver. So many years ago, now, Sam couldn't even remember how many. He could remember her eyes and her smile and the way her hair shone in the low light as he tucked her into bed. He could remember the sound of her voice and the touch of her skin and the quick nervous way she moved. And he could remember her mother, Donna, struck down by the same car.

They'd been shopping.

Twenty-four years ago. Twenty-four years, five months, three weeks, two days and . . . he counted on his fingers . . . eleven hours. Something like that. If it would do the trick, Sam would wait until hell froze over. But nothing would bring them back.

He looked down at the still water. Black as Hitler's heart. Tons of it, just in that lock alone. But not enough to drown in. Sam Turner had drunk that much, maybe twice as much as that, straight from the mouth of a whisky bottle. And he was still alive.

He caught an hour in bed, then had a slow breakfast, and took the best part of an hour to go through the shit, shave and shampoo routine. Wouldn't do to arrive at the office looking like he'd been on the tiles. Even if he had.

Geordie and Marie had been in early and gone out again to continue their inquiries. They'd each left a file on his desk, transcripts of interviews with residents and traders in Micklegate and around Brownie Dyke.

Celia took one look at him and said, 'Couldn't you sleep?'

Sam laughed. 'If you only knew how long it took me to put my make-up on this morning,' he said. 'And you see right through it.'

'I work for a detective,' Celia told him, 'and I do the reception work in this office, meet all kinds of people every day of the week. It sharpens your perception.' She placed a cup of coffee in his hand. 'There's the reports from Geordie and Marie,' she said. 'And there's some mail. I'll bring it through in a moment.'

Sam reached across his desk for Geordie's file. Then looked up again at Celia, who hadn't moved. 'What?' he said.

'You didn't answer my question. Couldn't you sleep?'

'Bad dream, Celia. I tried to ignore it but it kept coming back.'

Celia shook her head. 'That poor woman,' she said, 'Mrs Bridge. She'll have to live the rest of her life knowing that someone did that to her boy. To lose a child is bad enough, Sam. But to have someone mutilate him like that . . .' She walked towards her own office, and Sam watched her back, realizing suddenly that Celia was no longer young. 'I couldn't sleep myself,' she said. 'I don't think I'll ever sleep again till we've found the man who did that.'

He spent what was left of the morning going through the reports from Geordie and Marie. Neither contained any startling revelations, but they were both still out there in the field, doing the legwork. He took Celia over to Betty's for lunch, and they had lasagne with a really wicked sauce.

Back in the office, Sam was putting his coat on to go over to the Scottish Widow's neighbourhood when the telephone call came. Celia usually answered the phone, but she was over by Geordie's desk when it rang, so Sam picked it up quickly. The background hum signalled a call from a mobile phone.

He couldn't make out what the first voice said. 'Ugh, Gog . . .' Something like that, then another voice, a voice further away from the mouthpiece, said, 'Give it here.'

There was a bang and scrambling noises, as if they'd dropped the phone between them. Sam said, 'Hello,' again, into the receiver.

'Sam Turner?' asked the second voice, now closer to the mouthpiece, and obviously with a firm grip of the telephone.

'Yes,' Sam confirmed that he was himself.

'We want the tape.'

The guy, whoever he was, had obviously been to finishing

school, you could get that much from his telephone manner, but there was still a rough edge to him. A recent graduate, perhaps? 'Sorry,' Sam said. 'You're gonna have to be more explicit.'

'The fucking tape,' the voice said. 'We want it.'

Sam shook his head. 'You say please, now, or I'll put the phone down.'

But the voice, the guy behind the voice, was not going to let himself be led astray. After a pause, he said, 'We want the tape.'

'Sellotape?' Sam said. 'Tape measure, maybe? Are you sure you have the right number?'

There was a short silence on the line, maybe that was how long it took the guy on the other end to interpret Sam's words. Then he got back into gear. 'Listen, fuckhead, we know you've got it. So you can be a volunteer now, or we'll come and take it off you.'

'I'm looking at my knees,' Sam said into the mouthpiece. 'They're starting to shake.'

'Your fucking knees won't have any caps on if we don't get that tape.'

Then the phone went dead.

Sam took his coat off and sat at his desk.

'What was all that about?' Celia asked.

'Maybe we'll find out soon,' Sam said. 'Couple of guys just made an appointment.'

But they didn't keep it. Sam waited in the office until after five and no one came. The telephone rang every five minutes or so, mostly with queries that Celia fielded herself. Once or twice it was someone who needed to talk to Sam. But the guy who wanted the tape didn't ring back at all.

Sam left the office, then went back again and unlocked

the floor safe under his desk. He took out his 9mm Glock and slung it in a holster under his arm. He unlocked the bottom drawer of the filing cabinet and took out an eighteen-round magazine and slipped it into his jacket pocket.

He stood by the door to the office for several seconds debating with himself if he should put the gun back. He almost never carried it in the street. But just this once it felt right. Must be something about the phone call. Not what the guy had actually said, maybe more what he hadn't said. But Sam listened to his intuitions these days. It was a time to wear a gun. He hoped he wouldn't have to use it. But if he did have to use it it would still be quicker, cleaner than the slow institutionalized violence of the State. The same State that had now turned the rehabilitation of offenders over to the private sector, so the care and penal processing of human beings became subject to the profit motive.

Sam went to an AA meeting after work. It was snowing. Half snow and half rain. Freezing wet stuff sprinkled down through the cosmos by a god who had forgotten what it was like to be human.

Two women spoke before Sam. When his turn came around he said, 'My name is Sam and I'm an alcoholic. I've been dry for eleven months. I haven't had a drink today and I don't want to have a drink today. When I was drinking regularly I would occasionally become disgusted with myself, or I would get frightened. And then I'd say, "To hell with this, I'm going on the wagon." It never worked. I'd say I'm never gonna drink again, or I'm not gonna drink for a month, or a week. Whatever I promised myself would put me under more pressure, and the only way I could relieve the pressure, the only way I knew how to relieve the pressure, was to have a drink.

'I don't do that any more. What I do is, I don't drink today. I'll do anything to avoid having a drink today. To hell with tomorrow, that might never happen. But today there's me, and today I'm not gonna have a drink. And that's the contract, me and the drink. Just us two. And I'm not touching the drink today. I'm leaving it on the shelf. I'm not making a promise to my friends, to the people I work with, and I'm not making a promise to anybody in this room. I'm just talking to myself here. I'm doing this for me. I'm not having a drink today for me.

'How I got started on this eleven months ago, I didn't tell myself, "You're gonna give up drinking for just one day." I don't think I could have managed that then. What I did was give up drinking for just one hour. I told myself I could hold on that long. One hour. And I did it. It was easy. So easy I told myself I could do it for another hour.

'I did it twenty-four times that day. Didn't sleep a wink. Just avoided having a drink for twenty-four hours.

'I can only talk about today. I can't tell you a thing about tomorrow, or next week, or next month. I can't claim I'll be sober for ever. All I can say is that I'm sober now, and it feels good. I'm enjoying it.'

It was the convention when someone stopped speaking that the others would say 'thank you', and the people closest to Sam did that. Everyone was silent for a few moments and then a newcomer used the opening lines: 'My name is Leonard and I'm an alcoholic.' He was painfully thin, with a wispy beard, and had been to the past three meetings without opening his mouth. He was sharing his life story now, giving it out to the group like a gift. Sam closed his eyes. Leonard's life had been nothing like his own. Leonard had been born into an upper-middle-class family, and had attended several private schools. It had been a long, slow and painful journey from the post of junior teacher at Winchester to an AA meeting at The Friends' Meeting House in York. It was a story of privilege and the incapacity to live with it. A story of failure and a descent into alcoholism. A story like Sam's own, like everyone else's in the room.

A story that wasn't over yet. Because the last page wasn't written.

After the meeting Sam went over to Leonard to thank him. 'If you need to talk any time,' he said, 'or anything at all, give me a ring.'

'Thank you,' said Leonard in his cultured voice. 'I might very well do that.'

The snow had stopped coming down but the wind was sharp as a razor as Sam made his way across the park to Marie's house. There was always the dread now that he'd find her cutting herself, or even already cut up beyond recognition. The night he'd seen her attack herself with the apple corer, she wasn't in any way going easy. The sharp end of the thing had gone deep into her flesh, and she was pushing and twisting it with all her strength. In his time on the bottle Sam had witnessed plenty of bar brawls and street fights, and the attack Marie had made on herself was no less aggressive than any of those.

She was waiting for him. She showed him through to her sitting room and sat him down in front of a salad bowl full of potato crisps and several thinly sliced Mars bars.

'We're gonna eat?' Sam asked, smiling.

'I don't call this eating,' Marie said.

They looked at each other and without speaking, they both sat. 'My therapist is called Anna,' she said. 'I told her what happened, that you found me cutting myself. She thinks you can help, if you want to.'

'Anything, Marie. Just say the word.'

'We've been talking about involving someone else for some time. The problem has always been who that someone else would be.'

'When you say "involve",' Sam said, 'what do you want me to do?'

'Just be there. Listen. Sometimes talk it through with me. At the moment I've got everything internalized. What we've been trying to do is get it out. Then it might be possible to work with it.'

'Are you going to tell me what you mean?' he asked. 'I mean, I wanna help, but I'd have to have something concrete to work with.'

'Sam,' Marie said, 'my father sweet-talked me into a sexual relationship with him when I was seven. That went on for eight years. It was a secret between him and me. We were a completely normal family on the outside. My mother stood on the sidelines. I don't know if she knew what was going on or not. I think she suspected it was happening.'

Sam shifted in his seat, wondering if he should say something. But Marie was off again, telling her story. 'We were a conspiracy of three people against the world,' she said. 'If the world got even a whiff of what we were up to we wouldn't have been allowed to continue as a family.

'So we lived the secret, we kept it tight.

'I loved my father. Even the sex. Not all of it, of course, I didn't like the size of him, or the violence, when he forced me to do things I didn't want to do. Things that hurt. But I liked the quiet bits, when it started off, when it was just touching and cuddling and being warm and cosy together. Does that shock you?'

Sam shook his head.

'I didn't want him to do the painful things to me,' she said. 'But I didn't want to reject him. He said it was all right. I didn't blame him and I didn't blame her. I blamed me.'

Sam sat forward again. 'But you don't still do that?' he said. 'Now you're older. Surely you can see that it wasn't your fault?'

'That's what I'm trying to explain,' she said. 'Father, and mother, and the child that I was, they're all part of me now. Father is the aggressor, the one who hurts me. It's him who cuts me, or who forces all that food down my throat like he used to force his prick.' She got out of the chair and walked to the door. She came back and stood behind the chair, gripping the back of it with both hands. 'Do you understand, Sam?'

'Yes,' Sam said. 'I think so.'

'Mother is another part of me,' Marie continued. 'She's the part that can't stop me getting hurt. She's supposed to stop me cutting myself, or eating the food, but she can't. She sees it happening and she's paralysed. And the rest of me is the child that was in the middle of it all. The victim.

'I understand it now. In my better, my clearer moments, I can sit back and see exactly what is happening. But there are other moments when I lose sight of it all. That's when I go out and buy the Brie, or I reach for a knife.'

'And is that where I come in?' Sam asked.

'I *am* getting on top of this, Sam. But there are times when I'm numb, and other times when I'm ashamed, or consumed by guilt. Then it'll be good to know you're there. Someone who knows but doesn't judge.'

He got out of the chair and went over and held her close. There was a sense of the closeness she had enjoyed with her father. And it seemed like he'd just taken on another job. One he couldn't refuse. Sam held Marie tight and silently hoped that he was up to it. The job he was doing for Mrs Bridge, tracking the killer of her son, and the job he was doing for Jeanie Scott, tracking the killer of her ex-husband: these both seemed simple and straightforward compared to the task Marie had just handed him.

Walking home at two in the morning Sam did a slight detour and cut across St Helen's Square. He looked up at the office window, now in complete darkness. When he reached the corner of Betty's he turned round and went back to the steps leading up to the office door. The door was open, only a crack, but it was definitely open.

That's why he'd made the detour. That's why he'd walked back from Betty's corner. Some kind of sixth sense had been at work. Sam didn't really believe in a sixth sense. But he didn't have time to cogitate. He pushed the door open and made his way up the stairs. Everything was pitch black, but he knew the stairs and the passage above intimately.

When he got to the top of the stairs he breathed easier. If someone had been inside the building, they didn't seem to be still around. He walked along the passage, feeling in his jacket pocket for the keys to his office. He got them out, but didn't need to use them, because the door to SAM TURNER INVESTIGATIONS was hanging off its hinges.

He flicked the light switch and gazed at the chaos inside.

Someone, as promised, had been searching for a tape. Everything in the office had been thrown into a jumble in the centre of the floor. Celia's computer, Sam's stereo tape deck, even the filing cabinet had been upended. Desk drawers and broken chairs had been thrown on to the pile, and files and papers and books had been ripped apart and added to the chaos. Even the desks had been turned over or pushed on to their sides. One of them had had all its legs smashed off. The telephone was in a million pieces.

Sam picked up a piece of paper and, using a pen from

his inside pocket, he scrawled a note to Celia, telling her that the office had been broken into, so she wouldn't have a heart attack when she got there in the morning.

Then he closed the inner door as well as he could, locked the outer door and made his way to Celia's house, where he slipped the note into her letter box.

Then he went home to bed. Didn't expect to sleep at all. But as is always the way, he closed his eyes and slept like a baby until he heard Geordie filling the kettle in the morning.

CHAPTER 14

Sam had told Geordie what to expect in the office, but he was still surprised when he got there and found everything trashed in the middle of the floor. Barney ran to the spot in the office where his basket used to be. But whoever had been in there had no respect for anyone's property. Barney's basket was in the heap together with all the other stuff. The thing about Barney, though – one of the things about Barney – was that he wasn't a materialist. He was one of the least materialistic people – well, dogs – that Geordie had ever met. Geordie hadn't actually met a whole lot of dogs, only perhaps two or three, two he could remember at this moment in time, and as far as he could recall neither of them was materialistic either. But he hadn't known them that well, they having been the property of other people.

Barney was not actually Geordie's property. He had started off being Geordie's property when he was a puppy. Then, because he had been a homeless dog, and Geordie had been a homeless person, what Geordie had done was, he had adopted Barney. But that was some time ago now, and since then Barney had become as much Sam's property as Geordie's. So what Geordie thought was, that Barney was not anyone's property. He was more like a companion animal. He was more like Sam. If Sam had been a dog instead of a man, he would have been a companion animal as well. Not somebody's property. Geordie couldn't imagine Sam being anyone's property. So why should Barney be?

The reason he wasn't materialistic, though, the way you could tell that, was that he knew his basket wasn't there any more, where it should be, and he obviously didn't know where it was. But not only did he not make any kind of fuss about it, apart from that pathetic glance he gave Geordie – and you couldn't count that glance, because he was really good at pathetic, it was almost as if he'd been trained in it. What he did was, he turned round in a complete circle and sat down exactly where the basket would have been if it had still been there. Then he let his front legs go down and rested his head on them. Saying, in effect, OK, so I used to have a basket, and now I don't have a basket any more, but I've still got the place it used to be.

Still, you could think what you liked about personal property and companion animals and materialism, but at the end of the day none of that was going to extract all the bits and pieces of the office out of this jumble and put them back together and in the places they had been ripped out of.

Celia came up the stairs while Geordie was still thinking about starting the clean-up. She stood in the frame of the doorway, looking at the door which Geordie had lifted out of the frame and placed against the wall. 'Goodness,' she said. 'I didn't think it would be as bad as this. I don't know if I've got the stamina for it.'

'Hard to know where to start,' said Geordie. 'I suppose we could make it into two heaps, one for stuff that needs throwing out, and one for stuff we might still be able to use.'

'Why've they done this?' Celia said. 'Why would anyone want to do this?'

'It must be connected with the telephone call yesterday, about the tape.'

'Is that what Sam said? All this mess because someone thinks we've got a tape.' Celia moved forward into the room, slipping her coat off her shoulders and putting it on a hook on the wall where the surveillance camera used to be.

'The camera,' Geordie said. 'It'll have recorded whoever came through the door. Unless they took it away with them.' He got down on his knees and started searching through the mound of office furnishings and parts of electrical equipment. Celia couldn't get on her knees, but Geordie was aware of her on the other side of the mound searching through the debris for the camera or the VCR.

The surveillance camera had been the idea of Gus, Marie's husband. Gus had been Sam's partner, and had been a good friend to Geordie when he first joined the firm. But the other thing Gus had been was an electronics wizard. He built computers and small bugs that could pick up conversations and transmit them to a remote recorder. He also built a scanner, which Geordie had inherited, on which he could listen to police broadcasts. The trouble with that was, Geordie didn't understand the codes they used when they talked to each other: 10–62, or 10–20, or whatever it was. Do you copy? Copy what? Geordie couldn't understand why they didn't just talk plain. Gus could understand all the codes, and he would listen in to the police talking and he'd translate it as it went along, so you could actually understand what they were talking about.

Another thing Geordie couldn't understand was when he listened to the scanner and he picked up police broadcasts, and he couldn't understand what they were talking about, he would feel like going to sleep after a few minutes. Well, he could half understand it. But what made it complicated was, when he listened to the shipping forecast on the radio, he couldn't understand that either, because he didn't know where any of those places were: Dogger Bank, Cromarty, force seven, fading . . . It was exactly like listening to the police, except with the shipping forecast he didn't get bored and want to go to sleep. With the shipping forecast he never wanted it to end. He could just sit there and listen to it all over again.

So how do you explain that? The only way you can explain these things is to admit that you can't explain them. The most you can say about it is that it's probably a force of nature. Something like that. An ecological necessity.

And what Gus had said, before he was killed in the line of duty, was that one day, maybe not tomorrow, maybe not the next day, but one day, someone would break into the office. And if we had a camera trained on the door we'd be able to identify who it was. That's when Gus had put the camera on the wall and hooked it up to the VCR. And after Gus had been killed Geordie had not gone to the funeral, because he didn't want to be spooked.

But what he had done instead was to make sure that Gus's camera was switched on every time the office was left unattended. And every month he'd fitted a new tape in the

VCR, because Gus had said that was the best thing to do, because tapes wore out after you'd used them a few times.

And he picked the camera out of the mess now, and saw that whoever had broken into the office had not just ripped it off the wall; they had given it a good bashing on the wall or on the floor, so that the end where the lens was was squashed and the lens was smashed. It was all that was left of Gus, and Geordie doubted very much if it would ever be used again.

'The recording part's here,' Celia said, bending low and tugging at the VCR. It moved slightly, but was caught up with something else, so she couldn't pull it clear of the heap.

Geordie put the camera down and went to help Celia. He picked up the VCR and saw that the whole of the front facia was missing. He pushed the button which usually released the tape, but nothing happened. By pushing back the entrance flap he could see that the tape was still inside, but he couldn't see if it was damaged, and he couldn't get it out.

'I've got a screwdriver in my bag,' Celia said.

That was one of the things about Celia: she was just about ready for any situation. A screwdriver in her handbag. Who would have thought of such a thing? She handed Geordie a tiny bundle. When he unwrapped it he found it was a small oilskin containing dozens of parts lined up in individual pockets. There was a central handle, and all the other parts – corkscrews, knives, scissors, Phillips drives – fitted into the handle and then you could use it.

He found the right drive and fitted it to the handle and began unscrewing the tape bay of the VCR. In a couple of minutes it came away and he was able to extract the tape, which looked undamaged.

Geordie and Celia both looked around the office, as if

they expected to find something they could play it on. But there was nothing.

'We could take it to my house,' Celia said, re-wrapping her oilskin and placing it back in the right compartment of her handbag.

'What about Sam?' Geordie said. 'He won't know where we are. I'll give him a ring.' He turned to where the desk used to be, the desk with the telephone. But there was no desk and no telephone on it. Just space.

Weird. Weird feeling, trying to get your head round the fact that there was nothing left. It wasn't even an office any more. You couldn't operate it like an office, to use the telephone, say, or to sit at a desk and make out a report. It was a big untidy space, didn't even have a door.

'I'll ring him from the phone box,' he said. Geordie waited for Celia to put her coat back on and then went down the stairs in front of her. That's what you did with old ladies, and women and children. If you were a man, you went down the stairs first, so if they fell they'd fall on top of you, and that'd be softer for them than falling all the way down the stairs. Problem with it was they'd probably flatten you, especially some of the bigger ones. Marie, say, if she fell on you, Jesus, you'd wish you'd never learned any fucking etiquette.

When he thought about it Geordie couldn't remember where he'd learned that particular piece of etiquette, going down the stairs first. And he knew if he ever mentioned it to Sam, Sam'd say it was a load of sexist crap. He'd probably say it in just those words as well, say that women were quite capable of getting up and down stairs without the help of some lame-brained guy who'd picked up a bit of eighteenth-century etiquette from his children's home.

And what'd probably prove the point was that Geordie didn't know if it was right to go *up*stairs in front or behind them. Because if you were going upstairs behind them you'd be able to see up their skirts, you wouldn't be able to stop yourself from looking, and that can't be right. OK, so if they fell down the stairs you'd be there to give them something soft to land on, but ninety-nine times out of a hundred they don't fall down the stairs at all – Geordie had never known one to fall down the stairs on top of him, thank God – so ninety-nine times out of a hundred you got to look up their skirts, and that didn't make you into a gentleman. Or, if you did it the other way round, and went upstairs in front of them so you couldn't look up their skirts, then that made nonsense of going downstairs in front of them. Jesus, when you thought about things like etiquette, instead of just accepting them, it got really complicated.

But he was glad that he knew about it, especially this time, because Barney was running downstairs and then up again, weaving in and out of both his and Celia's feet, and one of the times he did it Celia stumbled. She didn't actually fall down, but Geordie anticipated her faltering and felt her hand on his shoulder to steady herself. He quickly told Barney to go play with the traffic, and apologized to Celia for the dog's behaviour.

But Celia laughed and said it wasn't Barney's fault, it was the fault of old bones.

Celia put the tape into her VCR and pressed the play button. But all they got was white snow. She fast forwarded it for a few seconds and tried again. White snow.

'Do you ever clean the recording heads?' Geordie asked.

'I've got something to do it with,' she confessed, 'but I haven't done it for about a year.'

'Maybe we should try it?' Geordie suggested. 'That could be the problem.'

Celia agreed and went in search of the cleaning equipment. She returned with a cassette labelled PUREVISION and a small container of fluid. She read the instructions to Geordie, who put five or six drops of the liquid on the tape and placed it in the recorder. They ran it through, but when they tried to play the tape from the office they got exactly the same result as before: white snow.

When Sam arrived he suggested adjusting the tracking on the video recorder, and they both watched him do it. 'I'd read about that in the instructions,' Celia said. 'I read it twice and I couldn't get the words to stay together in my head. But watching you actually do it, it makes complete sense.' When he'd finished, Sam rewound the tape and pressed play. The machine whirred into action and Geordie appeared on the television screen.

'That's me,' he said. 'How'd that happen?' But then he realized himself, so no one had to answer the question for him. 'That's last night,' he said. 'Just after I've switched the camera on, and that's me putting my coat on and going out the door. And now I've gone.' He laughed. 'I've seen this movie before,' he said. 'Shows the inside of the office after we've all gone home. Goes on like this for hours.'

The television screen showed the door of the office, from the inside. The tape whirred away, but nothing else changed. Just the door. Sam picked up the remote and fast forwarded the tape. It didn't seem to make any difference at first, because there was nothing moving. And then there was something moving, but the tape was going too fast to see what it was, and before Sam could slow it down the picture had vanished altogether, and they were back to white snow again.

Sam rewound the tape slowly, and then played it back again at normal speed. What they saw was the door come away from the frame. Then there was a guy standing in the frame, looked like the Terminator. His shoulders were nearly as wide as the door frame. Both the guy and the door frame looked unhinged. You couldn't tell which one of them was most in need of repair.

'Jesus,' Geordie said.

'Big guy.' That was Sam.

'Goodness,' said Celia, 'he broke the door down with his bare hands.'

They watched in silence as the giant looked up into the eye of the camera. Geordie thought the guy was looking right at him. Then they saw him reaching up towards the camera. They watched his hands get bigger and bigger. And the whole office turned upside down, and right after that it all went back to white snow again.

Sam whistled through his teeth. Geordie felt numb, and thought he must look dumb sitting there on Celia's couch shaking his head from side to side. Celia got to her feet and walked to the kitchen. 'I'm going to make us all a nice cup of tea,' she said.

Sam pointed the remote at the recorder again and rewound at the slowest speed. He played it. The guy had one of those Gorilla Wear shirts with short sleeves and a cap to match, and he wore striped baggy bottoms which finished about four inches above his trainers. There was something wrong with one of his legs, like he was deformed. Sam rewound the tape again, and finally paused on the face of the guy as he reached up for the camera.

He was dark-haired and had a fixed grin on his face, like a mask. Huge mouth, open all the time, a flycatcher. He was really intent on what he was doing, going for the camera, but when you saw him like this you were really glad he was going for the camera and not for you. What he'd done to the camera, smashed in the nose of it like that, Jesus, Geordie was really happy it wasn't his own nose.

The mouth. You had to look at his mouth, and not only because it was huge. Everything about him was huge. But the mouth was set, somehow, as if it only had the one expression. Like it had been cast in metal or porcelain, some material that had no plasticity. It wasn't like flesh. Except at the corners. At the corners of the mouth, and dribbling a little along the upper chin, were flecks of saliva.

Sam moved the tape on a second and froze it again, and now you could look beyond the guy's lips, into the darkness of his mouth. And back there, round his tongue, weaving in and out of the gaps in his teeth, was more saliva. What appeared to be great rushes of it. 'What is it, Sam?' he asked.

'Dunno, Geordie. Can't say for sure, but it looks to me like the guy is foaming at the mouth.'

'Jesus, Sam, he's terrifying.'

Sam said, 'Yeah.' And you could tell he really meant it. He wasn't just saying it for the sake of saying something. The guy on Celia's television put the shits up Sam as well.

Celia returned with a tray, tea for Geordie and herself, coffee for Sam. She glanced at the image on the screen as she shared out the cups and saucers. 'He was not made for climbing the tree of knowledge,' she said.

Geordie laughed because that was the kind of thing Sam might say, and just not the kind of thing that Celia usually said. But they rubbed up against each other, Celia and Sam. So sometimes she said what he might say, and other times Sam would say something that you'd expect to have come from Celia.

What Sam said now was, 'He wouldn't win any beauty contests, either.' And all three of them laughed, not because

Sam was so funny, but because they wanted to laugh, to ease the tension. That face on the television screen was something you could joke about. You could keep it at a distance. But they all knew that it had come closer than that when it broke into the office. And there was a good chance it would come closer still. Geordie didn't want to think about what might happen then. And he knew that Celia didn't want to think about it either. Sam stopped laughing first. He kept a smile on his face, but it was only for show.

'Just so we're all on the same wavelength here,' Sam said, 'somebody tell me what's going on. Geordie?'

One thing you could be sure of, if Sam asked you what was going on, he probably knew very well what was going on. What he really wanted to know was if Geordie knew what was going on. 'A guy rings up and asks you for a tape,' Geordie said. 'The same night some guy breaks into the office. I would say it's the same guy.'

'Maybe.' Sam looked at Celia.

'Jeanie Scott's house was broken into,' she said. 'There could be a connection.'

'Yeah,' Sam said. 'Because Jeanie came to us straight after her house was broken into. If we assume they were looking for a tape in her house as well as in our office, what kind of tape would that be? Geordie?'

Geordie shook his head. 'The only tapes I know about are music tapes,' he said. 'But we can't be sure.'

Sam and Celia both turned their heads back to the television screen, still showing the face of the guy who looked like the Terminator. 'Oh, Jesus,' Geordie said. 'Video tape.' Then it came to him in a rush, what Sam was driving at. 'Jeanie Scott was married to the guy who worked the camera. So what happened was the guy who worked the camera had a tape, and this guy, the one on the television, wanted that tape. First he thought Jeanie might have it, then he followed her to our office and thought she'd given it to us.' Geordie stood and walked to the television, then back again to his chair. 'That's it. Is that it, Sam?'

Sam nodded. 'We might be able to get more out of it yet,' he said. 'When I got the telephone call there were two voices, not one.'

'So we can't jump to conclusions,' Celia said. 'Our friend over there,' she nodded at the image on the screen, 'he isn't working alone. It might not be him that broke into Jeanie's house.'

'And don't forget what happened to Cal Pointer, Jeanie's ex-husband,' Sam said.

'He was shot,' said Geordie. And he looked at the screen again and realized that he might be looking at the face of a murderer. 'Him and the other guy. They were both shot.'

'For a tape?' asked Celia.

'No,' said Geordie. 'You don't shoot somebody for a tape.'

He looked at Sam and Celia, expecting them to agree with him. They both looked back at him, and neither of them said anything. Suddenly Geordie didn't know if he was right or not.

'What *do* you shoot somebody for?' asked Sam.

Geordie tried to think about that for a moment, but then he realized that it was one of those questions that don't need an answer. He'd had it in an English lesson. Couldn't remember the word for it. Celia would know it exactly, the word for that kind of question. But he didn't want to ask her, didn't want anyone to tell him. He wanted to remember it himself. Began with R. Ridiculous question, or rhinoceros question, something like that.

Sam picked up the handset again and wound the tape

back to where the Terminator first appeared in the doorway. 'Look at the size of him,' Sam said. 'You don't get as big as that without working at it. This guy's done some serious training.'

'Body building, you mean?' said Celia.

'What do you think?' Sam countered. 'Shoulders like that don't grow normally. Look at his biceps, his arms altogether. I reckon this guy spends most of his time in a gym.'

Celia waved the coffee pot at him. 'Your little grey cells are working, Sam.'

He shook his head 'no' to the coffee pot. 'Geordie, this is one for you,' he said. 'Go round the gyms. Look around, ask around. Somebody'll know this guy. He's distinctive. Find out what you can about him without getting close. I want to know where he trains, and I want to know where he lives.'

'Rhetorical,' Geordie said, because it just came into his head. 'I knew it'd come to me. Rhetorical question. Not rhinoceros.'

Sam and Celia exchanged a glance.

'Did you hear what I just said?' asked Sam.

'Yeah, ask round the gyms,' said Geordie. 'I'm not deaf, Sam.'

'Only when you start going on about rhinoceroses . . .?'

'Not rhinoceroses,' Geordie corrected him. 'Rhetorical. You asked a rhetorical question. I just couldn't remember the name.'

'Jesus,' said Sam. 'Can we talk about gyms?'

'I'll get on it now,' Geordie told him. 'I'll copy all the addresses from *Yellow Pages*. Then I'll start on the legwork. Won't come home till the job's done.'

'Just one thing,' Sam said. 'Something to remember. This guy is dangerous. Don't get close to him. When you've got an elephant by the hind legs and he's trying to run away, it's best to let him run. Remember that.'

Geordie got to his feet. 'I'll remember that,' he said. He walked towards the door. 'Elephants, rhinoceroses,' he said. 'Christ, can we all try sticking to gyms here?'

Geordie picked up a copy of the *Big Issue* outside Waterstone's. He'd always bought it off Tombo in the past, opposite Woolworths, but a couple of weeks back Tombo had disappeared. If it'd been South America he'd have *been* disappeared. But in England people didn't *get* disappeared. They just disappeared. Like they were volunteers. Or were they?

So now he bought it outside Waterstone's from a woman called Pat. Only this time there were three of them. Pat, another woman and a young guy who Geordie had seen selling the paper in Coppergate. They all had copies of the *Big Issue* for sale.

Geordie gave a pound coin to Pat and took the paper from her. 'Seen anything of Tombo?' he asked.

'No. Nobody has. We're gonna put something in the mag. He wouldn't just go without telling anyone.'

'Tell me something else,' Geordie said. 'Why're there three of you all selling the paper in the same place? You get lonely by yourselves?'

Pat shook her head. ''S'getting too dangerous. These two were both threatened on Friday. These blokes come up to Sita here, and they said they'd break her legs if she didn't give 'em all her money.'

'They had a hammer,' said Sita. 'There were three of them. I jus' gave 'em all the money.' Sita had a ring in her nose. She wore a pair of raggy jeans, and she'd wound a cloth around her legs to give extra warmth. But you could see it wasn't enough.

'They tried the same with me,' said the young guy, 'but somebody interfered. A tourist, I think it was. Then the police came.'

'So we're sticking together,' said Pat. 'Seems like the best thing to do.'

'Yeah,' Geordie agreed. 'A hammer. Jesus, it's getting like Chicago here.'

Back in the office Sam began sorting through the rubbish. That's what it was now. Rubbish. Yesterday it had been the collection of tools with which he earned his living. Now much of it was useless. Celia said she had a back-up of the computer's hard disk, so most of the accounts and the records of past and current cases would be retrievable. But that meant buying a new computer. This one would never work again, the monitor screen was a jagged black hole and the keyboard had lost most of its teeth. Both telephones had been stamped into oblivion.

Sam thought back to several conversations with Celia.

'Have you got round to getting the place insured yet?'

'Not yet, Celia.'

'I think you should, Sam. You never know.'

'Yeah. I'll get some quotes.'

'I got you some quotes, Sam. They're on your desk, bottom of your in-tray.'

'Oh, yeah. I'll have a look. Later.'

Trouble was, he didn't look later, or ever. He'd thought about it from time to time. Well, not thought, exactly, but it had come up in his mind. And he'd thought that you couldn't insure against destiny, against fate.

Trying to recall the thought patterns now. How could anyone be so wrong? It was true that nothing could have insured him against the death of his wife. If he'd been insured for a million against that it would still have destroyed him. No one, nothing could have brought Donna back, and that would have been the only kind of insurance he would have looked at. A celestial policy. Sam dropped the flattened telephone back on to the floor and felt a familiar lassitude take over his body. A celestial policy, endorsed by the hand of God. The same good Lord who had taken not only Donna, his wife, but the two-year-old scrap of humanity who clung to her hand as they crossed the road. Bronte, Sam's daughter, had been flung fifty feet through the air by the impact. A hit-and-run driver doing ninety in a built-up area.

Insurance? Who's gonna insure you against that? Show me the policy that takes into account a cold universe ruled by an insane creator. Someone, something, some alien intelligence that gives life and a beautiful, innocent promise only to snatch it back and away without a breath of explanation.

You had to think from time to time how ludicrous it all was. How that anger against God never dissipated. Sure, sometimes it receded into the background. But it was never far off. Sam had lived with it for over two decades, and it was still capable of consuming him. If God came down from Heaven today, Sam'd poke him in the chest looking for answers. And when he didn't get the answers he needed, he'd fight. God could do his worst. Bring on the heavenly host, all the ugly crew of Archangels, Thrones, whatever His henchmen were called. Sam'd put up a better fight than old Beelzebub had ever been capable of. He didn't think he'd beat them. But they'd know they'd had a fight, he'd put the boot in hard before they whisked him away. To hell with the Queensberry Rules. They'd need a first-aid kit and a stretcher or two after it was all over. Cold compresses, iodine and a good supply of paracetamol.

He looked up, through the window, at the clouds. Ground his teeth together. 'Don't fuck with me,' he said.

And half a minute was sliced off his life before he saw the funny side of it and relaxed into a smile. Still would have been better if he'd listened to Celia, got the place insured. As it was he was gonna have to go cap-in-hand to the bank, borrow enough to get the office up and running again. Take another cut in wages. It was either that or a bottle of whisky. He'd decide later, after due consideration.

That face. The face of the character on the video. Some people who are retarded look benign, and others look dangerous. The face of the character on the video looked retarded dangerous. You looked at that face and you wondered what it would take to stop him. You might try a lot of things if you had time. In theory the guy could probably be stopped in a number of different ways. But one thing you wouldn't bother with, unless you were an incurable optimist, you wouldn't spend a lot of time reasoning with him.

You looked at him and you could see something was really wrong. It was like he had the DNA, all the necessary, but it was as if the code had been made up in some foreign country. Like with those leaflets that tell you how to put wardrobes together. But it's a Taiwanese wardrobe for export to England, and the guy who's writing the code, he doesn't speak English English, he speaks Taiwanese English. You get the picture? When the wardrobe's finally built by some schmuck in the Cotswolds, it falls over whenever he hangs his jacket in it.

Sam went down to Betty's and the *maître d* gave him a selection of cardboard boxes. He lugged them all back up to the office and looked around for the telephone. But it was a move which didn't contain a lot of joy. He went back down to St Helen's Square and rang Celia from a pay phone. 'If I left the sorting out of the office to you and Marie would that be sexist exploitation?' he asked.

Sam met the secretary of the Traders' Council who had been responsible for Cal Pointer and Geoff Harper's employment. He was a tall thin man called Joseph Rockwell. Ears like a radar dish. Sam smiled and spoke respectfully and introduced himself. Joseph Rockwell smiled in return and told Sam his name and they were on their way towards mutual trust and respect. Maybe it would not result in a beautiful friendship, but it now had the possibility. Both of the dead men had had previous experience and good references. Geoff Harper was an ex-policeman and had worked as a security guard at Sainsbury's for several years before moving over to the Micklegate Control Room. Cal Pointer had been in the army and spent several years in Northern Ireland. He was an expert in surveillance techniques, and had had a special interest in CCTV since its inception. Giving this much information seemed to exhaust Joseph Rockwell.

'What I'm most interested in,' Sam told him, 'is if any sections of tape are missing.'

'The police have taken all the old tapes,' Rockwell told him. 'We heard back from them that some sections were missing. But we don't know why, and we don't know which sections.'

'When do you record?' Sam asked. 'Not the whole twenty-four-hour period?'

'No. We record from 8 p.m. to 2 a.m., 4 a.m. Fridays and Saturdays. That never varies, so whatever the police have found missing will be from those times. In addition to that the operators can start recording at any time if they think something is suspicious, or if something blatantly obvious is going on. We've had break-ins in the middle of the day which good operators have got on tape. Evidence like that, well, if you can take that into court you have no problem getting a conviction.'

True, but the guy also recognized that crime was not really being controlled by the cameras. Rather it was being displaced. The robbers and the muggers moved on to another patch which wasn't covered by a camera. And at the same time they found ways of getting round the technology. 'We've had cameras shot out,' Rockwell said. 'Thing is, if you're in the control room and a camera goes dead, you don't immediately think it's been shot, you suspect the technology. By the time you've gone through all the checks, the people who shot the camera have moved in and done whatever it was they'd planned. Ram-raided the jewellery store and now they're long gone.'

Sam left him in his big office. A lone typewriter was clacking away somewhere in the building – no one would ever repair it when it got sick. Modern technology had pushed it towards the edge of the shelf. If it was a lucky typewriter it would have a future – in a museum.

Faced with the prospect of returning to the office, Sam remembered that there were several traders in Micklegate who Geordie had been unable to contact. He decided to track them down. What had happened more than once was that when Geordie approached someone for information, they gave him the run around. Businessmen were the worst offenders. And thirty-something businessmen were dedicated Geordie evaders. Women were the opposite, often keeping Geordie tied up for longer than the questions should have taken. Women gave him cakes, family histories, talked about their marriages. Geordie took it all in his stride, believing the thirty-something businessman when he told him he had an important appointment just as much as he believed the woman who told him her cakes would build him up, make him strong.

But no one evaded Sam Turner. Even so, by the end of the afternoon he hadn't actually unearthed any real new information. He was cold and damp from occasional flurries of snow. Vowing, for the third time in a row, that the next man he talked to would be the last of the day, Sam walked into a used-furniture warehouse and introduced himself to the proprietor.

The man was large. Big bones amply covered with rough, white, lardy flesh. He had a belly which wobbled from side to side when he walked, and a bottom which did the same as it followed him around. He still had several of his own teeth. They were ground down and they were black, but anyone could see they were originals. The man had acne so bad, the only way to cure it would be to skin him. And to top it all he'd chosen *Essence de Urinal* for his aftershave.

Above his chair in the office was a small painted sign which read: CLAUDE WHITE, PROPRIETOR. This was just as well, because after Sam introduced himself, even though he waited, the man didn't get around to introducing himself.

He was busy taking ex-jukebox singles out of one box and placing them, in no particular order, into another box. Although the aftershave was strong, Claude's razor hadn't done a particularly good job on his face. There were clumps of hair at two points on his chin, and another under his nose. But maybe it wasn't a nose. It was in the right position but looked as though it had been replaced with one of his internal organs, his liver maybe, or a kidney. Something that needed a whole network of external blood vessels. Whoever recommended the surgeon was no friend of Claude White's.

He wore black boots with no laces, charcoal-grey

trousers that might once have been part of a Burton's suit and which were held up with rope, and an angora jumper with holes at both elbows. The jumper was tight at the neck and shoulders as if borrowed from slimmer times. Sam told his brain to smile at the man, but wasn't sure if the message ever got through to his face. He tried to keep an open mind. After all, who was he to judge? Claude might be a refugee in need of disaster relief, or he might be making a radical fashion statement.

C'mon, the millennium is looming, the firmament is in chaos, the end of the world is nigh. What does a private eye know about these things?

Claude finished transferring the ex-jukebox singles, and sat down heavily in a chair with half of its upholstery missing. He scratched at a patch of hair on his face with the broken black nails of his left hand. He looked at Sam and nodded towards another chair. The chair looked as though it had carried heavier than Sam in its history, but might not manage it this time. Still, no point in upsetting the man, he was obviously trying to communicate.

When Sam got the weight off his feet, Claude unscrewed the top from a flask and poured something brown and cold into a couple of cracked cups. Sam looked around for the saucers, teaspoons, sugar bowl and cream jug, see if he could help with the tea party, but it was going to be informal. He put the cup to his lips and tipped it so that a minute amount of the liquid entered him. He could now add 'bitter' to the descriptors 'brown' and 'cold', but couldn't put a more definite name to it.

He unfastened the buttons on his coat. Claude had a wood-burning stove in there that gave off a searing heat. At first it was pleasant, coming in off the frozen street, but after a few minutes you wanted to put more space between yourself and the stove than the tiny office allowed.

'D'you know Marnie?' Claude asked.

Sam nodded his head. He remembered a Hitchcock movie, but didn't think Claude would remember it. He let the man speak.

'Used to be gorgeous,' Claude continued. 'She's hideous now.' He looked away, up towards the rafters of the warehouse, and for a while there Sam thought he'd lost him. Like the guy had started in on the meaning of life. But he was only pausing for dramatic effect. 'Something's eating her away,' he said. 'Ate up all the gorgeous and left hideous behind. Ate up her brain as well. Don't know where she is. Sometimes she seems to know, you think she might be talking sense, then she starts screaming. Out of it.'

Sam interrupted. He didn't want to hear about Claude's love life. Didn't even believe he had one. The only thing Claude ever took out on a moonlit night was his teeth. 'Marnie? I don't know who she . . .'

'. . . I'm telling you,' said Claude, asserting the authority of the one who knows the answers. Sam pushed himself back into the chair. OK, Claude, he thought. I'll sit it out.

'She'd been about all afternoon,' Claude continued. 'Total mess. Stockings with great holes, the hem of her coat hanging down. There've been days when I've asked her in here, given her a drink, something to eat. But it's like feeding an animal, you know, if you've seen a dog or cat that's been kicked about. Wary, know what I mean? Eyes are never still, like she's worried you're gonna jump her.'

He shook his head. 'There might've been a time I'd've jumped her. But not now. Not for the last ten years. She's rotting away.

'I'd seen her go past on the other side of the road, then here she was coming back up this side. If it'd been earlier I'd have asked her in, but it was late. Later than I'm usually here. Dunno what I was doing, something kept me going. Whatever it was, I'd finished and I wanted to get home. So I watched her go past the entrance, and I was gonna come back in here and close up when she stopped on the pavement. Something was wrong about her, and it took me a minute or two to work out what it was. She didn't have a coat on. When I'd seen her go past earlier she'd had the coat with the hem hanging down, but now she didn't have a coat at all. She had a cardigan, I think it was. And she had it draped round her shoulders. It was cold. And I thought I might have something in here would keep her warm, so I came back inside to look out a new coat for her.

'I found something, and when I got back to the entrance she was moving on to the road. I didn't know what she was doing for a minute. Then I realized she was taking a crap. Right there, in the middle of the fucking road. I couldn't watch it. She'd been such a beautiful woman. It would've been different if I hadn't known her. But I really fancied her, you know. Used to dream about her. There've been nights I've followed her round the pubs – she used to sing sometimes, on the microphone, "Smoke Gets in Your Eyes", "Danny Boy" – just to be near her. I can remember the smell of her, when she was young, the perfume she wore. Jesus, I couldn't watch her taking a crap in the street.'

Claude looked around, and he reached behind him, pulling a threadbare red coat on to his lap. 'This is it,' he said, 'the coat I was gonna give her.' He held it up for Sam to see the imitation fur on the collar and cuffs. 'Dunno what it is,' he said. 'Fucking beaver lamb, something like that.'

'What time was it?' Sam asked. 'D'you know?'

He shook his head. 'Real quiet. Six, could've been later.

Seven o' clock. She was giving the V-sign to drivers, people were blowing their horns, and Marnie was squatting down there snarling at them, waving her arms around, falling over. Jesus. This cop arrived in a squad car, one of the babies they've started employing now. Still got bumfluff on his chin. Marnie could've eaten him for breakfast. And he's like, the cop, you know, he's got the belt with the radio and the truncheon and the torch and the handcuffs and the notebook. But the notebook, it's not a notebook any more, it's like a whole Filofax. The guy's so weighed down he can hardly walk. But even without any of the kit there's no way he's gonna be able to do anything about Marnie taking a crap in the middle of the road. So he's back to the car, and he just sits there behind the wheel and waits another ten minutes for reinforcements.

'Finally they arrive with a couple of women officers and a van, and they bundle Marnie in there and away. When they'd gone I walked over to the side of the road, and she'd left a little steamer behind on the cobbles. All that fuss over one blind eel, couldn't've been more'n about three inches long.'

'Do you remember seeing a kid about the same time?' Sam asked. 'Young boy, mixed race, maybe thirteen, fourteen years old?'

Claude shook his head. 'Only other thing I remember is a car. Real sporty job. Shortly after they took Marnie away there was a squeal of brakes, and these two guys get out. They were like body-building types. But I didn't pay it any mind. I was away home.'

'Can you describe them?' Sam asked. 'Or the car?'

'They were body builders. You could see that. Sporty clothes. Thick necks and huge overdeveloped shoulders. Night time this area turns into something else. You get all sorts. I thought they might be connected with one of the clubs. Bouncers, something like that. I think one of them had blond hair. And the car was white, two-seater job. But real sleek. Long and low, and with an engine that roared.'

'Anything else?'

After a long pause Claude said, 'Licence number. It wasn't a regular number. I can't remember what it was, but it wasn't normal.'

'A custom number?'

'Yeah, if that's what it's called. Custom number. Like a guy's name. Millionaires have them, something like CHARLES 1. That wasn't it. I can't remember the name, but it was one of them – custom? – numbers.'

Sam gave Claude one of his cards. 'You've been a great help,' he said. 'If you think of anything else, give me a ring. Especially if you remember anything about the registration, or the two guys.'

When they got to the street Claude shook his hand and said, 'That was another thing she used to sing, "Stranger in Paradise". Remember that song?' He half closed his eyes and reached for the opening note. 'Hold my hand, I'm a stranger . . .' He let it fade away. Grinned at Sam. 'She was a better singer than me.'

Ain't that the truth, Sam thought, as he walked back towards town.

CHAPTER 15

Everybody you meet, Sam thought as he made his way to meet the woman from Scottish Widows, they've all got an area of their lives they want to block out. There had been something about Claude White, something in his voice when he talked about Marnie. A wistfulness. A longing back to a time when something could have happened but didn't.

With Marie it was the opposite. Something had happened to Marie that she wished hadn't happened. Claude was trapped by an illusion, she by reality.

What about Sam Turner, superman? Had he escaped all that? Jus' call him Mister Very Well Adjusted. A fine specimen of British manhood, standing six foot two in his socks and afraid of nothing but closing time.

What Sam had been looking for was that numbness, that feeling when you've already started drinking, but before you get sloshed. That feeling called normality. You feel good, relaxed. Like being married, alone with your wife. Or when you're with friends and someone's just made a joke, and you're all laughing together. That. That moment.

Normality.

Drinking was always about that. About the anticipation of achieving that. Instead, you abuse your body. You abuse yourself. You want to hurt the world, so you hurt yourself. In Marie's case Sam can see the connections. In his own case he knows he'll only ever see what he wants to see.

Childhood abuse and self-abuse are essentially the same thing. When we abuse ourselves we abuse that in us which is most vulnerable: the child.

Jeanie said, 'What did you mean, when you said you were an alcoholic?'

'It's a weakness. An attempt to empower myself. When I drink, when I begin drinking, it gives me the illusion that I'm in control. After I've been drinking for a short while I can't read any signals accurately. Signals from other people, even signals from my own body or mind. I don't function properly. I don't work.'

She was disconcerting. He'd told her he was a wreck and

she just sat there gazing up at his eyes. She looked at him with undisguised admiration. Sam didn't know what he was supposed to do with that. He only knew that it pushed all his buttons.

Ricardo, the owner of the restaurant, returned and placed a Coke in front of Sam, ice clinking and cracking on the surface. He placed a glass of white wine in front of Jeanie. She reached for it, but then hesitated, contented herself with fingering the glass.

'Go for it,' Sam told her. 'Don't hold back because of me.'

She lifted the glass and brought it to her lips. Sam held up the Coke in a toast. 'Cheers,' he said, and drank a quarter of the glass.

'Is there a reason?' she asked, still looking up into his eyes. 'Some kind of trauma that makes you do it?'

'I go to AA meetings,' he told her. 'There are as many reasons as there are people. Some drunks are easy to read. They're looking for love, they're lonely, they've never had a really close relationship. Maybe they've had a hard time as kids. Whatever, the booze is a substitute for them. You can see the connections all the way along the line. With others it's not so obvious.

'Some people, maybe most people, can walk into a pub and have a beer, leave a couple of quid on the bar. Life's not like that for me. After that first drink I put my wallet on the bar, everything I've got in the bank, my car, my house, my wife and family if I had one, my health, eventually my life.'

He lifted the Coke again and took a swallow. He placed the glass back on the table. He smiled at her. 'You can leave if you want,' he said. 'If you're not sure about getting involved with a schmuck like that.'

She was still looking up at him. He couldn't tell if some

of her admiration had been dulled. He thought it should have been.

'What you said before,' she said, 'about how everyone has a part of themselves they want to block out, that they can't face.'

'OK,' Sam said. 'You've listened to me. It's your turn.'

They left it for a while when Sophia, Ricardo's wife, arrived, and served up the tortellini. Ricardo made the pasta dough himself, and stuffed the rings with chicken and cheese. Sophia divided them equally between Sam and Jeanie, then disappeared for a moment into the kitchen for a ragù Bolognese. She returned one last time with a dish of Parmesan. Sam refused his sprinkle, but Jeanie wanted everything.

'This is good,' she said, tasting the Bolognese. 'This is very good,' she said after one of the tortellini rings. 'Do you bring all your conquests here?'

'Is that what you are? One of my conquests?'

She looked at him. She licked her bottom lip. She didn't answer the question. She reached for her glass and took a sip of the wine. She let Sam's eyes go for a moment. Then she looked back at him, still keeping the wine glass close to her lips. 'I don't want to be conquered. I want to be independent. I live alone and I like it that way.'

'So do I,' he said. 'But life sometimes gets lonely.'

She smiled and shook her head. 'Living alone is like death by drowning: a really delightful sensation after you cease struggling.'

Sam returned her smile. She had eyes that were pale blue, and deep enough to wade in.

'I couldn't imagine living with someone else,' she said. 'Not permanently. Every minute of every day. Do you understand what I mean?'

Sam lied. He said, 'Yes.'

CHAPTER 16

Ben didn't like it when Mama came into the Monster Gym looking for servants. He didn't like it at the best of times, but he especially didn't like it on a busy morning when everything that could go wrong had already gone wrong.

When half the equipment in the gym was loaded up with muscle and being worked hard. When the supervisor was having a day off because his granny had died and he was booked to help carry the coffin. When Gog was upstairs in bed with another headache and crying because he'd begun to develop bitch tits and acne. When the guy who worked the till had rung in with 'personal problems' that everybody knew was a hangover from last night's boozing, so Ben had had to find somebody else to work on the till who had no idea how to work a till because he'd never worked one before, and who didn't understand money and anyway couldn't tell his ass from his elbow. When half the customers were complaining that they'd got the wrong change, and the other half were complaining that they hadn't got any change at all. When the heating was on the blink, and then in the middle of it all she comes waltzing in loaded down with parcels and carrier bags. And she was dressed to kill with high heels and a chinchilla coat down to her ankles, but open at the front so the whole world could see she'd got a dress on that was so short you should've been able to see her knickers. But you couldn't. So God was sometimes kind. And she was loud with it, her mouth full of plums, as she explained how she couldn't possibly get all those parcels across town to where she'd parked her car in Sainsbury's because she was too tight to park it in one of the cash and flash car parks near the shops. And Ben would've liked it best if the heavens had opened up and the hand of God or the devil or one of that crew had come down to Earth and scooped her up and away, out of his gym. But that didn't happen and what Ben had to do, he had to smile at her because she was the boss's mother. And he had to listen. And he had to pretend he didn't mind.

'Oh, my,' she said. And she called him Benjamin, which was not his name, and which he wasn't even christened as. But it was no good telling her that. 'Oh my, Benjamin, I'm so glad you're here. I was panicking out there with all these parcels, wondering how I'd ever get them back to my car. Then I thought: Benjamin! The gym! And here I am.' She stopped then, to give him a brilliant smile, then half turned and gave the same smile, collectively, to all the glistening customers who should've been working the equipment, but who had given up to gawp at the unbelievable woman.

Ben avoided all eyes but hers. She tainted him. His customers all knew that he knew her, and that he was, therefore, a prick. He looked up, but Heaven remained impervious to his plight.

'I've got an enormous problem, Benjamin,' Mama continued. 'I'm here now, but I absolutely must be somewhere else about ten minutes ago. So what I'd like to do, if it isn't too much trouble for you, is leave all these parcels with you, and then, if you wouldn't mind, drop them off for me at the house. No rush about it, any time in the next couple of hours.' Beaming smile. 'I knew you wouldn't mind. You're an absolute treasure.'

And she dropped all the parcels at his feet, turned on a high heel and left.

And Ben hated her.

She talked and dressed like a girl, but she wasn't one. She was an old broad. Youth had been a habit of hers for so long she couldn't bear to part with it.

The customers gave him odd looks for the next hour, but the worst of the morning was over. He got the heating fixed, and eventually the guy on the till seemed to work out how to do it without pissing everybody off. In fact he got so good Ben wondered whether to keep him on instead of the other guy who had 'personal problems' every other week.

Before lunch he got Gog out of bed and left him in charge, while he loaded Mama's parcels into the car and took them round to Franco's place. She wasn't in, so he left them with Doc Squires who lived in the same house, but in his own personal rooms.

Ben was glad she wasn't there. He simply couldn't deal with the woman. He had to deal with her because she was the boss's mother. But it was always a problem. One of the things was, she always wanted to know the furthest end of a fart. She couldn't leave anything alone. It was more like Franco was her husband than her son. She was like a wife flapping round him. She did the books, kept, apparently, immaculate accounts. She said that Franco would never be caught out like Capone, go down on an income-tax fraud. That couldn't happen, because she could account for every penny that came in, and every penny that went out.

How Franco could put up with her, that was what Ben couldn't understand. There was one time when Franco was going out, Ben couldn't remember where, but there was Franco, and Ben, and Gog, and there was somebody else, and they were in the hall at Franco's place, just going out the door. And she'd come down the stairs. 'Franco, darling, you're surely *not* going out into the world in *that* shirt.'

It hadn't been a question. There was no question that she was asking him. She was telling him. Any woman, anybody, who'd said that to Ben, Ben would have strangled them. There would have been no question about that. But what did Franco do? He said, 'OK, my love. Memory's going.' And he walked up the stairs to his room and changed his shirt. And Ben and the other guys, they just had to stand about in the hall and wait for him.

She was a liability. She was someone you could really enjoy hating.

Ben and Gog had worked for Franco since the day Gog left school. Before that Ben had worked in the firework factory, which is where he learned about explosives. Every year on November the fifth Ben and Gog had better fireworks than anyone else. That was because Ben made his own.

When Gog left school Ben couldn't go to the firework factory any more. There was no way he could have left Gog at home on his own all day. Gog would've got into all sorts of trouble. So Ben'd given up his job, and on the very first day they'd walked the streets, knocking on doors, doing odd jobs. Until they'd knocked on Franco's door, and Franco had answered it himself.

He didn't have any odd jobs, didn't want the leaves raking in his garden. What he wanted was a couple of bouncers for a new club he'd just opened, The Starlight.

'You seem like a couple of enterprising boys, to me,' Franco said. 'And enterprise should be rewarded. That's what I think. That's what made this country great, and it's what'll make it great again. As long as there are people around who recognize it.'

Ben still smiled when he thought about the club. The Starlight had been the beginning of a great career. It had been busted by the fuzz and closed down later, but by that time Ben and Gog were an established part of the organization, and Franco kept them on the payroll.

After The Starlight, they became debt collectors. That was in Nottingham, when Franco moved over there, and they moved over with him. Franco used to lend money round the estates. He'd lend it to anyone. No security required. With Franco you only had to ask. That showed enterprise, asking Franco to lend you some dosh. And what Ben and Gog did was, they went round all the people who'd borrowed the money, and they collected the interest. Vigorish, they called it in the trade. The job was a doddle. All you had to make sure was that you got the money. No excuses allowed. If somebody couldn't pay they were showing a lack of enterprise, and Franco had no time for that. If somebody said they couldn't pay you smacked them at least six times. Each. Ben smacked them six times and Gog smacked them six times. If they didn't pay the next week you kicked them at least ten times. Each. And the third week you showed them the Ref. The Ref was an iron bar. A heavy iron bar, nearly five feet long. And they always paid. Almost always. Ben could only remember two guys who'd forced them to use the Ref. It really made a mess. Ben couldn't imagine anyone being so unenterprising. Even really stupid people got enterprising when they'd been shown the Ref. Ben himself, if someone showed him the Ref, he'd get very enterprising. After you'd had a session with the Ref you were never gonna be any good to anyone. Not even to yourself.

They'd done good on the debt collecting. So good that Franco took them off it and put them on his personal staff. That didn't mean being in the house with him. There were only three or four people around Franco who got that close. But it meant that you got the responsible jobs. What Ben and Gog had to do was mainly clumpings.

How Franco described their new job was like they were James Bond. He'd laugh, 'cause the whole thing was a joke. 'You're the double os,' he'd say. 'You're double o nothing and Gog's double o zero. The fucking deadly duo.'

And everybody laughed. A rich man's joke is always funny.

If someone in the organization went bad, if they had their hand in the till or they fucked up in any way at all, it was Ben and Gog who would sort them. Or if someone who wasn't in the organization, maybe someone in another organization, or even a nobody, upset Franco in some way, or they upset Mama, it was still Ben and Gog who would have to sort it out.

Often it was someone who had upset Mama. Because what happened was, Mama upset somebody else, and then she'd go to Franco and say she was upset because this guy had upset her, and then Franco'd call in Ben and Gog.

What Franco wanted in cases like these was for the guy to be really sorry. So Ben or Gog or both of them together might break a few of his fingers, or an arm or a leg. There was a scale to it. Depending on the size of the upset. Sometimes you didn't have to break nothing at all, maybe do some burning with a cigarette, if it was one of the girls. You wouldn't have to mark her face, not do anything to her that might stop her earning. Just give her a night of pain. Something she'd remember next time she thought about creaming money off the top.

Torturers. Ben had suddenly thought about it one night, when they'd broken this guy's two big toes. He'd told Gog. 'We're torturers, Gog. Like in the war. Or in movies. We torture people.' They'd been stood over the guy with the toes, and he'd passed out when they broke the last one. And Gog had smiled and got a log and a hammer. And what they did was, they got the guy's trousers down while he was still asleep, and they put his balls on the log. And then they waited for him to wake up.

And when the guy opened his eyes, Gog showed him his

balls on the log, and then he showed him the hammer, and the guy was really very sorry that he'd upset Mama.

Things had quietened down at the gym by the time Ben got back. There were a number of lads in the alley doing drugs. Most times Ben would have gone in among them and chased them off, but he was worried about Gog, and went straight inside. The kids were between eleven and eighteen, and they were on anabolic steroids, the same as Ben and Gog, except they were unsupervised. They might take between five and ten times the recommended dose and usually combined four or five different brand names. They put on muscle, no doubt about that. They got where they wanted to be in the short term, but in the long term they would probably end up with a host of illnesses: hardening of the arteries and enlarged prostates. But they also gave the gym a bad name, doing it out in the alley. Some neighbours might complain, then the police would be round. Ben would have to think of a way of moving them on.

Gog said he didn't have the headache any more. But he still had the bitch tits and the acne and he thought his balls were shrinking. His eyes were wild looking, and he was having trouble keeping saliva in his mouth. It kept dribbling down his chin, and he wiped it away with the back of his hand.

He followed Ben around, not saying much, but watching whatever Ben was doing. When Ben picked up the telephone Gog got agitated, muttering to himself. Ben had to ask him to get out of the office so he could concentrate.

Whenever the telephone rang Gog would come galloping into the office. He didn't answer it. He never answered it anyway because no one would understand what he said.

But whenever it rang he would come running. He'd hang around while Ben dealt with the call, and then later, when Ben had been in the gym to change some towels, he found Gog in the office chair shaking the telephone, and listening to it as though there might be somebody inside it.

'What's wrong with you today?' Ben asked. 'You're like a cat on a hot tin roof.'

Gog said he thought the telephone had rung.

'How could you *think* the telephone had rung?' Ben said. 'Either it rings or it doesn't ring. If it'd rung I'd've answered it. You never answer the telephone anyway, because people don't understand Gogspeak. That's how I know something's wrong here, Gog. Because you're in the office shaking the fucking telephone and generally acting up and acting odd, and getting on my fucking nerves.'

Gog hung his head and said how would Ben like it if he got spots.

But Ben had had his fill. The day had been bad enough already. He'd had too much to deal with. 'I don't want you feeling sorry for yourself, Gog. I don't want you following me around all the fucking time. I also don't want to find you shaking the telephone and complaining. There are things to do in the gym, and you know what those things are. You move your ass in there and do those things, while I see to the things I have to do here in the office. OK?'

Gog said yes, that would be OK. And he was sorry. He went to the gym and did his jobs. When the telephone rang he didn't come to the office. He stayed in the gym. He wiped down the equipment. He sorted the weights. When he'd finished doing everything that needed to be done he worked out some on the bench, pressing up to 250 lbs.

'OK,' Ben said. 'I'm gonna phone this Sam Turner guy. You wanna come and listen?'

Gog wiped himself down and followed Ben back to the office. Ben punched in the numbers and held the mobile to his ear. He smiled at Gog while he waited, and Gog smiled back. They'd had some words, but they were brothers. They loved each other.

It was the old lady who picked up the phone. Ben had seen her going in and out of the office. Together with Gog he knew everybody who went in and out of that office. Where they lived as well. Watching the detectives, they called it.

'Put Sam Turner on.'

'Who shall I say is calling?' the old lady asked.

'Who the fuck you like,' said Ben, giving it back to her, the years of breeding in her tone, the cultured voice. The self-satisfaction, the arrogance, the weakness, the decadence. 'Just get him.'

She didn't do it immediately. She hesitated. Ben could see her there, on the end of the line, pursing her lipsticked lips, thinking of something to say. Probably going to tell him to mind his manners, something like that. Don't be rude, young man.

He intercepted before she could get to it. 'Don't fuck about, lady. If I'd'a wanted to talk to you I'd've rung the cemetery. Put Turner on the line, and put him on now, or I'll come round there and show you the Ref.'

That did it. She put the phone down on the desk and he heard her call over to Sam Turner. You only had to mention the Ref for people to start being reasonable.

'Sam Turner,' the guy said. He didn't have to say that. He had the kind of telephone voice that once you'd heard it you'd know it again. Ben didn't like his voice. Didn't like anything about him. 'Specially he didn't like that the guy just picked the phone up and said: Sam Turner.

'If you work in an office,' Ben told him, 'if you work in

an office you should know how to use the phone. You don't just say: Sam Turner, like you was the Queen, or the fucking Queen Mother. This is Sam Turner speaking. You could say that. Or something else, there isn't a fixed way of saying it. But you don't just say your name, like fucking Jesus, God or somebody.'

'This is Sam Turner speaking,' the guy said, coming on funny. 'Is this the CBI consultancy service?'

'Listen, birdshit. You've strayed off your turf. You're asking the wrong questions and you're asking them in the wrong places. Whatever it is you think you're into, forget it. If you like what happened to your office so much, it can be arranged for the same thing to happen to your house.'

'I didn't realize we were getting so close,' the guy said. 'You sound worried. And you should be, 'cause we're not gonna give up.'

'I'll tell you what,' said Ben. 'I'm telling you to give up, but in a way it's breaking my heart. You know why? 'Cause if you give up we'll have to leave you alone.' He stopped there and gave a little laugh into the mouthpiece, giving the birdshit guy the chance to think about it. 'In your case that would be a pity. We don't want to leave you alone. What we want . . .' Ben looked over at Gog, and they nodded at each other, '. . . is for you to force us to make your life a total fucking misery.'

But the guy on the other end was unstoppable. 'Do what you have to do, dumbbell,' he said. 'You and the other dumbbell. We've got you in our sights now, and we're gonna stop you. That's a promise. A guarantee. You can't do anything about it.'

'How's this, then,' Ben said. 'We start off terrorizing that old lady you got in there. The one just answered the phone. Shit, if somebody pushed her over on the road that'd be enough. After that we go for the Scottish broad, the one you're fucking every other night. Maybe we give her one on your night off, sport? How'd that grab you?'

'You're not above holding a grudge, then.'

Ben ignored him. The guy was all mouth. 'And when we've finished with the women, there's always the young kid with the dog. A boy and a dog, together, in a cellar with us for a couple of days. The thought makes my mouth water, Sam. Don't mind if I call you Sam, do you? Only we seem to be getting along so well.'

'Sam's my name,' the guy said. 'It's printed on the window of my office, and on the door. But you're giving yourself away, pal. I know you can read now. So you've had an education, like maybe a Ph.D. in weightlifting? What else? All the style and subtlety of a fruit machine. And about as much intelligence.'

'Clever sod, aren't you?' said Ben.

'Comparatively.'

'Yeah, yeah,' Ben said, and closed the flip-down mouthpiece on the mobile. He looked over at Gog who was sweating profusely. He did have acne. His face was erupting, and he had his head in his hands and was swaying from side to side, his face contorted with pain. 'Is it bad?'

Gog didn't admit it. He shook his head and tried to smile. But you could tell he was in agony.

'I think we're gonna have to clump this Sam Turner character,' Ben told him.

CHAPTER 17

Sam shaved with the bathroom door open. Barney ran constantly back and forth from Sam in the bathroom to Geordie at the kitchen table.

Sam was feeling good. His face was glowing after a day out on the bike with Jeanie Scott. They had cycled out to Selby on the cycleway, downstream along Terry Avenue and past the Knavesmire. Not met one single mugger, robber, child molester or murderer all day long. In Selby they'd walked round the market and bought Cox's Orange Pippins and a French stick and double Gloucester, which they'd shared with some ducks outside a pub near Cawood.

Jeanie had asked him about his alcoholism and he'd managed to talk about it without sounding pathetic. She'd been interested in the workings of AA, and he'd told her about the Twelve Steps, tried to explain how they worked.

'The way you talk about it,' she said, 'it sounds like some kind of religion.'

'It's not,' he said. 'There are believers and unbelievers. AA's open to anybody.'

'What about surrendering to a Higher Power?' she asked. 'That's got to be God.'

'I suppose it is for some,' he agreed. 'But for me the Higher Power is AA itself. Not the organization so much, but the spirit of it. The being of the group. When I tried to kick alcoholism by myself I couldn't raise the strength. There wasn't enough of me. But with AA I can keep it at bay.'

'You mean you're cured?'

He shook his head. Non-alcoholics didn't understand. 'No,' he said. 'There isn't a cure. I'll always be an alcoholic. At the moment I'm a sober alcoholic. With the help of AA I'll stay a sober alcoholic.'

She got quiet then, for several minutes. They exchanged the odd word, talked to the ducks, but really she had gone inside herself to digest it, try to work out how she felt about it. Later she said, 'There must be something special about a group like that.'

'Yeah,' he said. 'Unbelievable.' He wanted to tell her there was something special about her, but it sounded like a come on. Now, with his reflection in the bathroom mirror, he realized it would have been a nice thing to say, the kind of thing people liked to hear. But at the time he couldn't say it. He couldn't say it and he blamed her for it, that she would think it was too much of a come on. When in reality he couldn't say it because Sam Turner couldn't say it. Couldn't say it because he was a mean bastard.

He could watch and wait for Jeanie Scott to turn herself inside out over his alcoholism, and when she'd gauged his expectations and reactions microscopically, felt her way around his emotional landscape and ended up putting each foot exactly right, he couldn't even say thanks in a way that would have mattered.

Sam cut his throat with the razor, winced and reached for the towel to stem the flow of blood.

'Is she the one?' Geordie asked when Sam came out of the bathroom.

'D'you mind running that train through the station one more time?'

'The nurse. Jeanie. The Scottish Widows woman. Is she the one? D'you think you can manage to keep her?'

'Keep her?'

'Oh, Sam, you know what I mean. D'you like her? I don't know the words for it. Are you gonna get it on together?'

'Yeah, Geordie. I like her. That doesn't mean we're gonna have a life-long relationship. I'm not thinking of getting married, settling down, having kids. I just like her. None of those other things follow on from that. Not necessarily.'

Geordie sat Barney down on his back legs and stroked

the dog's head. 'It does with other people, Sam. With normal people. They get married and have kids and stuff like that. I know you don't like it, but that's because you're not normal. You get a woman and when I look the other way, or I take Barney for a walk, I get back and you've lost her or she's gone off with somebody else. I've never heard of anyone like you before. It's like you can't hang on to a woman for more than a few days before she's gone off you or you've gone off her. I think maybe you pick the wrong ones to start with. They're usually too young for you. You should start looking for a woman that's about your own age. I don't know, maybe somebody who's been married and her husband's died, she's had a family and they've all grown up and gone away and she's feeling lonely. That'd be really good for her as well.'

'Jesus,' Sam said, fingering the cut on his throat. 'This woman, does she make apple pies all day long, have my slippers warming by the fire when I come home?'

''Spect so,' Geordie said. 'Something wrong with that?'

'No.' Sam walked over to the tape stack and ran his finger down the labels. 'It's just a pleasant prison dream that I don't want anything to do with.'

'There's Janet's *Imagine* tape,' Geordie said. 'You could play that.'

'OK.' Sam took the tape out of its container and slipped it into the machine. 'I really wanted something for a cut throat, but this'll do for the bit that's crippled inside.'

Geordie cocked his head on one side for a moment, so him and Barney looked like twins. Then he said, 'Crippled inside? Hey, that's pretty good. No, I mean it, Sam. For an old guy like you that's really very good.'

'What about you and Janet?' Sam asked. 'Can we look forward to the sound of wedding bells and the patter of tiny feet?'

'None of your beeswax.'

'Well, *that's* consistent,' said Sam. 'My love life is public property as far as you're concerned. But I'm not even allowed to ask you a question.'

'I don't think Janet sees me as husband material,' said Geordie.

'You're just a stud, are you?'

'Stud? No, Sam, I'm not a stud.'

'Sorry. Just a horsey joke. You would think about marrying her, then?'

'Yeah,' said Geordie. ''Course I would, Sam. She's a great woman. And I like talking to her, I mean, like a friend. You know what I mean? We get on together great, 'cept she's more brainy than me. More intellectualistic, like.'

'You reckon?'

Geordie shook his head. 'No doubt about it. She's got eight GCSEs. An A in Maths, Bs in English and Geography.'

Barney reached up and licked Geordie's face.

Sam chuckled. 'Married life isn't so bad after you get so you can eat the things your wife likes.'

Geordie was supposed to laugh at that, so he laughed at that.

'Y'know what I think you should do?' said Sam. 'I think you should take on a case of your own. Next thing that comes up, you should run it yourself. Something that's interesting, and not straightforward. You'd feel better about yourself if you had your own cases.'

'Maybe. What we gonna do about the cases we've got on right now?'

'Carry on like we started. Work at it till we get a result.'

'What about the threats?'

'These guys are fresh out of the primordial slime. There's

an incipient intelligence, but no hint of morality, no feelings beyond their own self-consciousness. We take them seriously. But we take them.'

They listened to the tape for a few minutes. Geordie got to his feet and filled the kettle, set it on the hotplate. Sam joined him and took cups down from the hooks. 'There's nothing wrong with your intelligence, Geordie,' he said. 'You're as bright as anyone else around here. All that happened was you missed out on some schooling. And being homeless didn't help. But the stuff you missed can be put right. If you can't spell, who cares? That's not to do with intelligence. You can learn all that stuff.'

'I know, Sam. It's just that, well, fuck, I hope Janet'll wait for me, till I catch up with her.'

'She'll wait if she's got her head screwed on the right way, Geordie. And if she doesn't she'll be a bigger loser than you.'

'If I get the A level and lose Janet, the A level won't seem so important.' He paused a moment, seemed to listen to the tape. 'But at least I'll have an education. They can't take that away from you.'

Sam smiled. 'That's why they don't give you one in the first place.'

Whenever he walked that part of the river now, Sam expected to see another duck being gang raped. Maybe even the same duck. But it hadn't happened again since the first time. Perhaps it was an aberration. Not an everyday event within duck culture. He hoped not. It would be something to hang on to. If it was true he might become a naturalist. Retire from the mean streets and fade into a pantheistic heaven on earth.

Why not? Couldn't happen to a nicer guy. Still, don't hold your breath.

Marie wore a black dress. It fitted her, too. She was always saying that her clothes seemed to shrink more than other people's, but this dress fitted her. There was a smell of freshly baked bread.

'We might be dealing with a paedophile,' Sam said. 'Might even be more than one. They tend to run in packs.'

'You're thinking about Andrew Bridge? The way he was mutilated?'

'Yeah,' he said. 'D'you think you can handle it?'

Marie smiled. 'Because of my background? You might say I have certain qualifications.' She put plates and knives on the table. 'The Belgian. The one who kept those kids in a dungeon. What was he called?'

'Marc Dutroux. He had a statue of the infant Jesus in his garden.'

'Yeah, Dutroux. When I read about that, the things he did, I didn't sleep all night. Just sat up thinking about those poor kids. When I hear about anything like that, I have to think I was lucky.'

'He wasn't alone,' said Sam. 'He made a career out of it. And there are others like him. UNICEF reckon that trafficking in children is the third most lucrative illegal trade. Drugs, weapons and kids. In that order. Paedophilia is a multimillion-dollar business.'

'There's a part of me would rather work on a drugs case, or a weapons case, anything. A straightforward murder. But it's not a coincidence that this comes up now. Where shall I start?'

Sam shrugged. 'Wherever. Talk to the homeless kids for a start. Try the rent boys. Follow your nose.'

She sat him down at the table and served up a basket teeming with white buns, sesame seeds on the top. 'I made this as well,' she said, placing a dish of red salmon pâté on the table.

'It's great,' Sam said, breaking into one of the buns. 'But you shouldn't have bothered.'

Marie shrugged. 'Keeps me occupied. While I'm sifting flour, cutting up vegetables, I'm not cutting myself up.'

'How are you, Marie? I don't mean with the cutting, I mean altogether. Since Gus's death. How are you managing? We used to talk about nothing else. Now it hardly ever comes up.'

'It's true,' she said. 'We did talk about it all the time.' She smiled. 'I've been through the processes. I've forgotten them all now, the stages you're supposed to go through. The grieving. Loss, anger, all that. I've come to terms with it. I'll never see him again. Sometimes, from time to time, the fact of it comes swinging through the night at me like a giant club. But most of the time I accept it.'

'I miss him, too,' Sam said. 'In the same way. I go for months when he doesn't enter my mind, then when it comes it's like a punch in the back.'

They sat together quietly. Sam had another bun. Marie had three. 'The dead leave such spaces,' he said eventually.

'I'm still trying to unload my father,' Marie said. 'And my mother.' She took a deep breath. 'He was called Stanley, my father. When I first started to cut myself I used a Stanley knife. I used to call it Little Stanley. I would put it in my mouth. I'd suck the knife with the blade attached, not cutting myself at first. I'd stay like that for several minutes before I started twisting the knife around. I'd end up gagging on the blood. That was what would stop me.'

'The beginning,' he told her, 'when you had the blade in your mouth, but didn't do any cutting, before you got started, that's just like getting a drink. I'd do that sometimes, exactly like you described. I'd buy a shot and put it on the bar and look at it. Might sit in front of it for an hour. Then down it, and twenty more in the next couple of hours.'

She smiled at him. 'We should've got together earlier.'

'Have you seen your therapist again?'

'Yes. We're working on shame.'

'I know that one, too,' Sam said. 'People are always talking about it at AA meetings.'

She reached for another bun but changed her mind. 'It's not easy. All women know shame, anyway. Feeling ashamed and being a woman sometimes seem like the same thing. I'm beginning to see that my shame isn't me. And as I get to understand that more, to know it more, it becomes possible for me to take it on. What we hope – what I hope – is that I'll beat it. Put it behind me.

'What I'm doing now is remembering the shame. I'm forcing myself to relive it. I talk to my therapist about it. I share it with my good friend Sam Turner.' She smiled, and Sam smiled back at her and nodded his head. 'And they listen to me, take away some of the burden. Not all of it. It's my burden and I have to bear it.

'But I am beginning to see things differently. I even think of my father differently. There's a kind of love for him, compassion, because he was also ashamed. Oh, I'm not going to say I forgive him, or that it wasn't his responsibility. It *was* his responsibility. He hurt me.

'But because my therapist listens to my stories and doesn't get up and walk away, and because my friend Sam Turner listens to it all and comes back again for more, then I have to recognize that there is a sense in which I am loved. And if these other people, who are not me, love me, then it might be possible for me to love myself.'

Sam scratched his chin.

'That means you've got a question,' Marie said. 'When you scratch your chin.'

He grinned at her. 'I'm transparent, then?'

Marie nodded.

'You told me that your father committed suicide. Put his head on the railway track. But in the past you told me he died of cancer . . .' Sam let his words die away. He'd been going to ask her which story was true, but in asking the question the answer became obvious.

'Yes, he killed himself,' she said.

Before he left, Sam stood at the door with Marie and asked, 'Do you think anything else about your father?'

She thought about that for some time before she answered. 'There's what I said tonight, that feeling of compassion. Lately I've had another thought. What happened between us was in a way unique. Exploitative, certainly; secretive and traumatic, ultimately damaging and violent. It has scarred my whole life, all of our lives. Don't get me wrong, I wish it hadn't happened. But between him and me . . . my father and me . . . I wonder if it was a love affair.' She gazed off into the distance.

Sam walked to the Volvo, unlocked the door and slid behind the wheel. Felt in his pocket for a cigarette, then remembered that he'd given that up, too. Through the windscreen he watched the river playing with the reflected light from the city. There was a thin covering of ice close to the banks.

He thought about the face on the video and how things were never quite what you expected them to be. As he held the picture in his mind, the vacant stare, the brute face, the bovine head, he heard Marie's thoughts about her father. After a lifetime of discovering over and over again that it wasn't so, he still found himself returning to these childhood concepts. Marie's father had looked nothing like the face on the video. Sam had seen photographs of Stanley, and he had been a tall, slim, handsome man. He'd been a freak, sure, he was ugly inside. But if you passed him in the street you wouldn't see that. If you met him at a party you'd never guess what he did in his spare time.

By the same token, then, the face on the video didn't have to belong to a demon. Just because it was physically repulsive, stolid. There was an imperative to damn it, the person behind it, because of its asinine expression.

He conjured it up again. Held it before him on the windscreen. The fixed grin, like a mask. The huge mouth, open all the time, waiting for a fly. Sam'd sent Geordie round the gyms but it struck him now that it might be useful to check out the psychiatric hospitals. Someone as obvious as this would be known. He wasn't another Stanley. He was in a league of his own. This guy, someone like him, if you saw him coming towards you on the street, you'd cross over to the other side.

The image on the windscreen shifted slightly.

It was like an advert Sam'd seen on the TV, a technique they used sometimes, where two images merge into each other. Morphing? Something like that. There was this guy who had a migraine and was down in the dumps, looking like he was gonna top himself. Then he took some new pain killer, and another guy, the same man but looking really happy, walked on to the screen and inhabited the body of the first guy.

That's what happened on the windscreen, except it was reversed. The first image had been infused with something that Sam had placed there. There was an element about it that was sympathetic. But the new image, the image now inhabiting Sam's first projection, had nothing sympathetic about it at all.

It was hostile.

It was moving and breathing without the help of Sam Turner's imagination.

It was gently humming to itself and frothing at the mouth, pushing against the front of the car so that the vehicle bounced up and down on its suspension.

Sam shook his head, hard. But nothing changed. This was not an image. This was the monster who had destroyed his office. This was a guy who was beyond reason. He watched as the man leant over the bonnet and grinned at him. He said something, or at least moved his lips. But Sam couldn't make out the words.

Then he pushed himself away from the bonnet of the car and walked round to the driver's door. Sam hit the lock, fast, and sat there behind the glass while the face came up close to the window. 'Gog,' the mouth said. 'Ugh. Gog.' And the mouth was actually on the glass, the lips puckering up and making a kiss. When the face moved back an inch or two a trickle of saliva ran down the window. It wasn't much, but there was a hint of human intelligence there. The guy laughed loudly as he brought his head down against the glass. Then again, as though he was about to ram his way into the car with his forehead.

The glass held, but the violence of the man's movements roused Sam into action. He felt in his pocket for the car keys. This was no time for any kind of heroics. Just get it together and move the hell out of here. And do it fast.

While he was searching for the keys the face disappeared towards the rear of the car. No keys in his right jacket pocket. That pushed a panic button, he might have left them at Marie's house. Sitting on that low table, next to the basket of buns. But he was in the car, must've had the keys to open the door. Keep calm. Sam thought of opening the door and making a run for it, but his hand closed over the keys in his left jacket pocket, and he fumbled with them to find the one that fitted the ignition.

He found it and was aiming for the ignition when the car lurched forward. Sam fell back into the seat and then forward on to the steering wheel. The keys spun away from his grip and fell to the darkness of the floor. Felt like they landed somewhere near the clutch pedal, and he tried to locate them with his foot. A small voice in his head, getting louder all the time: Stay calm. Don't panic. The only way to manage this one is to be cool. If you get desperate you'll get dead.

But the car pitched forward again as the guy behind it utilized all his strength. It felt as though he was lifting the back wheels off the ground and then walking forward, a metre at a time, propelling the car over the track towards the icy river.

The guy was getting louder, too. Shouting and laughing. None of the words made sense, they were mainly grunts and hard, guttural sounds. Almost a series of commands, directing the action. Again the car bounced forward. The track disappeared, and Sam realized that the next push would have him almost into the river. He forgot about the keys and reached over into the glove compartment for his Glock 17. His fingers wrapped themselves around it, and he transferred it to his right hand while he searched for the magazine.

Another lurch forward, and this time Sam's head hit the roof of the car as the front wheels went over the bank. There was a screech of metal on stone as the undercarriage of the car came down on the edge of the concrete path. Sam looked through the windscreen, directly at the black water. The car had jammed itself on the brink. But the maniac behind it was shouting and screaming to himself, talking himself into giving it the final push.

Sam found the magazine and pushed it into the gun. He opened the car door and rolled out on to the path just as the madman heaved the car over the edge. The car hit the water nose first and stayed there, its back wheels spinning uselessly in air. The monster who'd launched it over the edge came forward stupidly to have a look at his handiwork, the same silly grin on his face. If he'd had any, Sam would have thrown him some meat.

Sam laughed briefly and loud. He laughed in reaction to the stress, but also in spite of it. The sense of the ridiculous got to him. What was he supposed to do now? Faced with a mammoth, some long-extinct beast? He realized with a shock that conservation wasn't uppermost in his mind at this stage.

The monster stole a last glance at the car, then turned to Sam and took a step forward. 'Gog Ugh,' he said.

'Yeah,' Sam agreed. 'You really know how to brighten up the day.'

Sam didn't think it was that bad a joke, he was still savouring it when the guy's huge hands tightened around his neck. He pushed the Glock into the guy's stomach and pulled the trigger, but nothing happened. You had to squeeze, not pull. Squeeze it slowly. But it was already too late. He felt himself lifted off his feet, saw in a flash the insignificance of man, the spiralling, gurgling nonsense of creation. He was being swung round by his neck. He was like a rag doll, light as air in the hands of this gigantic madman. He could see the muscles bulging on the forearms of his tormentor, and beyond them the biceps and massive shoulders. Finally, framed there, at arm's length, was the crazed, lumpy face with eyes as compassionate as a hungry mosquito's.

Sam imagined he would be swung round and round like that until he came apart. Until his head was freed from his body. But another thought must have fought its way through Gog's cognitive faculties, because he stopped swinging and pushed Sam on to his back. Then he stepped forward and sat astride him, coming down heavily, sending all the air out of the detective's body. Sam gasped for oxygen, taking in great gulps of it.

At the same time he remembered Geordie's new word. Brobdingnagian. But he forgot it again immediately. There are situations in life where language is no help. That was something he'd forgotten to tell Geordie. If he came through this one, he'd make sure the kid knew that.

But the word wouldn't go away. Brobdingnagian. It was a huge, unwieldy word, and it slowed everything. Shifted the speed of everything down. Gog's heavy arms reached upwards to the sky, then came lumbering down. The target was Sam's face. But the descent was so staggered that he felt the pain of impact long before it actually happened. The edge of one of the gigantic hands broke the bridge of his nose, the other caught his eye and sent a rush of blood to swell that whole area of his face.

Then those heavy arms were reaching up towards the sky again, slowly, adagio, like the presentiment of a funeral procession. Sam lifted his own arm, his right arm, feeling the weight of the Glock still gripped firmly in his hand. Less than a kilo, though it felt like a ton. He pointed it at the frenzied face above him. He shouted something inadequate: 'I'll shoot you.' But the retarded monster didn't even hear him. Sam shouted: 'Stop. Now. *Stop*.' He waved the gun.

Gog hesitated. He looked down at Sam's face, and his

great mouth fell open. The eyes glinted, but they were unseeing. The face seemed to consist of mouth alone. A slimy, bubbling orifice. Saliva, oozing from those lips, splashed on to Sam's head. The mouth was a yawning cave. There were stalactites there, hanging from the vaulted roof of the cavern. And it was a tunnel, leading back into the interior of this monster who was poised to crush the life out of Sam Turner. A throat, a gullet, a sanctum. At once the mouth became death itself. A blackness from which there was no return.

A movement above caught Sam's eye, and he realized that the great fists were once again beginning their descent. In a second, less, in a fraction of time they would be pounding the life out of him. He steadied the Glock, directing it at the crater, the black hole.

The Glock 17 has no conventional safety catch, but it will only fire if the trigger is pulled correctly. Sam concentrated on that, squeezing the trigger slowly. He heard the report and watched the short recoil. At the same time he saw a puncture appear at the back of the gaping void. He looked into the recesses of that mouth, and for a moment after the recoil of the gun he saw the night sky. The 9mm bullet opened a hole in the back of the monster's neck, and for a brief instant the heavens shone through.

Then the whole weight of the body flopped down on top of Sam, and he felt his mouth swell with blood.

There must have been a time of unconsciousness. A short period. A few seconds, maybe a couple of minutes. When he was conscious again Sam managed to heave the body over to the left and wriggle himself free. He stood uncertainly, taking a couple of steps back, away from the river. The great hulking body of the man he had shot was limp on the path. Sam holstered the Glock and staggered off in the direction of Marie's house.

He had no feelings or thoughts as he went. Occasionally his mouth filled with blood, and he spat it on to the grass. In the distance, from the town, there was the sound of merriment gone sour. Late drunks, unwilling to end the night and face the morning. White-knuckle city.

'Oh my God.' Marie took him by the arm and pulled him inside. She kicked the door closed and led him through to her sitting room. It seemed smaller than when he'd left, less than an hour ago. Still an aroma of fresh bread, the essence of salmon. There was something different about Marie; he looked at her and realized that she'd been in bed. She no longer wore the black dress, but a T-shirt, a long T-shirt, down to her knees.

She was holding his face gently, between both hands, turning it slightly from side to side. She caught his eye and shook her head. 'It doesn't look good. You should go to the hospital.'

'No,' he said, finding his mouth full of blood again. He couldn't talk. Marie gave him a bowl and he spat into it. He took a pen from his pocket and looked around for something to write on. Marie handed him a pad. 'I've just shot somebody,' he wrote.

He felt her stiffen, but the concern didn't leave her face. She shifted his position so that his head was slightly forward. 'I think your nose is broken,' she said. 'And your right eye is completely closed up. I can't even see it.'

He raised his arms in surrender. 'Coffee,' he wrote on the pad.

When she brought it through, he sipped the coffee. During the course of the next hour he told her what had happened. At first with the pad and pen, but after she'd taped his face and the bleeding had stopped, he could manage short sentences. But a pounding began in his head which was so violent it affected his balance. When he walked through the bathroom door he almost fell in the bath. He clung to the wall until Marie came to steady him.

She applied arnica ointment to his face, gave him something to dull the pain in his head. Three tablets in the palm of his hand. She wouldn't say what they were. He looked down at them; a fistful of dullers. She kept telling him she was a nurse. She knew what she was doing. If he wouldn't go to the hospital he'd have to trust her.

'Will you come back with me?' he asked. 'To the river. Then maybe to the police station.'

She nodded and went to get dressed.

They walked slowly along the track. The Volvo was exactly as he remembered it. Nose down in the mud of the Ouse.

'Insurance job,' Marie said. 'It is insured, Sam?'

'Yeah.' It was insured. But Sam was looking ahead, along the track, to the place where he had left the body. There was nothing there. He walked further, thinking perhaps he had made a mistake. But the moon was up, they could see for a couple of hundred yards along the track. There was no body.

Marie took his hand. 'You could have just wounded him. After you'd gone he came round and walked away.'

Sam shook his head. And it hurt. 'I killed him, Marie. There was a hole right through him.'

She gestured along the track. 'There's nothing here,' she said. 'If he was dead somebody must've found him. Called an ambulance.'

'No,' Sam said. 'The whole area would be cordoned off. There'd be police everywhere.'

He knelt down on the track where the fight had taken place. Looked at the ground. There were several scuff marks, but not a lot to go on. A quantity of brown stains, some of them droplets, a couple of them real smears. Sam didn't know which were his own and which the monster's, but there was blood on the tracks.

He got to his feet and tottered with a rush of vertigo.

She took his hand. 'Have you got any ideas?'

He didn't have any ideas at all. He felt weak. His legs kept buckling under him. 'I don't know if I'll make it back to your house.'

'You're gonna have to, big boy,' she said. 'There's no way I could carry you.'

He sat on her sofa while she made up a bed. Then he let her lead him to it. She helped him undress, untying his shoes and pushing him on to his back on the bed to remove his trousers. She brought the quilt up around his chin. 'Anything else?' she asked.

'If I'm dead in the morning,' he said, 'I'd like to leave my body to medical science.'

She smiled. 'I'll leave the door open. If you need anything, shout. My bedroom's next door.' She switched the light off and left.

Sam felt a warm blanket of tranquillity wrap itself around him. Outside it was raining to beat the band, and through the window he looked directly into the bowl of night. The cueball moon was propped up in the heavens by an invisible scaffold.

CHAPTER 18

'Celia, can you measure brains?'

'Goodness,' said Celia. 'I know very little about science, Geordie. I understand that they weigh them, after the owner has passed on, so to speak. There's no doubt that some brains are larger than others.' She was doing the accounts on her new computer, and Geordie had been in and out of the office several times already. He didn't want to stop her getting on with the accounts, but on the other hand he didn't want to be bugged by questions getting stuck in his head. That happened sometimes, you had a question and it got stuck in there, blocked up your brain completely. Geordie would feel panicky when that happened, like he would if he got something stuck in his throat. Best to keep everything clear.

'It's just that, I mean, not brains, that's the wrong word. What I was thinking, can you measure how good people are at thinking?'

'Intelligence,' said Celia. 'Oh, yes, that's something else again. There are IQ tests. Intelligence Quotient. They give you an idea around a mean for the whole population. That's a kind of measure. Is that what you meant?'

'Might be,' said Geordie. He went out of the door. He walked over to Sam's desk. Then he turned round and went back into Celia's office. She hadn't moved. She was still sitting at her new desk, but she hadn't transferred her attention back to the computer. It was as if she knew that Geordie would come back with another question. Like she was psychic. 'It's just that I was wondering,' he said.

'Yes, Geordie.'

'If two people like each other,' he said. 'Say, for example, there was this couple, this young couple. If I knew this young couple, or one of them, and he asked me to find out the answer to this question, or if the whole thing was just hypo, hypo . . .'

'. . . thetical,' said Celia. 'Hypothetical?'

'Yeah, like that. And this guy was wondering if it made any difference if their brains were both consisting of different intelligences. Like her brain, his girlfriend's, might have been bigger, or have more intelligence in it than his. What d'you think?'

'Whew,' said Celia.

Geordie smiled and scuffed his feet. 'Big one, eh, Celia?'

'Yes, Geordie. A big question.'

'Too big to answer?'

'No, I wouldn't say that. They could both take IQ tests. That would go part of the way to answering the immediate question. Would show which one of them was the brightest. The most intelligent. But from what you've said we are really dealing here with a much wider question than which one of these two young people is the most intelligent.'

'We are?'

'Yes. It seems to me that the young man, your, ah, friend, is concerned to know if a relationship is possible with a young woman of superior intelligence. Is that right, Geordie?'

'I don't know exactly,' Geordie said. 'I didn't talk to him all that long. We sort of spoke to each other about the brain size. He was just wondering, like.'

'I'm sure,' said Celia. 'I never married, Geordie. And there were many reasons for that. But as a teacher, and something of an intellectual snob, I would not have liked to spend a lot of time with a man who was not my intellectual equal.'

'You wouldn't? You mean if he was a bit thick, you would feel, like, as though he was underneath you.'

'Beneath, I think the word is, Geordie. *Be*neath rather than *under*neath. I'm not sure of my ground here. My job was concerned with education, so intelligence was important to me. To someone else it might not be a major factor. It's possible that what another woman would have looked for was a certain gentleness, maybe even a sense of humour. Overall intelligence might not have been so important to someone else. Do you see what I mean?'

There was a knock on the outer-office door and then the sound of the door being opened. Geordie turned his head as the voice of Dora, Celia's friend, came through to the office. 'Celia,' she called. 'Anyone at home?'

'Christ,' said Geordie. 'Just when we was getting somewhere.'

Geordie had been talking to people who ran gymnasiums. They were all men, he'd noticed after he'd only spoken to three of them. He had a private bet with himself that he wouldn't meet any women who ran gymnasiums. And he'd won that bet. But he'd also had another bet with himself after meeting the first three men that all the men he met who ran gymnasiums would be muscly. The first three were, really big-shouldered, muscly men.

But he'd lost the second bet. The fourth man he met wasn't muscly at all. The sixth and seventh men were, in fact the seventh man was nearly as muscly as the guy who had wrecked the office. But the eighth man was another weed.

It made you think. The muscly men, when you walked into their gym, they looked at you like you were a side dish they hadn't ordered. And the weeds, when you walked into their gym, their eyes glinted and they shook you limply by the hand. After a couple of minutes with them you'd check your wallet, see if it was still there in your back pocket.

Something else you had to think about, doing this particular job, was how it made you think about people in terms of muscly men and weeds. Normally you wouldn't think like that. People were just people. But the muscly men, nearly every one of them, looked down their noses at you if you weren't muscly too. And the weeds, if you'd just met them in a pub, say, or if you were introduced to them some other time, you wouldn't think they were weeds. It was the situation that made you think of them as weeds.

Geordie was glad he was in between. Glad he wasn't muscly, and glad he wasn't a weed.

That took care of the morning. He showed them all the picture he'd had made from the video. The close-up of the face of the monster who'd wrecked the office. Little bit blurred. No one recognized him.

He'd arranged to meet Janet for lunch in the arty café in Gillygate, and he got there five minutes early and drank three cups of coffee, but Janet didn't show. She'd said she might not be able to make it because she had an interview for a job in a bookshop, and she didn't know when she'd get away. After an hour Geordie ordered some soup and a roll and ate it by himself. He'd had breakfast alone as well, because Sam hadn't come home last night. Made you feel deserted when people deserted you. Maybe they'd run off together? Sam and Janet. Left him alone with Barney. Geordie wondered if Celia had gone as well, since their conversation about brains. And Marie. Everybody he knew in the whole world. All of them, just disappeared from the face of the earth.

He stopped himself asking the waitress for change for the telephone. He had a job to do. Ringing up everyone in the world wouldn't do any good. If they'd gone, they'd gone. Except he'd seen Celia already this morning, so at least she was still around.

He looked at his list of gymnasiums. The next one was just around the corner in Bootham. Sam wouldn't do that, anyway. Oh, he liked younger women, there was no doubt about that. But he wouldn't do that to Geordie. And Janet, she didn't fancy older men. Not at all; she thought they were creepy. She liked normal young men her own age, who weren't particularly muscly or weedy.

The gym in Bootham was different. The guy at the desk wasn't interested in talking to Geordie until Geordie showed him the photograph. Then he laughed. 'Gog,' he said.

'Gog?' said Geordie.

'Yeah. That's what they call him. Might be short for Gordon. I don't know. I used to work for them, him and his brother. They run a place in Acomb, called The Monster Gym.'

'Whereabouts?' Geordie asked, looking at his list. 'I don't have it down here.'

The guy gave him the address. 'Tell 'em I'm OK when you see them. 'Specially the blond one, Ben. He gave me the sack the other day, said I had too many personal problems. He'll be really worried about me.'

Geordie laughed. 'That's ironic,' he said. 'You're using irony.' He'd been working on English usage with Celia, and irony was the last thing they'd worked with. Celia had said that eventually he'd understand the difference between humour, wit, satire, sarcasm, invective, irony and cynicism, and Geordie had thought she was crazy. But maybe she was right. He'd just picked out one of them.

The guy didn't laugh, didn't think it was funny at all that Geordie had noticed his irony. He shook his head from side to side, a glazed look in his eyes. He sat behind the desk looking like a pigeon had just shit on his ice cream.

There was only one lad in the alley outside The Monster Gym. During the time Geordie had lived on the streets he had learned to be wary of situations like this. Street situations with strangers. Especially when the stranger was a junkie without a hit. But this time there didn't seem to be an alternative. The Monster Gym was closed. The notice on the door said it should be open, but the door itself was closed and locked. He'd knocked but couldn't get in.

He stood at the entrance to the alley and looked towards the lad. He was around fourteen at a guess, but big with it. He wore denims with Scotch plaid panels down the sides, a baseball cap and air-cushioned trainers.

'What's happening?' Geordie asked. He angled his head towards the entrance to the gym. 'I was supposed to meet somebody in there.'

The lad took a step forward. 'What kind of accent's that?' he asked. 'You're not from round here.'

'Round Newcastle,' Geordie said. OK, he'd go through the routine. There was a code, you couldn't arrive on somebody else's patch and start asking questions. You had to be accepted first.

'Good team,' said the lad.

'Football?' Geordie said. 'Yeah, they're doing well.' He played the accent, reaching inside himself for the shape of the vowels. It'd never worked for him before, but he sensed that it might be an asset in this situation. 'D'you support York?'

The lad laughed. 'No, they're crap. Leeds're better. If I had the readies I'd go there every week.'

'D'you play?' Geordie asked.

He shook his head. 'Used to play at school,' he said. 'Not now, though. Can't be buggered.'

'I still play a bit,' Geordie said. 'When I get the chance. But I wanted to do some training; thought the gym would be open.'

The lad came to the end of the alley and looked round the corner. 'It should be open,' he said. 'But the door's been locked all morning. Even the blokes who work there couldn't get in. They was kicking the door earlier on, but they've gone back home now. Home, or the betting shop.' He took Geordie by the arm and pulled him a little closer. 'You got any gear with you?'

'Gear?'

'Pills. Roids.'

'Oh, steroids. No.' Geordie knew the lad'd be into something, but hadn't thought far enough to guess what it was.

He let go of Geordie's arm. 'We had some EPO last week,' he said. 'And there was some Clenbuterol about. But there's been nothing for the last couple of days. D'you have a source?'

'Not in York,' Geordie said. 'Newcastle's easier.'

'Yeah, I bet. What do you use?'

Geordie frantically cast about for his knowledge of drugs. The only one that came to mind was insulin, and he didn't think that was a steroid. 'Oh, I'll take anything,' he said.

The lad smiled and slapped him on the arm. 'Yeah, like me,' he said. 'If it doesn't move or scream.'

'Who runs this place?' Geordie asked, certain now that he had passed all the tests. A slap on the arm meant all but total acceptance.

'Couple of brothers,' the lad told him. 'Well, the main one is called Ben. There's another one that has something wrong with him. He's like mental, you know. Two sandwiches short of a picnic.'

'Something wrong with his leg?' asked Geordie.

'Yeah, that's him. And he can't talk. Just sounds, but nothing that makes any sense.'

'Have there been other days when they've been closed?' Geordie asked.

The lad shook his head. 'They've always been open before.' He seemed to lose interest from one moment to the next. 'I've gotta go somewhere,' he said. 'See you.' He walked out of the alley and away down the street.

'What's your name?' Geordie shouted after him.

'Tone,' the lad said without turning round.

Geordie watched him go, then turned his attention to the gym. It was silent. He heard a footstep behind him and spun round expecting to see the monster from the video tape. But it was the lad who'd just said goodbye.

'Nowhere to go,' he explained.

'D'you ever go to watch Leeds?' Geordie asked, reminding Tone that they'd been through all the preliminaries. But that wasn't necessary. He was accepted.

'I watch 'em on the telly,' Tone said. 'I can't afford to go to Leeds. There was a kid from Leeds used to hang around here, but he got killed.' He stood back and watched the reaction on Geordie's face. He wasn't disappointed.

'Killed?' said Geordie. 'When was that?'

'Last week. They found him in the river.'

'Andrew Bridge?' Geordie said.

'Yeah, Andy, that's right. He used to get good gear, a lot of it. Did you know him?'

Geordie shook his head. 'No. I read about it in the paper. When they found his body.' Geordie would've liked to get a pad out then, and write down what Tone was telling him about Andrew Bridge. But that wouldn't've been cool. He'd have to remember it all, keep it in his head until he could get it down on paper. Hope that he wouldn't forget anything.

They heard the turning of the key in a lock, the sound of the heavy door to the gym being opened. Geordie moved towards the end of the alley to get a look at what was going on, but Tone held him back. 'They don't like us being here,' he whispered. 'Wait a sec.'

Geordie waited a sec, even a couple of secs, after the door had been slammed shut. Then he peered around the corner and saw the lumbering gait of a very muscly blond-headed man. 'Who's that?' he asked.

'That's Ben,' Tone told him. 'He's the boss. The main one.'

'Thanks. See you,' Geordie said. And he left the lad behind and took off after the body builder.

But he made sure that he kept a reasonable distance behind the guy. He wanted to follow him, to find out where the guy was going. And why he was in such a hurry about it. He didn't want to get anywhere near close enough for those huge hands to grab hold of him.

Be observant, Sam would say. *Don't just follow the guy, really see him. He'll be communicating with you in all kinds of different ways. He'll be telling you who he is. What he's about*. Geordie watched the guy's back. He wasn't the one who had trashed the office. He had blond hair, but the guy in the video had dark hair. Even if he was wearing a wig, it still wasn't the same guy, because he didn't have a limp. He was about the same size as the guy in the video, but not so frightening. The guy in the video looked less than human, he was like a monster out of the movies. Old black-and-white movies like they showed on the telly. Boris Karloff, one of those. *The Hunchback of Notre Dame.* But this guy, the one who was legging it from Acomb Green along the Wetherby Road, he wasn't the same kind of monster. He was more or less the same size, but he seemed to have all his wits, and he had a face like a schoolboy. It was the face that saved him. It was odd for a man to have a face like a schoolboy, a face that gave him a wholesome air. Like he wouldn't really hurt anyone.

Geordie had met dozens of them. People who looked like they wouldn't harm a fly. You couldn't tell by the look of them. When Geordie had been homeless, when he had been vulnerable, there had been times when everyone was dangerous. It was as if his vulnerability had precipitated violent reactions. The only way to survive on the street was to learn that one, and learn it quick. Down at the sawdust end of western civilization you went home with someone who looked benign and spent the next month nursing the bruises from that one night.

The weird thing was, Geordie had sometimes thought it was worth it. To get off the street for a night, to be warm and dry, to have some proper food. You'd know the guy was a pervert, there was a one hundred per cent chance you would be fucked, and maybe a sixty per cent chance you'd be beaten. There was even a chance (ten per cent, fifteen?) that you'd be killed. And you knew all that, yet you still went with him. It seemed worth it then, to take those chances, because you couldn't stand the street any longer.

After you'd been fucked, or while you were being beaten, you'd go numb, filter it out. Think of the pork chop or the lamb and mint sauce that the guy used to soften you up. The wine, the hot shower. The open fire in the grate, the music from the stereo. For a while you'd been human again. Now you were being crucified. What to do about it? Lie back and think of England.

The guy hung a left into the driveway of a big house. You couldn't see a lot of it from the road. You could see the sloping roof of one gable, and further along there were some dormer windows. Geordie would have liked to write the period of the house in his notebook. Georgian, say, or Victorian. But he didn't know what it was.

The house was sheltered from the road by old oak and beech trees. Between these were several ornamental shrubs hacked into the shape of peacocks and ostriches, turkeys and owls by a gardener who had a bird thing. Geordie didn't venture along the drive. He walked slowly past the entrance which had large, ornate, wrought-iron gates. The gates were open but guarded by a pair of stone lions.

Geordie kept walking. The house disappeared from sight altogether, but then he got a different view of it through the foliage. It was an old house, and the steps up to the patio and entrance were flanked by huge stone urns. There was no sign of the muscly guy. Geordie didn't know if he'd gone in through this main entrance, or through something less grand round the other side. Geordie himself would never have approached an entrance like that. There was no way he would ever have got in through there. Might be a butler or something, would look at Geordie like he was something the cat brought in.

When he ran away from the children's home and needed work, Geordie had tried a couple of houses like this. Houses with entrances like this. If it was a man came to the door he would be told to get lost, that would be the best reception he could expect. If they really needed to prove themselves they'd threaten to set the dogs on him, or call the police. If it was a woman, a maid or a cook or whatever they were called, then they would be protective. They might tell him, no, in a low voice, then indicate that he should go round to a side door. He'd end up with a slice of bread and marmalade, or a job weeding a herb garden or washing some steps.

The muscly guy was in the house for nearly two hours. Nothing much happened in the meantime. After about half an hour a car came out of the drive, a white sports car, and tore off in the direction of town. But it was a woman driving. She didn't stop at the end of the drive, she hit the horn once and drove straight out. If anybody'd been coming down the street she'd have gone straight into them. Then an hour later she came back again. She drove like she owned the whole street. Maybe she did. People who lived in houses like this one owned the whole world.

The rich. Geordie hated them. Sam hated them as well. Celia said there was no point in hating people. There was enough hatred in the world. What we should be doing was learning to love each other. Geordie thought that Celia was probably right. But when he saw people come out of big houses like this and drive as though they owned the whole world he just hated them.

Then the muscly guy came out and Geordie followed him back to The Monster Gym, watched him go inside and heard the locks and bolts go into place. Geordie stood in the alley and wrote it all down in his notebook, times and everything. He kicked his heels there for another hour, but there was no further movement from the gym, and he started getting hunger pains. Barney would be waiting to be fed back at the house, and tonight he had a date with Janet. Time to call it a day.

'All the time we've lived together,' Geordie said, 'Sam's never done that. He always lets me know where he is.' Janet looked really good. She'd had her hair done. Geordie didn't know what exactly had changed about it, but *something* had. Made her whole face look different. 'And there's Barney to think about,' he continued. 'I'm supposed to be out all day checking on the gyms, so what would normally happen, Sam'd be looking out for Barney. But nobody's been looking after Barney. I left him some water this morning. But he hasn't been fed, and he hadn't even been out for a piss. He was bursting when I got home. He's only a little dog, he can't hold it all day.'

He looked at her again. What it was, she'd had her hair cut in different lengths. It still reached down to her shoulders, but it was layered so the bits at the front only came down to her chin. She was wearing eye make-up, and she had on a T-shirt and black jeans, a tattoo of a butterfly on her shoulder. He'd never seen that before. It suited her. There was a lot of her he'd never seen. Over the back of a chair was a charcoal suit, and he remembered she'd been for a job interview. 'How'd it go?' he asked. 'I went to the café at lunch time, but you weren't there.'

'I got it,' she said, smiling. 'Got the job. Start on Monday.'

'There you go,' said Geordie, coming forward and giving her a hug. 'I told you so. All that stuff about them giving it to a *guy*. I knew you'd get it. If I was doing the interviewing and had to choose between you and a guy, I'd choose you every time.'

'Yeah.'

'Often the women get the job 'cause they're cheaper. It's cheaper for the boss to take on a woman. So the guy doesn't get the job.'

'How d'you think that makes me feel, Geordie?'

'What?'

'That I might've got the job because I was cheaper than a man?'

'Don't think about it,' he said. 'It's not real. It doesn't say anything about you. It's just how the world works.'

'I don't wanna live in a world like that.'

Geordie shrugged. 'It's the only one we've got, Janet.'

'I want to change the world, Geordie. Don't you?'

He thought about it for a minute. 'Now I've got you,

and Sam, and Celia, and Marie, everything seems really great. I don't *not* want to change it. I just don't want to rock the boat. I don't want to start changing things, then find I've changed too much, and I can't get back what I've changed.'

Janet took his hand and pulled him towards her. 'I only want to change the things that hurt people,' she said. 'And I want you to help me.'

'Well, I'm gonna be there,' he said. 'Wherever you are, whatever you're doing, I'll be there. So if you're changing the fucking world, I'll be changing it too.'

'Great.' She kissed him hard on the lips. Then she stood back. 'D'you wanna eat? I've cooked this thing with red peppers and barley. I hope you like barley.'

''Spect I will,' he said. 'If you've cooked it.'

Janet brought a bottle of red wine to the table and handed Geordie a corkscrew. 'I hope you like this,' she said. 'I've got a bottle of beer if you don't.'

'Oh, I like it,' he said. 'We never have it at home because of Sam. But sometimes I eat with Celia and we have red wine there. If I go to Marie's house we have white wine, and I like that as well.'

She brought an earthenware casserole and stood it on a straw mat on the table. She removed the lid and stood back while the steam escaped.

'Jesus, that smells great,' Geordie said, finally getting the remainder of the cork out of the wine bottle. He looked over at her. She still had an enormous pair of oven gloves on her hands. Maybe it was the size of the gloves, but she suddenly looked small and thin and vulnerable. It only lasted a moment. Neither of them said anything, but something passed between them. He wouldn't have been able to say what it was.

'Pour the wine,' she said, sitting down. She served out

generous portions of the casserole. Geordie said all the right things. Like how good it was, how it was the best meal he'd ever tasted in his life. How he wished he could cook like that. How you could hardly tell there wasn't any meat in it.

Janet got up for a minute, and put both the cats out. Then she came back. And something had changed in the mood. Geordie nearly said something about Barney and the cats, that they should introduce them to each other. But he kept quiet. He could tell she was working up to something.

Only she didn't seem to get there. 'What is it?' he asked, eventually. 'Something I've said?'

She looked over the table at him, gave him a tight smile. 'Nothing we can't work out,' she said. 'I'm gonna make this new job work, Geordie.'

'Yeah, I know you are.'

'No. I mean, I'm really gonna work hard at it. I can do it, I know that. I could end up managing that shop. It's a piece of cake.'

'I think you could do it, too, Janet. What I said before about women getting jobs because they're cheaper, that was just talk.'

'I know,' she said. 'It's not that. It's the way you look at me sometimes, and the way you talk to me. Like I'm small. You know what I mean, Geordie, you look at me as if I'm a little doll.'

He smiled. 'I can't help it. That's how it seems sometimes. I want to put my arms round you and take care of you.'

'I don't want that,' she said. 'I'm not a pretty little thing.'

'You are, Janet.'

She pushed herself up from the table, then sat back down again. 'I'm not, Geordie. I'm tough. I'm a fighter.

I've survived by myself for a long time. And I can tell you, I've been in some pretty scary situations.'

Geordie reached over the table for her hand. She moved it out of his reach, but he lunged for it and held it tight. She narrowed her eyes at him, and he did the same back to her. 'I've been in some scary situations myself, Janet. I got through them as well. I can be tough when I have to be, just like you.' He released his hold on her slightly, but she didn't pull free. 'I've been fighting the world since I was twelve years old. When I met Sam and Celia I was still fighting mad. There wasn't no one gonna tell me to lower my guard. But I began to do it when I met up with them, and then when I met you I realized that I wanted to be . . . what's the word? When it's not so important to be strong any more?'

'Vulnerable.'

'Yeah, that's it. With you I feel I can show you the parts of me that are scared. I don't think you'll take advantage of me. And I want you to do the same. I won't take advantage, I'll take care.'

'But . . .' Janet began to protest. Geordie stopped her.

'I don't mean I'll take care of you like a doll, like a *pretty little thing*.' He opened his fingers and looked at her hand in his palm. She didn't take it away, so he closed over it again. 'I respect you,' he said.

'Do you?'

'Yeah. You're tough. You really put the shits up me sometimes. Other times I think you're all soft. That's what I like about you. That you're so many things. I'll never be able to get hold of you, to define you.' He opened both hands on the table. 'I don't have words, Janet. I jus' wanna be close to you.'

Janet held his eyes for a full minute. She got off her chair and came round the table. She took hold of his head and angled it up towards her. Then she kissed both of his eyes in turn before going for his lips.

On the walk home he tried to recall the butterfly on her shoulder, but he couldn't remember the colours. He remembered everything at once, the way they'd made love in her double bed, then gone back to the kitchen to eat the salad without their clothes, drunk some more of the wine.

Janet had insisted that he listen to John Lennon, and she put it on loud so they could hear it in the bedroom while they explored each other's bodies. Later she brought the steamed treacle pudding to bed, and they listened to Elvis Presley, Buddy Holly, Roy Orbison, The Big Bopper, Jimi Hendrix, Jim Morrison, Louis Armstrong and Freddie Mercury. All of those tapes Geordie had borrowed off Sam.

'They're all dead,' he told her.

'Jesus, all of them?'

'Yeah, all the greats are dead. That's what Sam says.'

Geordie was involved in kissing each of the ribs under her left arm. He stopped for a moment, to hear what she was saying.

'That's something I didn't know till tonight,' she said. 'All the greats are dead.' He went back to kissing her ribs, then came up for air again. 'And they're all men,' she said. 'You've brought all these tapes, and none of them are women.'

When they'd finished the wine she brought the bottle of beer to bed, and they shared that between them, both drinking from the neck of the bottle. They wrapped themselves around each other and listened to Janis Joplin and Jo Ann Kelly. Janet fell asleep. Geordie stayed awake and felt his arm and shoulder go numb. He watched both cats creep into the bedroom, then dragged himself free, dressed and walked out into the night.

He walked into Sam's flat and saw Barney had had some company. The dog looked at him with one eye, raised his tail slightly in a greeting, then went back to sleep. Geordie was about to go upstairs to his own flat when Sam called from his bedroom.

Geordie walked through and saw Sam sitting up in bed. Hardly recognized him. Sam's nose was twice the size it had been the day before, and the area around it, including his eyes, was black and puffy. Had a smile on his face, though, behind all the bruises.

'Jesus,' said Geordie.

'No, but I can take a message.'

'For Christ's sake, Sam. What happened to your face?'

'Make a cup of coffee,' he said, 'and I'll tell you.'

Geordie headed for the kettle. He looked back at Sam from the doorway. The guy was drained of youth. 'I don't wanna sleep, anyway,' he said.

'No,' Sam told him. 'I can understand that. Your face is filled with broken commandments.'

CHAPTER 19

'I'll sit here and you all stare at me for as long as it takes,' Sam said. 'Then when you've all done we'll start work.' He was sitting at his new desk in front of the window, and Geordie, Celia, Marie and Barney were examining his face.

'You look absolutely terrible, Sam,' Celia said. 'You shouldn't be here.'

'That's what I said,' said Marie. 'I wanted him to go to the hospital.'

Geordie perched himself on a corner of the desk. 'It's changed your voice,' he said. 'You sound like Mr Spock.'

Sam looked at the dog. 'Come on, Barney,' he said. 'Everybody gets to have a go this morning. What's your slant on Sam's face?'

Barney wagged his tail. He wasn't at all sure about the guy. The huge black nose, the puffy eyes, the voice of Mr Spock and the smell of Sam Turner didn't add up to anything he recognized, but everybody else seemed to be getting along with him.

'It's actually worse than it looks,' Sam told them. 'There's incipient brain damage and some of my internal organs are still haemorrhaging, I'm partially deaf and I've lost my sense of balance. But God didn't have my room ready.'

'And that jacket you're wearing,' said Geordie. 'It's like nineteen fifty.'

'My suit's at the cleaner's being scraped.'

Celia turned towards her room. 'I suppose if you can joke about it you'll survive,' she said. 'The brain is a wonderful organ; it starts working the moment you get up in the morning and doesn't stop until you get into the office.'

Sam laughed. 'Happens to Gene Hackman all the time,' he said. 'Every movie I've ever seen with Gene Hackman he gets walloped with something. But does he go to the hospital, or have a few days off work? No he doesn't. Old Gene knows there's a job to be done, and he gets on and does it. Us private eyes are not like mere mortals, you know. We're unstoppable, that's why we're private eyes. The more the bad guys beat us up, the more determined we get to stamp them out.'

Marie went over to her new desk. 'Definite brain damage,' she said. '*Non compos mentis.*'

'I prefer the wicked to the foolish,' Celia said from the door to her office. 'The wicked sometimes rest.'

Barney had gone to explore his new basket. Sam looked

at Geordie. 'You're all I've got left,' he said. 'My last hope. What's the verdict?'

'You've got a screw loose.'

'Good, everything's back to normal. We can get down to work.' He stood and walked over to the entrance to Celia's room. 'You've done a great job with the office,' he said. 'And you, Marie. How much did it cost?'

'More than we had,' Celia told him. 'The bank paid. But you'd better stay out of there. If the bank manager sees you looking like that he'll call in the loan.'

'Oh, I dunno,' Sam told her. 'You can make anything look good with the right lighting.'

He would, though. The bank manager, call in the loan. Sam had only swung it in the first place by telling the guy a joke. The old one about banks being made up to look as if they don't owe a penny to anyone. The bank manager had laughed. Never heard it before. He'd wanted to get rid of Sam as quickly as possible, so he could tell it to his assistants, and the only way he could get rid of Sam was to give him a loan.

'Yeah, I'll lie low for a while,' he said. 'If we keep up the payments they'll let it run.'

They spent the rest of the morning sharing their experiences and the results of their investigations over the past couple of days. Sam described his battle with the Terminator, how he had shot him, thought he had killed him, but then the body had disappeared.

'What about the car?' Geordie asked. 'What we gonna do about wheels?'

Sam looked at Celia.

'I've checked with the insurance,' she said. 'We can hire one, and they'll cover the expense. But only in retrospect. We have to pay for it ourselves, then claim it back from them.'

'How did you explain it to the police?' Geordie asked. 'A Volvo in the river?'

'I told them I parked by the river overnight. When I went for it in the morning they were swarming all over the place. They thought somebody had driven it over, and they had divers out looking for a body. I should have told them as soon as it happened, but I had a headache. Wanted to go to my room.'

'Yes,' said Marie. 'I thought of ringing them, but it slipped my mind.'

'But the guy you fought,' Geordie asked. 'Was it the same one who trashed the office?'

'Yeah. No doubt about it.'

'I found the gym,' Geordie said. 'I didn't see the one you fought, but I saw his brother. They run the place together. And I followed the brother out to a place on the Wetherby road. Some kind of mansion.'

'He didn't see you?' asked Sam.

'No,' Geordie said, offended. 'I know how to tail somebody by now, Sam. I kept well back, even you wouldn't have known I was there.'

'And the place he went to. You got the address? You know who lives there?'

'Yes, I've got the address. No, I haven't checked who lives there yet. Gimme a chance, here, Sam. I didn't have time last night, worrying about you and Barney, not knowing where you were. And I haven't even got to my desk this morning, listening to you and everybody talking.'

Sam held up his hands. 'OK,' he said, 'but things are hotting up all round. I think we have to be extra careful from now on. Geordie, you and me ought to work together. Celia and Marie should stay together, too. The guy threatened all of you when I talked to him on the telephone. I don't want anyone getting hurt.'

'But if they're watching the office,' Marie said, 'we don't stand a chance. They only have to wait till you and Geordie go out, then come in for Celia and me.'

'You won't be here,' Sam said. 'We're closing the office. Marie, I want you to move in with Celia. You can have British Telecom transfer calls. You only open the door to people you know.'

'When's this gonna happen?' asked Geordie. 'Are we on the run from these guys, Sam?'

Sam pushed himself up from the desk. 'We're starting now. No, we're not on the run. Jus' trying to get us some shelter from the storm.'

The table stood in a pool of light. It had been re-covered the previous week and the green baize had been swept after the last players left. Sam and Geordie placed the balls on their spots, taking care to polish each one before positioning it on the table. Six of the fifteen tables in the hall were being used. The dull tap of cue against ball, the sharp contact between ball and ball, and the occasional exclamation or snatch of quiet conversation were the only sounds.

Geordie and Sam spoke in monosyllables. When Sam tossed the coin he said nothing. Geordie watched the action, then said, 'Heads.'

Sam checked the coin on the back of his hand. 'You break.'

They'd installed Celia and Marie in Celia's house. After picking up the hire car they'd gone out to The Monster Gym and watched it for a couple of hours. The rain had come down, and there'd been no movement and no signal that anything was going to happen. Sam had sighed deeply and said, 'Fancy a game?'

Geordie had consulted his watch, noted that it was not

yet quitting time, then looked at Sam for a long time. Finally he said, 'You're not losing your appetite for this case?'

'I jus' wanna play snooker,' Sam said. 'This's like watching paint dry. I feel old and bruised and kicked about, and I wanna play a game and relax and take things easy for an hour. Maybe two hours. Long as it takes. When I come back to the case I'll feel better about it.'

Terry, the part-time kid behind the bar at the snooker hall, had handed over their cues, Sam's Barracuda and Geordie's Riley. He'd asked about Sam's face, examined it with an empathetic reflection on his own face. When they'd turned away to go over to the table he'd raised his voice, called after them. 'I know what it is, Sam. You sound like Mr Spock.'

Geordie sent the white down the table and skimmed off the right side of the red cluster. The cue ball hit the top and side cushions, narrowly missed the blue and finally came to rest an inch from the baulk cushion.

The brass fittings on the scoreboards gleamed with reflected light. There was a hush broken only by the collision of ball with ball and the odd spoken syllable.

'Sam.' Geordie's voice sounded far off, as though coming from a different dimension. Sam went to the table chalking his cue and weighed up the shot. By narrowly missing the yellow he could get through to a red on the right cushion. If he hit it right the red would go back into the pack. The cue ball should then come to rest on the far cushion. If it did it would be safe. If it didn't Geordie would have the chance of a pot into the middle. Sam walked round the table to see what it would look like if he got it right. He walked back to the baulk end, chalked his cue again, blew the excess chalk from the tip and got down on the shot.

He feathered the white ball once, twice, and was pushing

forward to make contact when he saw Gus out of the corner of his eye. Gus disappeared immediately, because he wasn't real. The tip of Sam's cue made contact with the white ball, and the white ball fouled the yellow.

'Four to me,' said Geordie. He put the points up on the scoreboard, and came to look at the table. 'You sure you're OK?' he asked Sam.

'Yeah.' Sam nodded at the table. 'Miscued. Play.' He glanced round the room. Gus haunted the place. At one time, before they'd started the detective business together, Gus had worked here. Sam would come round once or twice a week and they'd play together for an hour or two. Later, after the business had taken off and Geordie had arrived on the scene, they'd play three-handed.

There'd never be a time when Sam would be able to come here and not be reminded of Gus. Gus'd never made a fifty break. The forty-nine had been against Sam. Gus'd broken down on a simple red over the green pocket, any other time he could've potted it with the curly end of an umbrella.

'I don't want this,' Geordie said, indicating the balls. 'Can you take it again?'

Sam went back to the table. There was no safety shot on, so he got down quickly and potted a long impossible red and ended in perfect position on the blue.

Geordie shook his head in disgust. 'Fluke,' he said.

Sam potted the blue and got on a red just below the black. He wondered if it was right to call it a fluke when the fingers of a ghost guided the balls. Gus was still at it. He'd always be there, striving against hope for that elusive fifty break. It was Sam Turner taking the shots, but he wasn't taking them alone. There was another fleeting, ethereal figure looking along his cue, willing the balls into the pockets. The ghost of the Stonebow Snooker Hall.

He potted the red, the black and another red, but missed the blue off its spot.

'You can still do it, then?' said Geordie, going to the table, making ready to put a little break of his own together. 'Hasn't affected your sight.'

Or my heart, Sam thought. There was a part of Sam's heart that was indestructible. There had been times in his life when he thought it had been destroyed, but he'd always been wrong about it. Either that, or it had the capacity for regeneration. Resurrection.

It wasn't reliable. It was a heart after all. Not something you could trust. A part of a heart.

What he'd noticed, what he knew about it, was that during those times in his life when his heart had shrivelled up, or turned to stone, or been broken – whenever his heart had not been functioning – then he'd gone out looking for a drink. And the other side of that picture was also true, that when he was drinking, when he found himself crawling through shit and vomit, when he'd alienated all his friends, it would be that tiny part of his heart which would begin the process whereby he'd reach out for sanity.

Sometimes there'd be periods of bad luck. Times when everything that could go wrong did go wrong. The time when he was homeless. The time when that mad bastard mowed down Donna and Bronte. The time when he married Brenda, his second wife, and the time when he lived with her, and when she left him. All these things happened when his heart was dysfunctional.

He wondered if that was happening now. If that was why he'd met the monster down by the river, the one who'd destroyed his car and his office, and had tried to destroy Sam himself. The one who'd threatened to destroy all his friends.

But no, that wasn't what was happening. He could still get down and pot the balls. He could still find space in his heart for Marie and her problems. He wasn't on the verge of giving up, nowhere near it. He was alive and kicking and looking for a fight.

And one of the reasons was Jeanie Scott, the Scottish Widow. Because Sam knew that when he met a woman who was possible, as she was possible, that he would begin a process which was nothing if not positive. His heart, if it had ever wavered, would cease to be dysfunctional. It would start to grow.

When Jeanie saw him she couldn't help herself. Right in the doorway, there on the street, she took his bruised and broken face between her hands and kissed it tenderly. There was a salt taste, and a tautness to his skin. It felt as though the surface could barely contain the bruised muscle below.

She took both his hands then, and drew him through to her couch. She sat back and pulled him down next to her. She placed his head on her breast and held it there. She felt him shake, and lifted his chin expecting to glimpse that rare prize, male tears. But his face was dry. If there were any tears, they were internal ones. He was a disappointment.

Something changed for Jeanie then, in that moment. She had thought a lot about Sam Turner, and she had thought a lot about Michael Caffrey, her Irish boyfriend. Before Sam had arrived tonight she had been ready to tell Michael that she wouldn't see him again. But now she wasn't so sure.

Rationality. Thinking about things. It had all been so clear in her head. One of the problems with Michael was the culture gap, the difference between her proud Scottish spirit and his war-torn Belfast Irishness. There was also the fact that she had been married before, and at a time when Michael was still wearing short trousers.

She and Sam, on the other hand, were more alike. He had been married before, twice, and they had a wealth of shared experience, while at the same time there were enough differences to make it exciting.

She knew all this, and on the basis of it had come to a sound and sensible decision. Then she had put Sam Turner's head on her breast, felt him shake, looked down for the tears and found none. And that had changed her mind.

'What's wrong?' he asked.

She smiled. 'Nothing. Just thinking.'

He sat up and faced her. He reached out a hand and touched her face with the tips of his fingers. He looked into her eyes.

Jeanie looked back, but then blinked and averted her eyes, stared at her lap, the weave of her skirt.

He said her name and there was a sense of insecurity in his voice that had not been there a moment before. This was something she'd passed on to him, like a virus. She clenched her fist, angry that he made her feel guilt. That she made herself feel guilt. For God's sake, it wasn't a deadly disease she was giving him. He'd survive it. It was only life. Reality.

'There's someone else,' she said.

He didn't react, not even with his eyes. There was no sharp intake of breath, no sense of a dullness spreading through his body.

'Michael,' she continued. 'I knew him before we met. I'm still seeing him.'

'Seeing?'

'Yes.'

'And me?' he asked. 'Are you still seeing me?'

'Yes.'

'And Michael? Does he know about this?'

She shook her head. Her eyes looked past him, thousands of miles.

Sam put his hand into his jacket pocket, felt around in there as though he was looking for something. Something he'd lost. A cigarette. But he didn't smoke. He gave up searching for whatever was missing and shrugged his shoulders. 'It's serious, then,' he said.

Jeanie felt him move in the night, disengage himself from the tangle of arms and legs, the heat where their bodies had been clammed together. He sat up in bed, swinging his legs over the side. Sex had never been quite so good before, she thought, not only with him, but with anybody. It needed a touch of something to make it extra good – nostalgia, betrayal, treachery, shame.

'You going?' she asked, recognizing the drowsiness in her own voice.

'I've been deceived by the clown inside me,' he said.

He was quoting something. She couldn't remember what it was. She reached for the practical, the mundane, a mask that would divert him and at the same time give her refuge. 'Will you ring me?' she said.

'We're idiots, babe.'

Here it was now. The anger.

'I might have been born at night, but it wasn't last night.'

She was awake for an hour after he left. Then she went downstairs to the sitting room. She found the tape he'd lent her, read the titles of the songs: 'You're Gonna Make Me Lonesome When You Go'; 'Simple Twist of Fate'; 'If You See Her, Say Hello'.

When Karen, her daughter, woke her in the morning, Jeanie was sitting on the couch. The tape had come to an end and there was a low buzzing sound coming from one of the speakers.

'Why are you sleeping down here?' Karen asked.

Jeanie shook her head. 'Dunno. I'm an idiot, I suppose.'

CHAPTER 20

As soon as Geordie mentioned the mansion on the Wetherby road Sam had known who he was up against. Called himself Franco Tampon now, but his real name, his original name, was Frank Squires, and Sam had first met him in Manchester twenty years previously.

'You know him?' asked Geordie.

'Franco, Frank,' said Sam. 'He was dangerous and I was hopeless. He's probably more dangerous now. But this time round I'm not as incapacitated as I was back then.'

'You can tell me if you like, or you can talk to yourself in riddles and I'll jus' take Barney for a walk.'

'Whenever I see Frank, or hear the name Franco Tampon, it makes me think of two things. The first thing that comes to mind is reruns of *77 Sunset Strip* with that guy who played Cookie. What was his name? Used to park Cadillacs all day. You seen any of those?'

Geordie shook his head. 'Never heard of it.'

'The other thing he reminds me of is a twenty-three-year-old girl called Kitty.'

'This's gonna be a long story,' Geordie said. 'I'm listening but I'm gonna close my eyes. Don't think I'm asleep.'

'Frank's mixed up in local politics now,' Sam continued. 'Last I heard he was on the Millennium Committee. But the reason he reminds me of *Sunset Strip* and Cookie is that when I was in Manchester, I was in a more or less permanent alcoholic haze. Those were some of the worst days of my life. Anyway, some nights I'd end up in one of Franco's clubs because that was the only place you could get a drink after hours. There was a kid worked on the door of the club who parked people's cars for them. I didn't have a car at all, didn't actually have a bean. Didn't have a bike. Didn't have a pair of roller skates. Sometimes didn't have a pair of shoes, not where they both matched. Nearly always had a drink, though.'

Sam stopped talking and looked over at Geordie. The kid had his head back on the couch and his eyes were closed. He was listening, though. Concentrated better with his eyes closed.

'Kitty was a dancer,' Sam said. 'She danced in a bird cage above the stage. There was a period of about three weeks when I didn't drink. I'd go in the club and make a Coke last all night, just sit there watching Kitty doing her thing in the cage. Three weeks, between drunks, just long enough to meet and fall in love with her.

'I was no good to anyone, though. Least of all myself. I went into another drunk, and when I sobered up she'd moved on, gone, disappeared, like a hole had opened in the dimension and she'd been sucked through it, not a trace left behind. She left a real bitter-sweet memory.

'I still get it sometimes, when I think about her. Like now. I can remember the way her heart used to beat.

'And I remembered two things she told me about Franco, her boss. "He likes children," she said, when I asked about his women. And "He's a cruel bastard," she said, in connection with something else. Can't remember what. Kitty had been recruited from a children's home, that's how Franco did business.'

Geordie kept his eyes closed.

'It's always the same,' Sam said. 'It was Kitty who went away, Kitty who left. Sweet, sweet, Kitty. What remained behind was Franco. And he's been there, on the periphery, ever since. Only in glimpses. I see him sometimes standing by the railings to the school opposite the Minster, and I read about him in the local rag, when he's donated money to yet another worthy cause. It seems like the Manchester days are far behind him now, he's made his pile and become a kind of local hero. Except a leopard doesn't change his spots. And whenever I see Franco I think of Cookie, and I think of Kitty. And when I read about him in the newspaper I don't think about him as a local benefactor at all. I think of him as someone who prefers children to women and someone who is a cruel bastard.'

Sam was quiet for a while, and Geordie opened his eyes and sat upright on the couch. 'Didn't you go looking for her?' he asked. 'Kitty. She can't've just disappeared for ever.'

Sam shook his head. 'That's booze for you. She wasn't the only one I lost. I carried on drinking until I didn't have a friend in the world.'

'Jesus, Sam.'

'There was something else I heard. When I was looking for her one of the other girls told me that Franco had used her as a bribe for a local cop. Police inspector. They used to say there wasn't a cop in the city who didn't take money from Franco. But they got other perks as well. Kitty was one of them.' He fell silent for a moment, and when he spoke again his voice was softer. 'She was touched by the sixties. She liked sex but it didn't like her. She wanted gentleness, but she never got it.'

'And Franco,' said Geordie, 'was he ever stopped? Has he done any time?'

Sam shook his head. 'He was untouchable. Still is, apparently.'

'Does he run anything here?'

'The first clubs were here. But neither of them lasted very long. I don't think he's done anything illegal here since then. He keeps York clean, doesn't want anything to pollute the place he lives. He has all kinds of shit going down in other towns, but not on his own doorstep. He's an original, is Franco. He didn't get where he is by shaking tambourines.'

'This is too big for us, Sam,' said Geordie. 'This guy's like the fuckin' Godfather. He probably doesn't even have a record, he's got minders, and if they're into drugs and girls they've got shooters. I mean, we haven't really given them much trouble, and already they've destroyed the office and beat you up, they've put the Volvo in the river and threatened Marie and Celia. They've even threatened me and Barney. What're they gonna do if we really start to get in their face?'

Sam shook his head. 'Dunno,' he said. 'But I expect we'll find out.'

'Shit, Sam. You mean we're gonna carry on?'

'Yes. I know Frank, remember. He might think he's big, and the people around him probably believe the organization is invincible. But he's scum. I should've stopped him when we were younger. Would've saved a lot of people grief. But it's never too late to put something right.'

After Geordie had gone up to his own flat, Sam played 'Lay, Lady, Lay' quietly on his tape deck and tried to think about the Scottish Widow. But he couldn't get Frank out of his head. The guy had this thing about being Italian. He had dark hair and a swarthy, oily skin that reminded you of the Mediterranean, and the move from Frank to Franco was understandable. It was an affectation, sure, but you could understand it if you knew the guy.

What was more of a leap was the change from Squires to Tampon. Sam didn't know if Tampon was supposed to be an Italian surname. If it was, it surely wasn't one that Sam had ever come across. The only tampon Sam knew was a female sanitary product.

Maybe he was ashamed of the Squires name. Sam reclaimed floating pieces of information from the past, fragments. There was something about Frank's father having to go bankrupt.

That word shame. There it was again.

Sam saw Frank Squires, Franco Tampon, from time to time in the town. You live in a place like York, so long as you get out of the house, you'll see people you know on the streets. Frank looked not a whole lot different from when he was in Manchester. A couple of times, maybe three, Sam had seen him outside the Minster School, looking in on the playground, while the children in their red shorts and white T-shirts played ball.

But there was something else as well. Frank had a brother. Sam couldn't remember his real name, called himself Doc Squires. Not a doctor of medicine, some kind of academic. Was he an historian? There had been an article in the local press, Doc Squires accused of shoplifting, some months ago, maybe a year. He'd got off, said he'd forgotten to pay and the magistrate had accepted it. But the local shopkeeper had been outraged, said the guy was always coming in his shop, taking things without paying. This was the first time he'd caught him red handed, but he'd known the guy was robbing him for weeks.

Might be worth having a talk with that shopkeeper. Get Geordie to turn up the article from the press.

Sam thought he had most of the jigsaw now, all he had

to do was put the pieces together. The murder of the boy, Andrew Bridge, and the murders of the two CCTV operators were connected. They were linked by a tape, probably a video tape, which was missing, and by a couple of seriously disturbed hardcore body builders. There was the suggestion of drugs, anabolic steroids being sold by Andrew Bridge. There was a custom registration number and a sleek sports car. And in the background, and, if Sam's instincts were intact, not only in the background but in the very centre, there was Franco Tampon.

It didn't quite gel. It was almost there, but there was something missing. To find the missing piece meant digging around some more, and that meant risking the wrath of the bad guys. It meant putting Celia and Marie and Geordie at risk. Sam had to think about it. It would be irresponsible not to think about it.

The two cases were the same. If he solved one of them he would solve the other. Any moves he made now would lead to some kind of retaliation by Franco and his associates. Sam would go ahead and do whatever he had to do. Whatever the final cost, he wouldn't be able to stop himself. He felt a smile coming through to the surface of his face. 'Professional detachment,' he said aloud. 'That's my middle name.'

He'd do everything he could to protect Geordie and the others, but at the end of the day he'd go wherever the trail led. He was an alcoholic and he was dry. Dry as hell. If he gave up now, failed the Scottish Widow and Mrs Bridge, if he failed himself on this one, the rest of his life would be tied to a bottle.

CHAPTER 21

Tone's real name was Anthony Read, but he wouldn't answer to it. He would barely respond to Tony.

Geordie had introduced Marie as a private detective, told Tone that she was OK, and left them to it.

'Is this for real?' Tone said.

'Yeah.' Marie kept her smile in place, hoped she didn't look too uncool.

'You're a private eye?'

She nodded.

'A woman private eye?'

'Yup.'

They were sitting in the window of Pizza Express. Tone with an enormous deep-pan job in front of him with extra double everything available on the menu and a litre of Coke. Marie with black coffee, unsweetened, dammit.

'I've never met one before,' he said.

'A woman or a private eye?' Marie enquired, but it was a dead joke before it was born in this company. Tone gave her a look he might have been reserving for something that crawled out of the mozzarella.

'You gonna gimme some money?' he asked.

'I'll pay for information.'

'How much?'

Marie shrugged. 'Depends what you know.'

'Geordie said it'd be fifty quid, maybe more. You pay for as much as I can eat and a pack of fags.'

Marie shook her head. 'Tone, it's important we're honest with each other. Geordie told you twenty, not fifty. And he didn't mention anything about fags.'

'He said fifty to me.' Tone showed her a face that would never lie.

Marie got to her feet and turned to the door. 'OK, the deal's off.'

'Wait,' said Tone. 'He said twenty, but it's right about the fags.'

Marie continued towards the door. 'Get in touch when you can tell the truth,' she said.

Tone got to his feet and intercepted her. 'It's all right,' he said. 'Come back. It happened like you said. Twenty. No fags.'

'You sure?'

'I was trying it on. You'd think I was barmy if I didn't.'

Marie followed him back to the table and sat in front of her coffee. 'I wouldn't,' she said. 'The most important thing for me is that you tell me the truth. For absolute truth, no trimmings or exaggeration, twenty could be stretched to fifty.'

'What do you want to know?'

'I want to know everything you know about Andrew Bridge. Even the conversations you had together. Then I want to know the names and addresses of all the other kids who hang around The Monster Gym. And I want to know anything at all about you or the other kids being propositioned.'

'Propositioned?'

'Offered money or drugs for sex.'

'You're not the fuzz?'

'No.'

'But you're looking for bum bandits?'

'Just one'd do.'

'I'll tell you this to start with. Andy, the kid from Leeds who they fished out the river, he was deep into that stuff. He went to parties where there was acid and coke. He told me about orgies. I'd've gone for the drugs, but I didn't wanna get fucked.'

'Do you know any other kids that went to these parties?'

Tone didn't reply immediately. He seemed to have a thought that only slowly made sense to him. Eventually he said, 'Andy is well dead, isn't he?'

Marie nodded.

'Did they do it? The people at the parties?'

'Maybe,' Marie said. 'Do you know who they are?'

Tone shook his head. 'This is serious stuff, isn't it?'

Marie didn't answer.

'OK,' he said. 'I know someone else who's been to one of the parties. I'll see if he'll talk to you.'

Marie watched him polish off the remains of his pizza. She finished her coffee and looked him in the eyes.

'Is it worth fifty?' Tone asked.

Marie smiled and nodded her head. 'Yeah,' she said. 'If you get this friend of yours to talk I'll even throw in a pack of fags.'

CHAPTER 22

Ben had never had to deal with a body before. Not a proper body anyway. He'd got rid of bodies, bagged them up and put them in the river, or buried them on the moor. But they'd been scum, and anyway he'd always had Gog to help him.

This body was Gog. It wasn't a piece of shit like those others. It was his brother, and what it needed was a funeral. It needed flowers, wreaths, a preacher and hymns sung in church. It needed a white marble headstone with an angel on the top, little cherubs climbing up the sides and a kind of poem or inscription. How he was sorely missed by his loving brother, RIP.

Ben had done everything he could do. When he'd first brought Gog home he'd been alive. At least, Ben had thought so at the time. Now he wasn't quite so sure. Gog hadn't said anything, and he hadn't opened his eyes. Also, Ben wouldn't swear now that Gog had been breathing. His heart had been beating, his great heart, Ben had felt that as he carried his brother into the house. But the next morning there was nothing.

Nothing except leakage, which Ben had dealt with. He'd put an elastic band round the end of Gog's prick, twisted it round hard, which seemed to do the trick. Then he'd got a cork from an old cider vinegar bottle and stopped up the back passage orifice. He'd changed the bedding, then remade the bed and dressed Gog in his favourite pink skin-tone tracksuit. Nothing underneath it apart from his weightlifting belt. Gog didn't need underwear any more. Looked like Don Ross stretched out there, and Ben told him so. 'You look like Don Ross stretched out there, Gog. You know that. Don Ross, the Ripper?'

Gog didn't say anything back. That was par for the course. Gog never said much, but that didn't mean he didn't know what was going on. There's talkers and doers in this world, and Gog was a doer, not a talker.

Franco and Doc Squires and Franco's mother, they were all talkers. You'd've expected them to do something. When you think about all the times Gog had come through for them, then you'd think at least they'd be able to help with a church service. A decent burial.

But no. They didn't want to know. All Mama wanted to know was if they'd got hold of the tape yet. Franco, when he heard who it was shot Gog, he went all quiet and said he knew the guy, the detective, Sam Turner. It turns out that Franco knew him from Manchester. Maybe that's why he didn't want to do anything about it.

Doc Squires said he'd come down to the gym and issue a death certificate. 'Well, I'll have to bring someone with me,' he said. 'Someone with a licence to practise.'

'What?' said Ben. 'I thought you was a proper doctor.'

'Er, yes,' said Squires. 'I am. But not a medical one.'

'But you've been prescribing roids for us.'

Doc Squires appeared not to hear that.

'Better make it natural causes,' said the Bitch. 'We don't want any heat.'

'And find a tame funeral director,' Franco said. 'Have you got one?'

'Yes,' said Doc. 'Don't worry.'

They went on like that. Arranging things. Nobody asked Ben what he wanted, nobody thought how Gog might have liked it doing. What Ben would have found the most help would be if they'd all sat down together and tried to compose a poem for the headstone. But he didn't even get around to suggesting it. He couldn't get a word in edgeways with these people.

What it amounted to, though, what they wanted, all of them, was for Ben to finish the job on the detective. Franco was very keen about that. 'I don't want Sam Turner sniffing round my operations,' he said. 'I know what I'm talking about here. If that guy gets a hold of something he hangs on with his teeth. Just take the fucker out, Ben, and get it right this time.'

Yes, sir, Mr Tampon, sir. At your service, sir.

Ben would've taken the detective out anyway. It was the fucking detective who killed his brother. What did they think, Franco and the Bitch, Doc Squires? Did they think he was gonna let the detective off? Oh, excuse me, Mr Turner, this thing about you killing my brother. Well, I'm not gonna hold it against you. OK? All's fair in love and war. Gog knew what he was getting into, tangling with you.

And now he's paid the ultimate price. Don't worry about it. I know you just did what you had to do.

Back at the gym Ben sat at Gog's bedside. 'I'll get the detective first,' he said. 'Then I'll go after Doc Squires. After him I'll get Franco, and I'll save the Bitch for last.' He looked at Gog. Gog didn't say anything, of course, he was dead. But there was a sense in which he understood and approved. 'Called himself a doctor,' Ben continued. 'Prescribing all them roids for you. No wonder you got in such a state, your balls shrinking, all that acne. It was like he was just experimenting. And Franco and the Bitch must've known about it.'

Ben unplugged the telephone and turned it over. He unscrewed the bottom and opened it up. What fell out of there was something that looked like a monkey's finger. Ben didn't know why he thought it was a monkey's finger. It was not as if he'd ever seen a monkey's finger, or really knew what a monkey's finger looked like.

He picked it up to get a closer look, and then he dropped it and poked at it with a pencil, moving it around the desk, turning it over so he could see it from all sides. Eventually he put the pencil down and looked at the thing in front of him. The thing that had come out of the telephone. He scratched his head. He got out of the chair and walked round the desk. He sat back down again, and it was still there.

Ben sat with the thing in front of him for the best part of an hour. He thought. It wasn't easy, thinking, although it seemed to come easier to some people than others. No one in Ben's family had ever been too good at it. They could do it when they had to, though. Ben did it now, just sat there and did it. Thought and thought till he came up with an answer.

He walked into the bedroom and sat down by Gog's bed. He had the thing in a towel and he unwrapped it and placed it on Gog's chest. 'Gog,' he said, 'I found this shrivelled-up prick and balls in the telephone.'

No answer.

'It was Blu-tacked inside the telephone, only the Blu-tack must've dried up, and the prick and balls came loose, so every time I picked up the telephone I could feel this thing rattling about inside.

'This morning I thought I'd take a look inside the telephone, and when I opened it up this thing fell out, which I thought was a monkey's finger. But then I found out it wasn't a monkey's finger at all, after I'd had a really good look at it. Which is a pity, because if it was a monkey's finger I might not have blamed you.'

Gog didn't flicker an eyelid. If he'd been alive he'd've been giving himself away by now. He'd be denying it, saying he'd never seen a shrivelled-up prick and balls in his life, and did Ben think he was stupid or something, putting a prick and balls in a telephone. But he wasn't alive, so it was quite understandable that he didn't protest.

'And the last few days,' Ben said. 'You've been acting weird in the office, and one of the things you've been doing in there is shaking the telephone. So when I sat down to think about this prick and balls in the telephone I had to recall that picture of you shaking the telephone.' He sighed, reached out a hand and touched Gog's cold forehead. 'And in the end I put two and two together, Gog. And there's no way it could've been anyone else but you. Except there's just a couple of questions that I'm not sure about the answers.

'The first question is why did you Blu-tack a shrivelled prick and balls inside the telephone? And the second question is, well, I suppose it's two questions in one, really. Whose are they, and where did you get them from?'

Gog wasn't going to answer any of those questions. What Ben was left with, and he knew it even before he asked the questions, was a mystery.

He spent more time with the body of his brother. Gave the mystery more thought. But he couldn't fathom it. In the end he decided to make the bomb.

'We can do this together,' he said, placing the white ammonium nitrate crystals on the scale. 'Make up a little parcel for Sam Turner and leave it in his house. Slowly with this stuff, though, its very unstable.' He put it to one side. 'Now we need about twelve per cent of absorbent charcoal powder.' He poured a small mountain of the fine black powder on to the scale.

'Good. Very carefully mix the two together. Like so. And put them into a container.' The container was a family-size Ovaltine tin. 'Yeah,' Ben looked over at Gog and laughed. 'A big container.'

Ben placed the lid on the Ovaltine tin, and the tin into a black canvas sports bag. He reached over to the bedside table for his alarm clock and tucked that inside the bag as well. 'Let's see, enough wire? Yeah, should be OK. And I got a dry-cell battery downstairs.' He went downstairs and came back up again with the dry cell, put that in the bag as well.

'That should be everything,' he said. He began zipping up the bag, and then had another thought. 'Oh, shit, the blasting caps.' He took these out of the cardboard box and placed them in the bag. 'And that's everything. Detonator cords as well.' He zipped up the bag and tested its weight.

'It doesn't weigh a lot,' he told his dead brother. 'But it's gonna shake up that Sam Turner character. He'll be sorry he ever tried to mess with us.'

CHAPTER 23

'Get dressed and piss off,' Franco told the boy. He let a twenty-pound note float down towards the bed and watched the boy's hand come out from the sheets and wait for the money to land. A thin, white, bare arm and adolescent shoulders, but a coarse face, pock marked and spotty. Young, dumb and full of cum. He was another new one Doc had found in the town. New ones, always new ones. Never satisfactory. It took time to train a boy.

Franco turned on his heel and walked into the *en suite* bathroom. He had a black plastic chair in the shower, and he sat down there and let the water bite into his flesh. He missed Andrew, that's what it was. Andrew had been more than a boy, he had been like a lover. Not for long. It could've been a lot longer than it was if he hadn't also been a thief. If he hadn't also been a junkie. Or both, and worse.

Franco didn't know for sure. He knew that Andrew had been stealing anabolic steroids from Doc, which was bad. That alone would have been enough, if he was just stealing them for himself. But then Ben had found him selling the drugs to the kids outside The Monster Gym. Which was also bad. But it was the attempt to blackmail him that had caused Franco to lose it. That had certainly been enough. Franco was quick to violence. Everyone knew that. And once he started there was no knowing where he would stop.

The pity was that Franco hadn't worked his violence off before Ben and Gog brought Andrew back home. If they'd taken a bit longer about it, not found the kid and brought him back so quickly, Franco might have had time to get over it. Or at least he'd have had time to cool down some. As it was he was still fuming, and he'd started on the kid straight away. Throwing him around, beating the shit out of him. It was such a betrayal.

And Franco had gone too far.

He realized that now.

Because Andrew wasn't here any more, wasn't available any more. And Franco had to fuck other kids instead. Kids who were completely new, only in it for the money, and who didn't understand about Franco's needs.

The only people who really understood Franco's needs were Mama and Doc. It had always been like that and it always would be.

Franco had not known Doc when they were children. Not *really* known him. Doc was four years older, and had gone off to university when Franco was still singing falsetto. At that time it had always seemed to Franco that Doc was straight, a kind of clone of their father, part of the world of reliable, traditional values. He was a cert, and in going off to university to study history he confirmed that for him the world's compartments made absolute sense.

Nothing in the world made much sense to Franco at that time. Only several years later did he realize that he was a paedophile. He read about it in a newspaper. Paedophilia. It meant someone who sought out young stems, new shoots.

When he met up with Doc again, Doc was posing as a Doctor of Medicine. Doc had been posing as a Doctor of Medicine all his life. His nickname, Doc, was something he had picked up when he was seven or eight years old. Franco had called him Doc all his life. But they recognized each other then, when they met as adults, knew that they were more alike than any other two people in the world. They had both been fashioned from the same genes and by the same environment.

Of late Mama had seemed to want to spend more time shopping and driving too fast. She was always keen at the parties, but there had been a time when she'd share a young stem with Franco at any time of the day or night. Some of Franco's best memories of Mama involved the two of them offering a protective wing for a night to someone's neglected child.

Before Doc returned, when he lived alone with Mama, Franco had taken frequent trips to Thailand and become well known in certain houses in Bangkok. In one of these, situated next to a Buddhist temple with a coloured tile roof and gilded spires, Franco had been supplied with a young boy for cash. The payment included the removal of the boy's body the following morning.

When he told Doc about the house, Doc laughed and said you didn't need to go all the way to Bangkok. There was a Triad place down the Elland Road offering the same service. Plus they'd video it for you and around midnight they delivered free Chinese food to your room.

'Mr Julian.' Franco hugged the telephone to his cheek.

'This is Julian speaking.'

'Oh, no, I mean the old Mr Julian.'

'Who is this?'

'It's Franco. I need to speak with your father.'

The voice on the other end of the phone slipped a couple of degrees. 'My father's indisposed. How can we help you?'

'Indisposed? Tell him it's Franco. He'll speak to me.'

'He doesn't want to speak to anyone.' The young Mr Julian hung up the phone, leaving a buzzing sound in

Franco's ear. He looked at the phone. 'What the . . .?' he said. Mr Julian was Franco's boss. For as many years as he could remember, when he'd needed to get hold of Mr Julian, Franco picked up the telephone and talked to him. There'd never been a time when he'd picked up the telephone and not been able to get Mr Julian. Not until the last few days. This had to be a mistake. He pushed the redial button, and a moment later a girl picked up the phone.

'Mr Julian, please. It's Franco.'

'One moment.'

Then the young guy's voice. 'Julian.'

'Yeah,' Franco said. 'I need to speak to Mr Julian, your father. If you tell him it's Franco, he'll come to the phone.'

'Franco,' the young guy said, 'go to the other number and stand by.'

Franco got the buzz in his ear again.

He went to the garage and backed out the white Carrera. The other number was a public telephone on Clifton Green. He parked up against it and went inside the booth. He looked at the telephone for five minutes but it didn't ring. He left the booth and went back to the car. He opened and closed the car door and went back to the booth. The telephone still didn't ring. Franco shivered. He hadn't put a coat on. He was wearing a cotton shirt, checked red and black, open at the neck, and house shoes.

Why didn't the stupid little fuck ring the number?

He went back to the car and got in, closed the door. But now he wouldn't be able to hear if the telephone rang. He got out again and went back to the phone booth. He went inside and picked up the receiver, to check it was working. Then he put it back down again and waited. He could be patient. Franco had learned to be patient. And anyway, he'd get his own back.

When the telephone rang it was twenty minutes later. Franco's toes had frozen and were rattling about loose inside his shoes. His fingers were numb. In the tiny mirror above the telephone his nose was bright red. 'Yeah,' he said.

'Franco?' It was Max's voice.

'Max?' Max looked after the Manchester operation. In the old days he'd been Franco's right-hand man. He was still Franco's right-hand man. 'Max, what the fuck is going on? I rang Mr Julian, but that young prick won't let me speak to him.'

'You're out, Franco.'

'Out? What you talking about, out? How can I be out?'

'Old Mr Julian's had a stroke, he's paralysed. Young Mr Julian's taken over, and he wants you out. I've taken over here.'

'Listen, Max. I'm coming over there. I'll drive over now.'

'Don't do that, Franco. We go back a long way, but I still have to look after myself, after my own interests.'

Franco shook his head. 'Max, what're you saying? I don't know what's going on.'

'Listen and I'll tell you. Anything you were involved in before, I'm taking it over. Mr Julian, the young Mr Julian, doesn't like you. He doesn't want to see you in Manchester again. If anybody sees you in Manchester again, they'll tell me, and part of my job would be to put a bullet in your head. Is that clear?'

'Christ, Max. The guy doesn't *like* me. What kind of reason is that?'

'I don't have to tell you these things, Franco. But seeing you've asked, and seeing I've got a minute, it's the kids. We heard about the latest one they fished out of the river over there. And we heard it was another one of yours. The old Mr Julian thought you was just quirky. He used to laugh about it. But the young Mr Julian, he's a new man. He's got little kids of his own. He doesn't want perverts in the organization. So you're out.'

'Jesus,' said Franco. He couldn't think of anything else to say.

'No more questions?'

'Yeah, don't hang up on me, Max. Is there a contract on me?'

'No. I've told it like it is, Franco. You've just been fired.'

'But I know things, Max. I could go to the police.'

Max laughed down the line.

'OK, you know I wouldn't do that. I wouldn't even think of doing that. But what if I get in trouble? Don't I have any protection?'

The tone of Max's voice changed. 'Franco, I'm gonna hang up now. No, you don't have anything. You are an ex-employee of this organization. You didn't qualify for a golden handshake. You will not have a leaving party, and at the leaving party that you don't have, you won't be given a gold watch. You're on your own.'

Buzzzzzzzzzzz.

Ben and Gog had delivered Andrew Bridge to Franco at around seven o' clock that evening. He was already crying and saying how the blackmail thing was a joke. He was sorry he'd stolen the drugs off Doc. He was sorry about everything.

They'd messed him up some, Ben and Gog. He said Gog had stamped on his chest and neck, and his chest hurt. There was a cut on his face as well, looked as though someone had given him a back hander with a ring or a knuckle duster.

When he thought about it now, Franco thought the boy had looked vulnerable. He couldn't understand quite why he hadn't looked after him. Got Doc to strap up his ribs, Mama to bathe the cut on his forehead. He was sufficiently frightened. He would have been a good boy after that.

But at the time Franco hadn't been sympathetic at all. He'd wanted to kill the kid. He had killed the kid.

He'd taken him by the arm in the tiled basement bathroom and swung him round. Then let go. Andrew had spun into the wall and cracked his face against the tiles. He'd got to his feet again, swaying from side to side, a trickle of blood running down his face and neck. Franco had come forward and grabbed his head and smashed it back against the tiles. He'd done it repeatedly, watching the tears coming from the boy's eyes. Then the tears had stopped and Andrew had given him a long, cow-like, pathetic stare. Franco went on smashing his head against the tiles. After Andrew's legs had gone, and even after the hard feel of bone against tile had changed to mush against tile, Franco had carried on that same movement. Pulling the head forward and smashing it back again.

Then he'd tied Andrew's hands to the brass towel rings and gone for his knife.

Later he'd put the body in the bath and Gog and Ben had taken it away. Mama and Doc had swabbed down the bathroom.

Franco blamed himself. You always hurt the one you love.

It was the kid's own fault, but he was only a kid. Franco blamed himself because he was the adult. He shouldn't have let things get so bad that there was only one solution.

Franco left his car in the castle car park and cut through the Coppergate Centre on foot. He walked along Colliergate, then through to College Street and took the Queen's

Path to Deangate. He stood by the iron railings of the Minster School and looked in on the empty playground. He had been coming here all his life, and felt something like nostalgia about this particular spot. Even when there were no children playing it still felt good. Safe, somehow, and with a whiff of fascination.

Franco had heard, a long time ago, how a bull in the ring will always gravitate to a particular spot. Each bull has its own spot, patch of earth, on which it feels safer than anywhere else in the ring. No two bulls choose the same place. And people were like that, too. Doc's spot was a park in Stevenage where they had spent some time as children, and Mama's was Piccadilly Gardens in Manchester where she had been a teenager for twenty years.

But this was Franco's place. The Minster School. Or this particular part of it: the iron railings outside the playground. Franco had never ventured inside, and he didn't think he ever would. The children here were special, an important part of Franco's fantasy life. Other kids, all the other kids in the world were up for grabs. But not these. These were completely untouchable. Just for looking at, on the other side of the railings.

CHAPTER 24

Sam and Geordie looked up at the Norman archway of the Micklegate Bar. 'What're you saying?' Geordie asked.

'Traitors,' Sam said. 'If they had somebody was a traitor, they'd chop his head off and hang it on the Bar.'

'This Bar?'

'Yeah.'

'Not other Bars?'

'No, Geordie, they hung the heads on this Bar. This was the main entrance to the city.'

'Why'd they call it a Bar? What's it mean, Bar?' Geordie was aware that he was full of questions, but couldn't stop himself. There were things he could find out here, and he didn't want to let the opportunity pass.

Sam thought for a moment. 'I think it's short for barrier,' he said. 'Something that keeps people out, that's a bar, a barrier.'

They walked through to the other side, and Geordie looked back, tried to imagine the heads hanging there, blood dripping down the stone, the dead eyes staring at the tourists. It was a real fort kind of gate, bar. A square tower built over the arch with embattled corner turrets on either side.

'There must've been hundreds of people killed here,' he said. 'I mean in York.'

'Try thousands.'

'Yeah, if you count battles and wars, executions. But I was just thinking of murders.'

'I suppose,' said Sam. 'But why bring it up?'

'It makes me feel weird,' said Geordie. 'I mean, we live here, right? This is where we live and work, where we spend our time. And you walk round it, not today when it's freezing cold, but in the summer, say, you walk round York and the sun is shining and all the people are out in the streets, little kids running around. There's these cafés down here bringing their tables out on to the street, and it's like everything's normal.'

Sam looked over at him. 'Everything *is* normal.'

'I know, Sam. But you go and sit at one of those tables, and you don't think about it, but maybe somebody has been murdered there, right on that spot.'

'Why should they've?' said Sam. 'I mean, why would you think somebody's been murdered right on the spot where you're having your coffee?'

Geordie shook his head. You'd think Sam would catch on easier than this. But then again, that's Sam. If he feels like being awkward, there's no way round him. 'Because everything's so old, of course. I mean, this road, Micklegate, like how old is it?'

'I give in,' said Sam. 'How old is it?'

'A thousand years,' said Geordie. 'At least a thousand years old. Might be even older. When were the Romans here?'

'BC,' said Sam. 'At least.'

'See what I mean? You're walking along a street that was probably walked along by the fucking Romans. They used to kill Anglo Saxons for sport. Then after them came that other lot, Normans, and they killed people. And that's been going on since BC. So if there's been a murder, say one murder a year for a thousand years, how many murders'd that be?'

'Two hundred and forty-three,' said Sam.

'Yeah. And there's probably been more than one a year. Hell, we're investigating three at the moment.'

'Oh, you remembered that,' said Sam. 'Why we're here.'

'Of course I remember that,' said Geordie. 'What do you think, I've lost my memory?'

'No. I thought we were into some kind of history lesson. Like in school, or something. A quick tour of the history of York, from the Romans to the present day.'

'You're as hard as a tombstone, Sam.'

'But every other inch a gentleman.'

'You're quick. You've always got an answer, but you're like an ostrich.'

'Oh, God, I've been rumbled.'

'See what I mean?' said Geordie. 'You can't stand it if somebody else has the last word.'

Sam didn't reply. They walked side by side for a couple of minutes, right past the area they were supposed to be working in. Sam stopped outside a café. 'I'll buy you a coffee,' he said. 'To make atonement for being a complete bastard.'

'Tell me about it,' said Geordie. 'It's your money.'

Sam opened the café door and stood aside to let Geordie precede him into the warm and aromatic interior.

There's always this other side to Sam. Geordie was learning to be wary of it. But it wasn't easy, because it came at the oddest times. Exactly when you weren't expecting it. For six days of the week he's on an even keel. (Even keel! Look at that, bloody great cliché crept in there. If he'd written that in one of his essays, Celia would have drawn a red ring around it. *Even keel! What on earth does it mean?* Geordie knew it was something to do with boats and he knew why it was wrong to use it in the English language. Because it was trite. And that was a great word: trite.)

Anyway, whatever, he was on an even keel, and then on the seventh day he was a total grump. Mean. Mean and nasty. And when you pointed it out to him, he'd probably get meaner and nastier because you'd criticized him. What was supposed to happen was that Sam was mean and nasty to you, and you just had to take it.

And sometimes Geordie had done that. Just taken it. Because Sam was good to him the rest of the time. But when he'd got round to thinking about it, he thought, why should he? Just take it, that is. And he couldn't think of a good reason, so he'd stopped. Now, when Sam got mean, Geordie told him he was being mean.

Hell, if Geordie got mean, Sam would be the first to

point it out. And when Sam pointed out bad things about Geordie, like he'd told him about washing his feet, then Geordie learned it. Eventually he learned to wash his feet before they started smelling. Also, through learning that whole lesson about feet he also learned to change his socks every day, even though Sam hadn't mentioned that. See? Geordie had figured that out for himself, the part about the socks, because if you changed your socks every day your feet stayed cleaner longer.

But with Sam it could go either way. You tell Sam he's being mean and nasty, and he might be mean and nasty for the next couple of days. Or he might think about it for a few minutes and then say he's sorry.

Geordie thought it might be his age. Because he was a senile old bastard. But it wasn't that, it was something else inside him. A kind of demon. Something that made him lash out at the world because he didn't understand it. A sore spot. Something that made him grind his teeth in the night.

Most of the time Sam could manage it. Keep it locked away. And when he could do that he was great, he walked with a kind of spring, and he played loud music, he told stories and jokes, and he could be real serious and interesting at the same time.

Geordie found it strange, how someone could change so quickly. From one thing to another. But that was how it was. Nobody was perfect.

The guy who served them in the café was worried about Sam. Must be because of his face. Maybe it was the first time he'd served somebody with a black nose. He kept looking over, and a couple of times he touched the telephone behind the counter, just to make sure it was there if Sam started a fight or began throwing cups around.

Geordie whispered to Sam that the guy was worried and

Sam laughed. He seemed to ease up a little, as though the fact that he'd worried a café proprietor had made him feel better.

'You right, then?' he asked Geordie, getting to his feet. He felt in his pocket and let four pound coins drop to the table, about twice as much as the bill. He smiled at the guy behind the counter as they went out, an attempt to reassure him. But when he saw Sam's teeth the guy stumbled back against the telephone and knocked it off its hook.

They worked opposite sides of Micklegate. Geordie saw most of the people he'd seen before, and none of them told him anything new. He also met a couple of men and one woman who hadn't been available last time he'd called. But neither of the men remembered anything exceptional the day that Andrew Bridge disappeared, and the woman, an antique dealer, had been at an auction in Leeds.

When he left the antique shop Geordie saw Sam waiting for him on the other side of Micklegate. He crossed over, rubbing his hands together against the cold.

'Anything?' said Sam.

Geordie shook his head. 'Pneumonia.'

'I think I've got something. Follow me.' Sam turned and entered a large warehouse, stacked to the rafters with old furniture. He made his way to an office area, and Geordie followed. As they approached the office the temperature changed. When they actually entered it Geordie caught sight of a fat man loading blocks of dry wood into an already glowing stove.

'This is Geordie, my associate,' Sam said. 'And this is Mr White, the proprietor.'

'Call me Claude,' said the fat man, leaving the stove and shaking Geordie's hand. His smile exposed a range of yellow and black stumps that had been teeth back around the time of the *Belgrano*. He turned his attention back to Sam. 'You've had some kind of accident,' he said. 'I nearly didn't recognize you.'

'It's a disguise,' said Sam, keeping a straight face and touching his blackened nose with the fingertips of his right hand. 'We're incognito today.'

Claude took him seriously for about half a minute. He leant forward to get a good look at Sam's face, sniffed to see if he could detect any grease paint, then let his smile come.

'That's not a disguise,' he said, turning to Geordie for confirmation. 'You're having me on.'

Geordie smiled back at him. 'That's how he got the bruises,' he said. 'Telling jokes like that.'

'Yeah?' Claude thought about that one for a while. Geordie thought Claude was wearing the lamest shirt he'd ever seen in his life.

'Claude has a friend,' Sam said. 'Thinks she might have seen something.'

'Marnie,' said Claude, his face softening as he spoke the syllables of the name. 'An old friend.'

'An old *girl*friend,' Sam said. 'Isn't she, Claude?'

The fat man smiled and puckered up his lips in embarrassment. 'A man loses his illusions first,' he said, 'his teeth second and his follies last.' He looked down at his laceless black boots and tried to gain some control over his face. But when he surfaced he was still smiling, still puckering his lips, and he'd begun reddening up. 'She'll be here in a minute,' he said. 'She's in the ladies' room.'

When she came in Geordie thought Marnie was the ugliest woman he'd ever seen in his life. Claude had a beaut of his own, but if anything Marnie's honker was even more obscene. Claude's had a whole network of external veins feeding it, which drew your attention. Marnie didn't have that, what she had was exactly the opposite. Her nose had been starved of blood for a long time, and as a result it was withering away. It was a much darker hue than the rest of her features, being composed almost entirely of blackheads. 'Nearest you could get to a description of it,' Geordie told Janet later, 'was, well, it was like something a wasp would make. But not a regular wasp's nest. If you could imagine a wasp that'd always been a failure, a kind of black-sheep wasp. You know what I mean? From a broken home, and a mixed marriage, and it left home too early, before its parents had time to teach it things. Like it would build something like Marnie's nose and try to live in it.'

But that wasn't the worst thing. The teeth were even better. They were huge and white and Geordie had the impression that they didn't really belong in her mouth. She had thin lips, which she'd covered with dark red lipstick, kind of plum coloured. But she hadn't quite followed the line of each lip, so the plum juice gave the impression it was spreading outwards.

He'd seen her before. Hadn't known she was called Marnie, but everyone in York knew her. She used to hang around outside the Theatre Royal and swear at the traffic, often stepping into the road, oblivious of any danger. She would turn sharply when a driver braked to avoid her, give him the V sign, and then start slagging off the tourists as they queued for their tickets.

That was Marnie. Except there was something different about her.

Yeah, the teeth didn't belong in her mouth. The Marnie that Geordie had seen around the town didn't have any teeth. She had a shrunken face, her lips sucked into her mouth so far that her chin almost touched her nose.

She was dressed differently, too. The old Marnie wore a

shapeless coat and huge boots, and she trundled a couple of enormous shopping bags full of bottles and trash retrieved from waste bins. 'But today she was different,' Geordie told Janet. 'You should've seen her. She had on a white blouse, well, it was a kind of creamy colour, with long sleeves, and it had frills on the front and on the cuffs. Real posh. And then she had a maroon suit on, which wasn't new, but it wasn't old and raggy at all. If you'd've been wearing it, you'd've ironed it first, and then it'd've been OK to go to work in. And she had grey woollen tights on, that actually fitted her. When I've seen her before she'd have tights on but they'd be full of holes and they'd be wrinkled round her legs. Well, these tights weren't like that at all. They fitted her legs. They were her size. Could've even been new. And then she had a pair of red shoes, not the same red as the suit, but good shoes, you know. Flat heels.'

And she was sober.

He couldn't believe it was the same woman. He looked at Sam and Claude.

Sam didn't give anything away. You could never tell what Sam was thinking by looking at him. Mr Inscrutable. His feelings, if he had any, didn't make it as far as his face.

But Claude's feelings were all over his face. To look at Claude, if you hadn't seen the state of Marnie, if you didn't know what he was looking at, you'd think a fairy princess had just arrived in a golden coach. He beamed.

Geordie had heard about people beaming, but this was the first time he'd ever experienced it in the flesh. There he was, Claude White, second-hand dealer, proprietor of the Micklegate Furniture Emporium, struck dumb and beaming. If it was an act, he was one of the all-time greats.

In mid-beam he got to his feet and went over to her. 'Oh, my dear,' he said, putting his arm around her and guiding her to a chair next to his own. He lowered his voice, speaking only to her. 'You look lovely.'

No, Geordie thought, she doesn't. She looks *different*, Claude. But lovely's not the right word. Then he remembered about relativity. 'OK,' he said.

They all looked at him expectantly, and he smiled back at them. He hadn't meant to say anything. He'd said OK inside his head, and the words had somehow got into his mouth. He hadn't wanted to float them into the world. 'Nothing,' he said. 'It's all right.'

'That's Geordie,' Claude said to his fairy princess. 'And this is the other one I told you about, Mr Turner.'

Sam extended his hand, and Marnie reached forward and shook it. She didn't let go immediately, but looked into Sam's face.

'Yes,' she said, with difficulty because of the teeth. 'Sam Turner. Me old drinking partner. How's it going?'

'Fine,' said Sam. 'Since I gave it up. Trying to kill myself, that is.' He nodded at her and there was the suggestion that he squeezed her hand before he let it drop. 'How're you doin', Marnie?'

She smiled and nearly lost the top set of teeth. She pushed them back into place. 'I've been worse,' she said. She looked over at Claude and reached out a scrawny hand to him. 'I'm on an up at the moment.'

'You know each other,' said Claude. And then he laughed at himself. 'To state the obvious.'

'There was a time,' said Sam ironically, 'when we both had a problem with the drink. Times like that you don't really know anyone, or get to know anyone. You just tend to end up in the same places.'

Marnie nodded her head in agreement. 'But that's the past,' she said rather too hurriedly. 'Let's talk about today.' The top set of teeth came forward again, and she took them out and placed them on the table in front of Claude's chair. 'They hurt,' she said to Claude. 'They're not the right size.' Weird. Her top lip immediately disappeared inside her mouth, as though it had been sucked in by a nuclear-powered internal vacuum cleaner. And her face changed totally. If you'd had a picture of how she looked with the top teeth in, and you compared it with how she looked after she'd taken them out, you wouldn't know her.

The top set of teeth, on the other hand, you'd recognize them anywhere. Sitting there on Claude's desk they looked more like Marnie than she looked like herself.

'They're only temporary,' Claude said, picking up the teeth and holding them level with his eyes, peering at them. 'We'll get a dentist to measure you up. I'll make an appointment.' He put the teeth back down on the desk, left them there, on guard.

'Claude said you saw the boy,' said Sam.

She turned to him quickly. 'He was frightened,' she said. 'Waiting for his mother, and this car kept coming round, looking for him. We put him in a doorway, and I put my coat on top of him, then I stood in front of him.' She looked over at Geordie, then back at Sam. 'He was only a young 'un. Younger than him.' Her eyes flashed back at Geordie. 'He was a darkie, called Andrew. My father was called Andrew.'

Jesus, thought Geordie. Her father. He'd never imagined her having a father, parents. Never thought of her as being a child.

Then she was gone for several minutes. She stared up at the rafters, and a low moaning sound came from her.

'Jesus,' said Claude, getting to his feet. 'This happens.' He stood behind her chair and held both sides of her head. Gently, giving it some support, as though he was afraid it might fall off. The moaning gradually changed pitch, becoming a loud keening. Claude moved his feet around and looked over at Sam with a wordless plea for help. Sam didn't move, his eyes never left the old woman.

She was wailing now, like a lamentation, Geordie thought. For the dead? Her father? For those parts of herself, her youth and beauty, her past, which were for ever lost? Or perhaps for something else, something she couldn't even name herself. Something that the whole world had forgotten.

The sound stopped with a series of jerks. She took in gulps of air and looked around. Claude tentatively let go of her head. He moved his hands away, but left them hovering there, a couple of inches away. When her head didn't fall off he took a step back and sat in his chair again.

Marnie reached over and patted his hand. Then she picked up her story again, where she had left off. 'The lad was terrified. Andrew. I left him in the doorway. He was shaking, but my coat was over him, so I thought he'd be safe. I wanted to stop the traffic, cause a traffic jam, so those two in the car wouldn't be able to get round again. That would give the lad a chance to move. Or at least it would give him time. His mother was on her way.

'I squatted down on the road. And it worked at first. They were all blowing their horns at me. But somebody must've called the fuzz, because they turned up and hauled me away. I told them what I was doing. I told the first one, but he didn't want to listen, and he went back to his car and called for a woman fuzz. And then I told her, but she just pushed me into the back of a van. I even told them back at the police station.

'But the next thing I saw was the lad's picture in the evening press. Drowned in Brownie Dyke.'

'The two guys in the car,' Sam said, 'did you see them? Can you describe them?'

'Big boys,' Marnie said. 'Like strong men. When I was a girl, they'd've been in the circus, bending iron bars. I saw a couple of them once, lifting a tractor between them. Stupid thing to do.'

Claude's wood-burning stove was fairly jumping by now. Geordie felt a small river running down his back, and he looked over at Sam and saw him wipe a film of sweat from his forehead. Claude and Marnie didn't seem to be affected by it. Sam got to his feet and told them they'd been a great help. Especially Marnie.

They hit the street in time to stop Geordie's blood from boiling. The sweat on his face and neck turned to ice.

On their way back to the office Sam said, 'That clinches it, then. We thought we had two cases, but we've only got one.'

'You think the muscly men did all the murders?' asked Geordie.

'Looks like it, but the guy who gave the orders calls himself Franco Tampon.'

She was beautiful. That was the pity of it. Sam hadn't gone out of his way to sweep her off her feet. He had liked her right from the start, from the first moment he saw her. But he hadn't pressured her. He'd wanted to take it slowly, see what developed. See if there was anything there, a spark that he could nurture. Something he could start growing, and watch it bloom.

But Jeanie wasn't growing. She was confused, she didn't know which way to turn, to Sam or to the Irishman. He reached for the carafe and poured more wine into her glass. Sat back in his chair and took a mouthful of Vichy water.

'Have you told him yet?' Sam asked. 'About me.'

She shook her head, and her long black hair shimmered

and her dangly earrings flashed in the candle light. She wore a black blouse with a circular, black, lacquered clasp at the neck. When she looked at him he saw the regret moored behind her eyes. But he ignored it because he couldn't bear to live with it.

'We need to find the tape,' he said. 'A video tape. Cal must've left it somewhere. Can you look again?'

She shrugged. 'I've turned the house upside down. First of all, when they broke in, whoever they were, they left the place in a total tip. So I sorted everything out. And since then I've looked again, I've looked everywhere, Sam. If there was a video tape I'd've found it.'

'What about Karen's room? The last time Cal came to visit he went up there.'

'She'd have found it.'

'She's eleven years old, Jeanie. Are you telling me she knows where everything is in her room?'

Jeanie shook her head. 'She doesn't know where anything is, but it's such a small room.'

'OK,' Sam said. 'You're probably right. I'm only asking you to look.'

'I'll do it tomorrow. I'll take the place apart.'

He had an urge to reach out and touch her face, but he didn't do it. Once the air goes out of a balloon there's no point in pretending.

CHAPTER 25

When she had been a nurse Marie had thought she'd seen all the layers of British society. On a cancer ward it became increasingly difficult to tell the difference between an accountant and a cabby. Horizontal, pale and sick, with shit coming out of both ends, they all looked the same.

Later she realized that she never met the very rich. It wasn't that the very rich didn't get sick and die like everyone else. They did. But they rarely seemed to find their way on to an NHS ward. They were given personal attention to the very end, in the private clinics that were built exclusively for them.

After she left the caring profession and went to work for Sam as a private detective, she discovered more layers of society, specifically the underbelly, the remnants of the Thatcher revolution. Those who cashed in and thrived on the 'fuck thy neighbour' mentality. The criminal classes, many of whom were allowed to work within the law. But also those who were simply victims, who were placed outside the system and stripped of any rights or privileges of citizenship. The handicapped, the mentally ill, the old.

For some time now she'd thought that the bottom of the pile was represented by the sellers of the street-people mags in Coney Street or outside Waterstone's bookshop. They were the homeless, scratching a living built from the pennies of passing tourists.

But the boy she sat with in a passageway off Colliergate was in a class way below any of the high-profile vendors of the *Big Issue*.

Pete was nineteen years old and badly undernourished. His physical build was more typical of a twelve or thirteen year old, narrow shoulders, frightened, bulging eyes. Marie kept coming back to those eyes, and the depths they concealed. Depths of abuse? Of depravity? Yes, and more. Even the depths of an old wisdom, a knowledge that had no place or function in the years leading up to the millennium.

He was sitting on the remains of a tabloid newspaper, both of his legs splayed out in front of him. He wore a pair of battered trainers and his jeans were thin and torn around his legs. He had two sweaters, a red one and a green one, and a hat made of black wool which he'd pulled down low over his eyes.

His guitar was backless and had only three strings, one of them broken and tied together again over the the sixth fret. 'Guitar' was a misnomer, for this was no longer a musical instrument. Neither John Williams nor Eric Clapton would have had the ability to make it sing.

While he strummed away at it, Marie counted the coins on the rag between his legs. One pound forty-seven pence. An old woman stopped for a moment and added another twenty pence. One pound sixty-seven now, and going up. Two thousand years of constant and unending progress.

'You know what I thought?' she told Celia later. 'I couldn't get the thought of Dickens out of my head. Not that he would come back and make sense of it. Help us to get rid of it. Not that at all. What I thought was that it was time for another Dickens. A Dickens for the end of the century. The world seems to be full of writers and journalists, politicians who are all impotent. One Dickens could replace them all, one man or woman with heart and willpower and talent.

'Yes.' Celia knew exactly what she meant. 'Maybe it's you, my dear.'

'Not me, Celia. I can't write.'

But Celia shook her wise old head. 'You can do whatever's necessary.'

Pete was described over and over again in those great nineteenth-century novels of social realism. But Marie came face to face with him not through the pages of a book, but on the streets of one of the wealthiest cities in the land. And he wasn't the exception that proved the rule, he wasn't a lone example of bad management or misfortune. There was more than one Pete on the streets of York, and he was duplicated many times over in every city and town in the country.

'When I started off the places were called "orphanages",' he said. 'But they changed the name to "children's homes".

'Yes, I went to one of the parties. I don't know where the house is, but I can describe the inside to you. They had a white piano in the entrance, just when you go in the door. And I remember the bathroom, 'specially that. There are no windows, and there are two brass towel rings that he puts your hands through.'

Pete strummed on his guitar. He looked at Marie and gave her a brilliant smile, almost a perfect mask. Then his white face and bulging eyes were averted for a few seconds, before he snapped himself back into the moment.

'There's a shower in there,' he said. 'With a chair in it. You can sit in it and have a shower. Watch all the blood go down the plug hole.'

'And the man,' said Marie. 'Would you recognize the man who did it?'

Pete nodded. He looked off into some inner distance, and he began nodding his head, and he didn't stop.

CHAPTER 26

'You never seem to get any fatter, Geordie.' Sam had been watching him for the last few minutes. 'When I first saw you on the street, I thought you were the thinnest thing I'd ever seen in my life. Apart from Donna. She was even thinner than you. She put a bit of weight on after she'd been pregnant. But you don't alter at all. I'd thought, you know, after a while, three meals a day, you'd start filling out.'

Geordie looked up from his writing. 'It's genetic,' he said. He dropped his head again and went back to the letter.

Sam waited a while. Sang along with the man on the tape deck: 'Honey, why are you so hard?'

'What're you writing?' he asked.

Geordie looked up again. 'Two things,' he said. 'I'm writing two things. The first one I'm writing to this place called Watchtower, which you have to send two pounds, and they send you a book back which is about paradise on earth. And the second one I'm writing to is a firm that knows about why your hair goes thin, and how you can stop it.'

'Busy then?'

'Yeah, and I'm not getting very far with it, 'cause you seem to want to interrupt me all the time. I jus' get to thinking what the next word is, so it's a proper sentence, and I start looking it up in the dictionary, and you come up with another question. At this rate I'll be bald and in paradise before I get either of them finished.'

'Sorry,' said Sam. 'It just struck me about you being so thin.'

'I've written to this place that helps you get more muscly,' Geordie said. 'Going round the gyms and seeing all these guys with shoulders makes you feel like a wimp. So soon I won't be so thin any more. There's this stuff called MuscleForce from America. It's like a drink, but it's actually a food, and you can get it in strawberry or watermelon flavours. Others as well, I think, lemon and lime, and cherry. But I'm getting it in Strawberry. It's all these carbohydrates stacked up in a bottle, fructose, stuff like that, and you drink it, I dunno, maybe once a day or something. Anyway, what it does, it goes to work on your lean body mass and after a couple of weeks you look in the mirror and you've turned into a hunk.'

'And women in bikinis start following you around?'

'Yeah, I expect so.' Geordie smiled. 'Dunno. Some of 'em'd be in bikinis, others'd be fully dressed. 'Specially in this weather.'

'What about Janet?' asked Sam. 'I thought she was enough for you.'

'She is,' he said. 'I'm not drinking this stuff for the women in bikinis, you brought that up. I haven't told Janet about it, I jus' wanna see her face when I get all muscly.'

Sam left it a moment before he said, 'You worried about losing your hair?'

'No. It's really thick. It's just I was reading this thing, and it said your hair starts getting thin for all sorts of reasons. You don't have any control over it, so you have to massage it and put this cream on. I think it's cream. Maybe it's a shampoo.

'Even women use it, 'cause their hair starts getting thin with, well, when they get pregnant, and after they've had babies. And they use colours and have perms and all those things work against the hair. So what they do, they massage it and use this cream, and that keeps it healthy, and that's why you don't see so many bald women.

'Even Marnie has loads of hair. After what she's been through, using drugs, and living under stress, I reckon she must use this stuff. That other thing we talked about, the menopause, that makes your hair fall out as well, when you don't have a balanced diet.'

Sam walked over to the window and pulled the curtains tighter together. 'So, come the summer,' he said, 'you'll be unrecognizable. All lean body mass and thick hair. You could grow it long, make a feature out of it.'

'No way,' said Geordie. 'I don't wanna be a hippy. Janet doesn't like long hair, either. We think short hair's more natural for a man.'

'Really. And the guys with long hair, they're unnatural?'

'No, Sam. You know what I mean.'

'Yeah. OK. But I don't understand the paradise on earth bit.'

'I've never read the Bible. Have you? This book, it tells you all about the Bible without you having to spend the rest of your life ploughing through it. What I thought was, first I thought I'd just start on the Bible, read a bit of it every day, and see how long it took. But after a couple of days I couldn't face it any more.

'Celia said the King James is the best version to read, 'cause the language is nicer, so I started on that, but I can't concentrate on it. I'm half the time in the dictionary. So I had a go at the modern translation, where Celia says the language is crap, well, she says it's parochial. And it's easier to read like that, except it's really boring.

'So I thought I'd get this paradise on earth book. Seems like a way out. Even if it's a con, it'll only cost me a couple of quid.'

Geordie dropped his head again, picked up his pen. Sam listened to the man on the tape deck, who'd moved on to 'eyes like smoke' and 'prayers like rhymes'. When that song was recorded Sam Turner was nearer to Geordie's age now. Aw, but so much older then.

Ben shivered in the street where the detective lived. He watched the curtains move, and wondered if they would come out, leave the place for just a few minutes, so he could get in there and plant his bomb.

It had tried to snow earlier, and the wind was like a million whips. Ben kicked his feet in a doorway and wished he had remembered to wear gloves. He blew on his fingers. Thought about the cold body of his brother back at home. He transferred his bag to the other hand and blew on the ends of those fingers as well. Instant relief followed by instant disappointment.

Ben didn't know what life would be like without Gog. He'd tried to think about it, but had been unable to visualize anything. Gog had always been there. And Gog, being like he was, needing so much help, so much understanding, which the world didn't give him, he took up much more time than other people. Most people, you could just ignore them, or you gave them as much attention as they needed to get a response. Which wasn't much. Like in a shop, the woman behind the counter, you just had to listen to what she asked for, five pounds, say, or ten pounds. Then you gave her it, and she gave you your change. You might say thank you, or please, or if it started to get complicated you might have to say excuse me, or sorry.

But with Gog it wasn't like that at all. You really had to listen, not only because of the Gogspeak. It wasn't because you had to interpret everything he said, translate it into the English language, it was because even when you'd done that you still had to hear what it was he was *meaning*, rather than what it was he was *saying*.

Ben and Gog talked all the time before Gog died. Lots of the time they didn't actually say anything, not in words. But Ben reckoned he'd had the best conversations of his life with Gog. He couldn't think of anyone in the world he'd rather talk to than his brother. Even if it was famous people, like great body builders or film stars. If he could have three wishes and they'd come true, and it was, say, the three people you'd most like to meet, Ben would say number one, Gog, number two, Gog, and number three,

Gog. Even if it was a toss up between Gog and Robert De Niro. No contest. Ben wouldn't even flip the coin.

Gog would like this, just the two of them standing in this doorway. With a bomb in a bag, waiting for the detective to go out. Freezing cold. He'd love it. He'd say, 'You got the bomb, Ben?'

And Ben would say it was in the bag.

'It's in the bag, Ben?'

'Yes. I just told you, it's in the bag.'

'We gonna blow the fucking roof off, Ben? Can we watch it?'

'Yeah. We set the clock, then we get a good way off. We watch the detective come back. We see him go in the house, then all the lights go out, and we know he's gone to bed.'

'Yeah, Ben, he's gone to bed. The detective's gone to bed.'

'Then we wait.'

'What we waiting for, Ben?'

'We're waiting for the clock, Gog. For the time to come round.'

'What time's that, Ben? What time's the bomb go off?'

'We've set it for two a.m. That's the one in the middle of the night. We think the detective'll be back by then. We could've set it for midnight, but sometimes he isn't back at midnight. We know he's always back at two a.m. because we've been watching him.'

'Yeah, Ben. So, he's blown to bits in the middle of the night. There won't be nothing left.'

'The odd bone. Bits of skin.'

Gog would laugh at that. 'Fuckin' great, Ben. Blow the roof off.'

'Bring the house down, Gog.'

A car turned into the street and crept along the kerb, bringing Ben out of his reverie. Gog was dead. He was dead, finished. Nothing would ever bring him back.

'You going out tonight?' Sam asked.

Geordie put his pen down. 'I'm gonna see Janet later,' he said. 'She has to work late now. Doesn't even get paid for it. But if you want to be the manager you have to take all kinds of shit.'

'You work late sometimes. Hell, you've worked all night and not been paid.'

'That's different, Sam. I don't work for money. I work for you.'

'What's that supposed to mean?' asked Sam, watching his huff arrive and getting ready to climb aboard, before registering the smile on Geordie's face. But he still couldn't quite let go of it. 'You want me to pay overtime, you only have to ask.'

'You wouldn't be able to afford it,' said Geordie. 'Jesus, Sam, you're almost broke as it is.'

'I'd find it somehow,' said Sam. 'It's always possible to lay your hand on a few quid if you're careful.'

'That's not what I want, Sam. I like things as they are. But it's different where Janet works. It's like a big firm. The guys who run it, they don't know who Janet is. They don't know anything about her. So if she works twenty-four hours a day for a peanut, why should they care?'

'She's helping to make them even richer than they are already.'

'Yeah, she knows that. But that's because she wants to be a manager, and she's a woman.'

'Why does that make a difference? Are all the managers men?'

'I don't know,' said Geordie. 'But if you're a woman you have to work twice as hard to stay in the same place as a man.'

'Is that what Janet said?'

'Yeah.'

'Maybe she should look for another job, then. Not all companies think like that.'

'C'mon, Sam. There aren't that many jobs. And she's only just got this one.'

'She'll leave eventually,' said Sam. 'Guys who have a problem with somebody just because she sits down to take a pee, they're not gonna make it anyway. The end of the day she won't wanna waste her time on them.'

'I don't think so,' said Geordie. 'I think she'll get a job as a manager, then get an even bigger job. In the end she'll be running the whole company. She could do it, too. She's intelligent, and she's got will-power.'

The telephone rang and Sam walked over to pick it up. 'Hello.'

It was Jeanie. 'I've found the tape, Sam. It's got the boy on it, Andrew Bridge, and a couple of thugs, like the one who attacked you.'

'Where was it? In Karen's room?'

'Yes. Well hidden. She had this small box chair, when she was tiny. She doesn't use it now, and he'd put it under the cover.'

'I'll come round,' he said.

'Sam.' She hesitated. 'I'm going out later.'

'I'll just collect the tape,' he said. 'I won't interfere with your personal life.'

'Christ. Did I ask for that?'

'No. I'm sorry. It was out of line.' He wanted to put the phone down and walk out into the night. Drink some scotch. Forget about the tape, forget that the world contained people with ovaries. He wanted to let go of everything. It took the length of a couple of breaths before he got hold of it again. 'When are you going out?'

'About an hour.'

'I'll come now,' he said. 'And I'm sorry, Jeanie. It's the ostrich position. I seem to get into it more easily these days.'

He put the phone down and turned to Geordie. 'Jeanie,' he said. 'She's found the tape.'

'I gathered that. Are you all right?'

'I'll live,' said Sam. 'I'm OK, apart from the fast lip.'

'You'll never learn to curb it.'

Sam looked over at him. 'I'm living with a philosopher.'

''Fraid so,' said Geordie.

'D'you wanna come? I'm gonna pick the tape up.'

Geordie stood and walked to the door. 'Just get my coat,' he said. 'Take a leak, finish these letters, make an Easter bonnet. I'll be right with you.'

Ben watched them come out of the house and walk to the hire car. The detective first, buttoning his coat as he unlocked the driver's door. Then the skinny kid, wearing a leather jacket and a checked scarf.

The detective didn't get into the car, though. He said something to the kid, and the kid looked up at the sky, and nodded. Then the detective closed the car door and locked it. Ben thought they'd changed their minds for a second there, decided to spend the night in the house, not go out at all. But they didn't go back to the house, they walked off along the street together.

Maybe they were going to the local. It didn't matter, really. Ben would only need a few minutes to place his bomb, wire it up and set the clock. Then he'd be out of there.

He watched the two of them until they turned the corner at the end of the street, then moved to the rear of the house and looked at the door and windows there. The door was locked and probably had a couple of bolts top and bottom, so he didn't bother with that. One of the windows to the right of the door, seemed to be a kitchen window, looked like it would be easy. He opened it with a flat-bladed knife.

He pushed his bag through first, then clambered in after it. Caught his jacket on the edge of the sill and had to partly back out to get it loose. But then he was inside. The street curtains were drawn, so he used his torch. It wasn't a kitchen, but it was a kitchen area of a much larger room. Should be easy to find somewhere safe for the bomb.

His first choice was one of the cupboards next to the cooker. But he changed his mind and took the bag to the other end of the room. There was stacked stereo equipment and hundreds of tapes. Nearly all the tapes were American. And they were all old, sixties stuff, Ben guessed. But most of it he'd never heard of. Richie Havens, big grinning black face, hoping to take over the world, which they never would. Loads of them were by Bob Dylan, and the guy didn't keep them tidy, left them out of their cases and spread around on the shelves. And there were no CDs, not even a CD player. Just tapes. The guy was a cheapskate.

When Ben took a step back to make room for his bag he fell over a stool. He fell hard and hurt his back, strained something. He cursed, but then he cursed again and forgot about his back altogether when he heard the dog barking.

'I'm going back for Barney,' Geordie said.

'Christ, why didn't you bring him?'

'I thought we were going in the car,' Geordie said. 'He's not that keen on cars. Then when you said we could walk

I thought of going back for him, but he was sleeping upstairs.'

'So, he'll be OK,' said Sam.

'But I won't. I'll feel guilty, 'cause he's missed out on a walk. And he'll know we've been out walking and left him behind. It'll only take a couple of minutes.'

'Ten minutes. Twenty minutes altogether. Ten minutes back and then another ten minutes to get back to here. What if Jeanie goes out?'

'She won't,' Geordie said. 'She'll wait for us. And even if she does go out, so what? We'll get the tape tomorrow instead of tonight.'

'I don't want the tape tomorrow, Geordie.'

'Then you go on ahead. I'll go back for Barney and I'll meet you at Jeanie's or on the way back.'

'No. I'll come back with you. Barney'll think it's his birthday if he gets to walk with both of us.'

They turned around and walked back to the house.

'Something's wrong,' said Geordie when they got close to the house.

'Is that Barney?'

'Yeah,' said Geordie. 'What's wrong with him?'

'He wants to go for a walk.' Sam stood outside while Geordie opened the door and went upstairs for Barney. The little dog was kicking up a racket. Really pissed off at being left behind. The barking turned into a long whine when the dog saw Geordie, and Sam could hear Barney's tail banging on the floor. Sam thought of checking his own flat to make entirely sure that Barney wasn't trying to tell them something. But he didn't do it. Wanted to make sure he got to Jeanie's house before she went out to meet her Irish boyfriend.

Geordie and Barney came out on the street, and Barney leapt up at Sam, trying to lick his face. 'This is why we keep you, Barney,' Sam told him. 'You're the only one in the whole world greets us like we've just risen from the dead.'

Ben found a place for the bomb in the sideboard under the stereo equipment. He mixed in the fuel oil he'd bought on the way there. Give the thing a bit of extra oomph. The dog was barking its head off, and it was difficult to concentrate, but what he had to do wasn't complicated. The house was detached, and there were no near neighbours, so he should be OK for a few minutes.

But his back hurt as well, from the fall, and working in torch light only made everything more fraught.

He'd got all the makings spread out in front of him and was ready to put it together when the two of them came back. His first thought was to get inside the cupboard, pull the bag and all the bits and pieces of the bomb in after him, and close the door. Apart from there not being enough room in there, there wasn't enough time. If the detective had walked in he would have seen Ben, and what Ben was doing. There was simply no place to hide.

But that didn't happen. The detective didn't come into the flat at all. One of them, sounded like the kid, went to the flat upstairs and got the dog. The dog stopped barking and started howling like a wolf when they brought him down the stairs. Ben crouched by the sideboard and froze. He didn't move. He waited to be discovered, or for the two of them to go back out into the night.

And that's what they did. The dog was whining all the way down the street, and both of them were talking to it, calling it Barney, and saying how sorry they were that it had got left behind.

They weren't as sorry as Ben was, though. For a while there he thought the dog was gonna come bursting into the room with dripping fangs. Then when the two of them came back he thought the dog and the two of them were gonna come in and work him over.

But now, all of a sudden, it was completely quiet. The only sound was Ben's own breathing. He switched on the torch and placed the blasting cap in the Ovaltine tin. He ran the two wires back, one to the alarm clock, and the other to the dry cell. Then he connected the dry cell to the alarm clock, and sat back for a moment.

He reached for the clock and began winding the alarm. Three flashes took place simultaneously in his mind. There was the flash of recognition within Ben that he was not winding the alarm, but that he was *resetting* the alarm. There was the further flash of recognition that he'd already turned the knob too far and that the alarm was ringing. The third flash, coming very quickly on the heels of the other two, was that the bomb was huge and that it was activated, and that it was going to blow him to pieces.

Ben didn't try to run. He listened to the bell ringing, and he suddenly knew why Gog had put the kid's prick and balls in the telephone, and what he intended to do with them. And he felt his lips quiver and his eyes moisten. Inside his head he said, 'Jesus, Gog, roids aren't made out of pricks. The balls wouldda done on their own.'

And that was the last thought he had. And the last thing he said. Out of the corner of his eye he saw the ignition of the family-size Ovaltine tin, and there was no doubt about it. He had made a mistake.

When the house went up Sam Turner and Geordie were about a hundred yards along the street. A brick went past Sam's head, and the two of them were thrown forward by the blast. Barney began his whining again, as if to say, 'I told you so.'

Sam couldn't make his brain work. Somewhere beyond consciousness he knew exactly what had happened, but he couldn't hold the concept in his mind. Geordie reached over and took his hand, and Barney licked his face.

'You OK?' Geordie asked.

'Yeah, no bones broken. What about you?'

The tank of the hire car blew. The flames lit up the entire street, and Sam and Geordie went back down on their faces.

Sam sat up on the pavement again and Geordie did the same. They sat side by side and looked at the car and the few remaining bricks of their house. A fire was raging towards the rear of the house, where the back door used to be. Bits and pieces were still falling out of the sky. A shirt came down, like a parachute. Not a whole shirt, it only had one arm, and in the half-light Sam couldn't tell if it had been one of his or one of Geordie's.

'Christ, Sam, we only got Barney out of there just in time.'

Sam didn't answer. The enormity of what had happened was still not getting through to him. He could see the place he lived along the road, reduced to a heap of rubbish. There was no denying it had happened. But it didn't fit into reality.

Then a child's voice cried out in one of the houses, and reality descended like a cloud. It wasn't just their house that had been bombed. The other houses in the street were standing, but all of them had shattered windows, many had the tiles taken off the street side of their roofs. Some people had come outside, and from the cries and panic it was obvious that others were injured. Signs of the Apocalypse.

Sam got to his feet and went to a woman who had opened her door. She had an open cut on her cheek, blood running freely down her neck and staining the front of her dress. She looked up and down the street as Sam's feet crunched over the broken glass on the pavement. 'I'll ring for help,' he said. 'Where's the phone?'

The woman pointed behind her, to a hall table.

Sam picked up the telephone and dialled 999. 'An ambulance,' he said into the mouthpiece. He gave the name of the street. 'Lots of ambulances,' he said. 'All the ambulances you can spare. And quick.'

CHAPTER 27

'What was your connection with Ben Wills?' CI Delany, also known as the weasel, addressed his question to Sam and Geordie simultaneously. His sergeant, Sergeant Thompson, hovered in the background taking notes. They were in Fulford Police Station, and Geordie and Sam kept yawning.

'Never heard of him,' said Sam. Geordie looked at Sam, then at Delany, and shook his head.

'He must have been in your house,' said Delany. 'And both of you had just left the house. You were still in the street.'

'Was that who blew the house up?' asked Geordie. 'Ben Wills?'

'And himself,' Delany said. 'We still haven't found all of him. Bits and pieces are turning up all over the neighbourhood. His wallet was more intact. You must know something about him.'

'I've never met him,' Sam said. 'But we have been threatened over the phone. Maybe he's the same guy.'

'You've been threatened over the phone,' Delany said

sardonically. 'Your office was turned over, everything smashed up. Your car took a dive in the river. Your face looks like it's been run over by a bus, and now your house and your whole neighbourhood has been bombed. Why is it, Mr Turner, that I get the feeling you're not exactly being frank?'

Sam didn't reply. That was really very good, he thought. About him not being frank, Franco. Seemed a pity to waste the joke, but he restrained himself, let it go. He looked at Delany and shook his head. Stifled another yawn.

'I've got all night if necessary,' said Delany. 'If you don't want to go home, that's fine by me.'

Sam looked at Geordie and they both laughed. 'We haven't got a home to go to,' said Sam. He looked around the interview room. 'If you can put us up here for a few days, it'll be a great help. Not quite our style, but better than a tree house.'

'OK,' said Delany. 'Ben Wills, a local body builder, planted a bomb in your house. While he was so planting this bomb, he blew himself up. His brother, Gordon Wills, known as Gog, was found at his home, a flat above The Monster Gym in Acomb. Gordon Wills was dead, apparently from a bullet wound. We think from a 9mm automatic fired at close range.'

'Why are you telling us all this?' asked Sam.

'Because Ben Wills obviously didn't like you. I don't subscribe to the theory that he borrowed your house to commit suicide. I get the feeling that the bomb was really meant for you. Now, it wouldn't come as a great surprise to me to discover that Ben Wills was mad at you because you shot his brother.'

'Why would I do that?' asked Sam.

'Because he made a mess of your face.' Delany smiled. 'Am I getting warm?'

'You're only guessing,' said Sam. 'If you had any proof you wouldn't be talking to us. We'd be banged up in one of your cells and we wouldn't even know why.'

'You wouldn't happen to own a 9mm automatic, would you, Mr Turner?'

Sam stood and pulled out his trouser pockets. 'That's what I've got,' he said. 'All my worldly goods. My friend Geordie, here, is in exactly the same position. You can get a search warrant if you like, go through that pile of bricks we used to live in.'

Back on the street Geordie turned round on the pavement. Barney had been banged up in a cage in the police station, and he was so glad to get out he could hardly keep his feet on the ground. He was leaping up at Sam and Geordie, trying to lick their faces. 'He's never been in gaol before,' Geordie said.

'Bet they didn't read him his rights.'

'You could sue them for wrongful arrest, Barney.'

They walked along the Fulford road. Geordie kicked a stone along the pavement and watched it roll into the road. 'We're homeless, aren't we, Sam?' he said.

'Suppose so. At least, there's not a lot of point going home tonight.'

'So, what'll we do?'

'Can you stay with Janet? I'll bunk down in the office.'

'Yeah,' said Geordie. Then, 'I don't wanna be fuckin' homeless again, Sam.'

'Don't worry about it. We'll work something out. We'll have to make do tonight, but tomorrow we'll sort out something more permanent.'

'When you did that, in the police station, held your pockets out. Jesus, it's true, isn't it? I could do exactly the same. Hold my pockets out, and that's what I've got. I've got this leather jacket and a lead for Barney. I've got maybe six, seven quid in my pocket. And that's it. That's me.

'Like a few hours ago I had stereo equipment, records and tapes. I had a tuner and books and a basket for Barney. And we had food in the cupboard, a massive bottle of Coke I'd just bought at the supermarket, eggs and bacon and bread. Almost a full box of Weetabix. Socks and underpants and that red shirt with the buttons on the collar. Even dog food. I was set up, Sam. I had the whole world.

'And now I'm totally broke. Got nothing.'

'I had a hire car,' said Sam. 'But it's buried under my house.' Geordie didn't laugh, so Sam had to get serious. 'You're breathing, Geordie. You've got Barney, and me, and Janet, all your friends. Those other things don't mean shit.'

'And all my writing, Sam. My pens. All the stuff I've done with Celia. And I was reading *Heed the Thunder*, that Jim Thompson book. It was next to my bed, and I'd just finished that part where Sherman Fargo makes the shopkeeper laugh. Forces him to. Makes him laugh and cry at the same time.'

'You can buy another copy, Geordie.'

'I won't know the page number. I had that bookmark Celia gave me. It's all fuckin' blown up, Sam. Don't tell me I can buy another book, I don't want another book. I want my own book with the bookmark.'

Sam put his arm around Geordie's shoulders. 'Geordie, it'll look different after you've had a sleep. It's not the end of the world.'

'Feels like it,' Geordie said. 'That's exactly what it feels like.'

'You're in shock,' Sam told him. 'We're all in shock, Barney as well, that's why he was leaping around back there. Hell, we just missed getting blown up ourselves. But it'll be all right. We've still got our faculties. We just need to replace a few staples.'

'Staples,' Geordie said. 'Like a roof?'

Sam laughed. 'Yeah,' he said. 'And a clean pair of knickers.'

Geordie was quiet for a while. Then he said, 'And a toothbrush.'

'Is that a joke?'

Geordie tried to smile but it wouldn't come. 'Yeah, Sam, it's a joke, but life's a pig, innit?'

CHAPTER 28

The next day they watched the video on Jeanie's TV. It was all there. The chase along Bar Lane and Toft Green, with Andrew Bridge trying to put distance between himself and Gog, but Gog bearing down on him, stamping on his lower back once he'd pushed the boy over.

They saw the white Carrera arrive, and watched as Gog picked the boy up and folded him in two to fit him behind the seats. And Sam hit the pause button on the handset when the camera zoomed in on the car's registration number: FRANC O.

'They're all dead, Sam,' Geordie said. 'Andrew, the boy, and both the body builders.'

'Yeah,' said Sam. 'The only one still alive is Franco. The one who started it all, and the one who killed the kid.'

'You don't know that,' said Jeanie.

Sam looked at her and slowly nodded his head. 'There's lots of things I don't know, Jeanie. But that isn't one of them. Those two goons probably killed your husband and his friend, under orders from Franco. But I'd bet everything I've got that Franco killed the kid himself.'

Geordie laughed. 'We're not talking a lot of betting power here, though, seeing you ain't got nothing left.'

'Still got my snooker cue. Left it behind the bar at the Stonebow.'

'Oh, shit,' said Geordie. 'Mine was under my bed.'

Sam got to his feet and moved towards the door. 'Come on,' he said, 'let's go pick Franco up.'

Geordie followed, but Sam came back to Jeanie. 'Thanks for the tape,' he said. 'It clinches the whole thing. It's all we need.' He shifted his weight to the other foot. 'This should be all over by tonight,' he said. 'Would you like to go to Ricardo and Sophia's again, get something to eat, talk a little?'

Jeanie hesitated, some of the dismay of the Scottish Widow coming through. Sam was sure she was going to say no. But she nodded quickly and said, 'Yes, that'd be nice. I'm not doing anything.'

'Shall I pick you up?'

'You haven't got a car.'

'Yes, I have. Picked up another one this morning. They said to try and make it last longer than the other one.'

'No. I'll meet you there. Eight o'clock?' She smiled.

'Eight,' said Sam, returning the smile. 'Can't wait.'

Geordie drove the hire car out to Franco's mansion on the Wetherby road. It was drizzling and he had the windscreen wipers set to that now-and-then sequence. They drove through the gates and along the drive up to the front of the house. As they approached the door Mama came out in a silver fox, high-heeled shoes to match. The coat fell open momentarily, revealing more thigh and breast than a Christmas turkey.

'Can I help?' she asked.

Sam looked at her. It wasn't every day you met somebody wearing clothes that went out of fashion with sailing ships. 'Maybe,' he said. 'We're looking for Frank, Franco.'

Mama was obviously in a hurry, and she was irritated by having to deal with this. There was a sharp wind blowing along the drive, and she asked them to step inside while she found Franco. 'Who is it?' she said.

Sam turned towards her. 'Just say an old friend.'

She disappeared into the house. Sam and Geordie could hear her calling for Franco, but she didn't seem to be having much luck. She came back to the reception area and shrugged her shoulders. 'He was here,' she said. 'But I can't find him.' She had a smile stashed away especially for an occasion like this. 'I'm sorry,' she said. 'I'm supposed to be meeting someone for coffee. This is really inconvenient.'

'Life doesn't get any meaner,' Sam agreed.

But Mama wasn't listening. 'Maybe he's with Doc.' She knocked on another door off the hall, opened it and went in. 'Doc,' she called. 'Is Franco with you?'

Sam looked round at the place. The reception area alone was bigger than Sam's old flat. That was the flat he used to have, but didn't have any longer, since yesterday. There was an old suit of armour in one corner, which might have been assembled once, but was now reduced to a heap of sheet metal. There was a collection of paintings on one wall, bright and modern and expensive looking, but not by any name that Sam recognized. A grandfather clock. A white Bechstein. On another wall was an extensive antique dresser in dark wood. And above it a series of silver plaques. On the dresser was a stereo system in white wood, one of the huge speakers placed to one side, the other balanced on top of the Bechstein. On the same wall as the entrance was a lighted bar with a quilted front in pale blue leather. There were three high stools in front of it and a selection of chairs spread around the room.

Mama reappeared, followed by Doc Squires. Sam put the pieces of him together from an image composed in his imagination.

Squires had worked up a smile that went no deeper than his teeth. 'Franco isn't here,' he said. 'He went out about ten minutes ago. If you leave your name I'll tell him you called.'

He had a pussy tickler on his top lip. Doc possessed the secret of eternal middle age. His face had yet to grow a second chin, but was obviously making plans. The sickening thing was, even after the double chin had established itself the guy would still be a maiden's dream. *Hello* magazine's or *Cosmopolitan*'s idea of a maiden's dream. Some poor cow who'd been fucked over so much by the system all she had left was dress sense. That kind of maiden. That kind of dream. But definitely a maiden's dream, not Sam Turner's.

Oh, and the voice as well. It stopped short of plummy but could easily have made it if the need arose. With a voice like that a man could scatter a working-class rabble easier'n with ball bearings in a blunderbuss.

If he'd gone into politics, the guy would've been Prime Minister by now. Sam flashed him the glance he'd been reserving for a snake and walked away.

Above the door was a huge picture of Jesus, hands spread, eyes lifted to Heaven, seemed to be saying: 'Would you like to live here?'

Sam held the door open for Geordie to follow him, then

closed it quietly behind them so as not to start an avalanche of money.

Geordie whistled through his teeth. 'That place,' he said. 'When I see something like that I'm glad I've got nothing.'

'Yeah,' Sam chuckled. 'The place stank of bad taste. Frank Squires was always like that. You shouldda seen his clubs. He loves power first, then excess. People in Manchester used to say Frank was pissed off because he had four pairs of shoes and only one pair of feet.'

Geordie got back behind the wheel, and Sam climbed in next to him. 'What now?' asked Geordie. 'We wait here for him?'

Sam shook his head. 'Drive into town. Park in Lord Mayor's Walk. I've got an idea where he'll be.'

They walked along Minster Yard towards Deangate, and Sam nudged Geordie's arm and nodded up ahead of them. Geordie looked towards the school and saw a short man with slicked-back black hair standing by the railings. Small children beyond the railings were playing ball, setting up the characteristic shrill clamour, unlike any other sound on earth.

'That him?' asked Geordie.

Sam nodded, and stopped. 'Maybe we should split up,' he said. 'I'll get round the other side of him.' He crossed the road and increased his pace. Geordie hung back to let Sam get into position.

But as he inched forward, Geordie saw that Franco was not alone. On the other side of the railings was a small girl from the school, maybe seven years old. Red shorts and a white T-shirt, thin little legs and white plimsolls. Franco was holding something out to the girl, and the girl was reaching for it. Looked like a chocolate orange.

That's OK, Geordie thought, as long as he's distracted he won't notice us closing in on him. The girl was safe enough, on the other side of the iron railings. Franco was not liable to leap over to the other side and harm her.

He looked towards Sam, who'd got past Franco and would soon turn to begin a pincer movement. But when he shifted his eyes back to Franco, Franco had turned away from the railings and was walking across Deangate in the direction of the Queen's Path. The small girl was by his side, clutching the chocolate orange with one hand, while Franco held the other in a tight grip. Geordie looked back at the railings and saw that one of the uprights was missing. Franco had coaxed the young girl through the gap.

Geordie shouted to Sam at the same time as Sam turned and shouted at Franco to stop. Sam was running towards him, and Franco scooped up the girl and changed direction, heading for the door of the Minster.

Geordie tried to cut him off, but Franco had too much of a start, and disappeared inside the cathedral, scattering a covey of tourists in his wake. Sam reached the entrance at the same time as Geordie. 'You go in here,' he said, 'I'll cover the other door.'

Franco had turned as he went through the door, and Geordie saw his face for the first time. It had all the compassion of Arctic ice.

Sam ran off towards the west end of the Minster, and Geordie went through the door into the south transept. There was a scattering of tourists, but they were lost in the enormous space of the ancient sanctuary. To Geordie's right were a couple of tombs containing the remains of thirteenth- and fourteenth-century VIPs, behind him was the fourteenth-century rose window. To his left were the entrances to the foundations, the treasury and the tower.

Franco could've gone anywhere. He could be close,

waiting for Geordie to move away from the entrance so he could make his get-away. Geordie kept his back to the entrance and scanned the area, but there was no sign of Franco.

Sam came from the nave area with two security guards. One of the guards closed and locked the door behind Geordie.

'OK,' said Sam. 'He's in here somewhere. All the doors are covered. We just have to find him.' He took Geordie's arm and led him over to the left of the south transept. 'You choose,' he said. 'Tower or foundations; the guards will cover this floor.'

'Tower,' said Geordie.

'Wrong,' Sam told him. 'You take the foundations, I'll take the tower.' Then he was gone through the door to the tower.

'Cheers,' said Geordie. 'Sam Turner, democracy's last hope.'

Sam found himself on a narrow, spiralling stone staircase, seemed to go up for ever. Franco would've come this way, no doubt about it. He would never have chosen to go down to the foundations. Franco was a climber, he'd be heading for the heights.

The steps were high and taking them quickly put a strain on the backs of the calves, the thighs, after the first couple of minutes. Daylight began to show itself, and Sam came out at a crossing. To his right was an enormous lead-covered roof, to his left the open sky and the surrounding roof-tops. Ahead of him was a narrow gutter that led to another entrance and more spiralling steps. Sam covered the ground of the gutter in a bound and continued forcing his way up towards the highest point of the Minster.

He didn't stop to rest, realizing that the girl with Franco

was in danger of her life. But his legs were beginning to feel like jelly, and his lungs were a searing ache. He slipped a couple of times, saving himself with his hands, though the stone tore at his skin and opened up a flow of blood. He thought he must reach the top in a moment, but the steps continued spiralling upward without relief.

When he eventually burst on to the roof, Franco wasn't there. The roof area was enclosed in a metal cage, presumably to stop would-be suicides throwing themselves off. York and the surrounding countryside was spread out before him, but Sam didn't stop to take in the view. An icy sleet was coming down and the wind began to howl.

If Franco and the girl had been up here there was nowhere for them to hide. The cage enclosed the whole roof. Sam checked it out, pushing at selected spots, even trying to lift parts of it. But it was secure. His hands were torn more, and blood mingled with the rain and dripped from the ends of his fingers.

Far below, on the roof of the nave, a flash of red caught his attention. There were two figures down there, moving slowly towards the west end of the Minster. One of them was tiny, a child, the other was mighty in comparison, Brobdingnagian. Franco still had the girl by the hand, and was leading her along the top of the roof.

Sam plunged back down the twisting staircase. He would've liked to take the steps two or more at a time, but the confines of the tower made that impossible. It was all he could do to keep his balance, save himself from falling headlong down the steps.

He came out of the tower at the crossing and looked for some way to get on to the roof of the nave. At one end of the crossing there was a metal ladder fixed to the wall. Sam swung himself on to it, and climbed up to the roof. The rain was coming down fast now, and the ladder was greasy and slippery. The roof of the nave was even more treacherous. Over to the west he saw Franco and the girl. They were seventy or eighty yards ahead of him and the rain had slowed down their progress. Franco was on hands and knees, urging the child forward, pushing her when she didn't move fast enough.

Sam came up behind them.

The small girl was screaming, obviously terrified of falling. And her cries muffled the sound of Sam's approach.

When he was within ten or fifteen feet of them Franco glanced behind instinctively. He turned back quickly and grabbed at the girl, knocking her to one side. The girl slid away with a despairing cry, but Franco had her by the wrist. Franco snorted and turned back to Sam. 'Fuck off,' he said. 'Back off. Or I'll drop her.'

Sam froze. He went down on hands and knees and hung his head. 'OK,' he said. 'I'm going. Give me a minute.' He breathed heavily, with his mouth open, feigning more fatigue than he felt. If he made a leap for Franco the chance was that he wouldn't get to him before Franco let the girl go. The girl would slip down the slope of the roof, but there was a low parapet at the base of the slope, some thirty feet below, which would stop her from going over the edge.

Maybe.

If the parapet held.

Decision time, Sam said to himself. If Franco took the girl a few yards further along the roof, there would be no parapet to save her. If Sam backed off now, there might not come a better chance to save the child.

While he wrestled with the impossible equation, there was a sound behind him. Franco heard it at the same time and looked back along the roof, beyond Sam. Geordie had followed Sam up to the top of the nave, and was coming along the roof towards them.

'Get back,' Franco yelled, and Geordie stopped in his tracks. 'Tell him,' said Franco.

Sam shouted to Geordie, explained what was happening, and Geordie backed up to the ladder.

'Now you,' said Franco. 'I want you to get back to where he is, and then I want to see the both of you disappear down the ladder.'

'I'm going,' said Sam. He got to his feet, looked for a long minute into Franco's eyes, but didn't back away. 'Frank, it's over. Let the kid go, there's no way back from here.'

'Go piss up a rope.'

'I'm not going back without the kid.'

'It's up to you,' Franco said. 'But the kid's a goner if you take one step forward.' He glanced down at the girl. 'Tell him, Tilley. Tell the man I mean business.'

Sam didn't say anything. The kid was called Tilley. Whatever happened now, he'd always know that. The kid was called Tilley. He held Franco's eyes, hoping somehow to hypnotize the man. Paralyse him. A battle took place right there, in the eyes. A battle that Sam won, because he had nothing to lose. Franco gave up a degree of confidence. Some of his will-power was appropriated by Sam Turner.

Suddenly Franco's temper flared, he growled and began shouting at Sam, telling him to back off now, or the kid was dead. The hiss came into his voice. He was deadly serious, aware that he was cornered, but determined not to capitulate.

Watching him, Sam was reminded of the greatest distance in the world – the distance between Frank Squires' mouth and his ears. He waited until Frank was in full voice, then lunged at him with all the speed and energy he could muster. He saw the girl slide away from them, to the left, heard her reaching for an elongated note at least two octaves above middle C.

Sam had his hands around Franco's neck. The guy's skin was cold and wet, clammy to the touch, and Sam tightened his grip. Thinking clearly, what Sam wanted was simply to hold Franco where he was for as long as it took Geordie to get Tilley off the roof. He glanced off to the left to see if the girl had in fact been stopped by the low parapet.

She had, and she was now on hands and knees, using the parapet as an aid to lever herself up. Sam couldn't see Geordie, but sensed that he was making his way towards the child.

Franco bucked violently, loosening Sam's grip and causing him to lose his balance. Sam felt himself slipping away, down the slope of the roof towards the girl. He grabbed wildly at whatever came to hand, and found himself hanging on to Franco's legs. Franco kicked one leg free immediately, and used that freed leg to kick at Sam's hands.

Sam hung on to the leg despite the pain and managed to get up on his knees, then his feet. He made another lunge for Franco, throwing his weight forward, feeling the air escape from Franco's lungs as he landed on top of him. Whatever he had been hanging on to, Franco let go of it, and the two of them began sliding down the roof towards the parapet.

Sam knew it was impossible to fight gravity, and relaxed into it. As they slid he continued his fight with Franco, wanting to be on top when they came to a stop. In the back of his mind he was worried that they would land on top of the girl, and there was also a nagging fear that the parapet, although it had been strong enough to arrest her fall, would not be able to sustain the combined weight of two grown men.

But he shook both thoughts off. There was nothing he could do about either. If the parapet gave and he found himself in free fall he'd try to get one good last punch in, let Franco know that it was a hard life right up to the point where he hit the pavement.

As they continued to grapple on the slope of the roof, they reeled round and round, head over heels, like on a merry-go-round, the view spinning from sky to rooftop, ramparts, gargoyles, the tower, while all the while the rain pounded down around them.

Sam landed on his head. He had time to think, 'This is the last thing I wanted,' before his vision slipped away. He fought against it, hung on to his consciousness, but in his confusion Franco gained the upper hand.

There was a cry from the girl, and Sam saw Geordie lift her off her feet and make off with her back along the roof. Her red shorts were sodden, and Geordie looked like a drowned rat.

Sam was on his stomach, his legs and arms spread. There was a substantial flow of blood coming from a cut high up on his head. Some of it ran into his eyes, and he wiped it away with his already blood-stained hands. His vision was hazy, he could make out the red of the girl's shorts, and he knew it must be Geordie taking her away to safety. But where was Franco?

As if in answer he felt himself propelled forward by a violent kick between his legs. His chin scraped along the stone floor beneath him and all the air left his body as Franco landed another gut-wrenching blow to his balls.

And Sam was back in Manchester, in that club of Frank's. He was in the lavatories, and Frank's two bouncers were holding his legs apart. They had his head in the bowl and he tried to come up out of there, but didn't make it in time. He heard Frank pull back, and then he felt the impact as the boot landed between his legs. The force of it sent his head back into the bowl, and split open his head above the eyes. A thin trickle of blood joined the water and piss in the bottom of the bowl. '*I don't think he'll ask any more questions about Kitty.*' Then the boot landed again. Same spot, between the legs. And again. It just kept coming and coming.

It was raining hard and there was no pain any more. The boot was still coming in, but Sam wasn't thinking about it any longer. He heard Geordie shout the first time but didn't react. The voice seemed to be so far away. There was a hazy vision of a girl dancing in a cage. But when he heard it the second time, Geordie shouting his name, he picked up on the urgency of it. The toe of Franco's boot landed in his groin again, and he felt Franco steady himself, getting ready for an extra big one.

When he felt it coming Sam twisted away from the parapet and lashed out with his feet, catching his assailant on the knee. Franco couldn't regain control of his kick, and as Sam looked up he was aware that Franco wobbled for a second or two on one leg before he went over the edge.

Sam listened to a long wailing cry, steadily diminishing in volume as Franco flew down the Minster walls.

Missing you already, Sam thought as he slipped into unconsciousness. It was easy. No one was kicking his balls. And he was shagged, anyway, running up and down all those steps.

CHAPTER 29

A week later Sam knocked on Marie's door at nine-thirty in the evening. He'd got to the restaurant a little before eight and waited an hour for the Scottish Widow, but she hadn't shown. Sam was a private eye with a nose for these things. By eight-thirty he'd concluded categorically that she wasn't keen, and at ten minutes after nine he knew he wasn't going to see her again. He left the restaurant, making for Marie's house, walking small.

Jeanie'd visited him in the hospital. Once. Brought him some grapes and a Virago Modern Classic that never really got going, petered out after page ten. Maybe it was a sign.

Marie opened the door and stood aside to let him pass. He took his coat off and sat at the table.

'I thought you were seeing Jeanie tonight,' Marie said.

'Yeah,' he said. 'These things don't always work out.'

Marie went to the kitchen. 'I'll put the kettle on.'

He'd known she wouldn't show. He'd always known it, that a time would come when he would be sitting there, waiting for her, and she wouldn't come. When she'd told him about her Irish boyfriend he'd known for sure, but before that, right from the first time he set eyes on her, it had been obvious. A woman like that. What would she want with a guy like him?

The Irishman's name? Caffrey. Michael Caffrey. Michael and Jeanie were lovers. Those two had chosen each other, and they were going to have a life together. Sam Turner was going to stay single and try to live. Something he knew all about.

'Did you eat?' Marie asked.

'Ricardo gave me some pasta. I'm not hungry.'

'Did you love her?' she asked.

Sam shook his head. 'I thought so for a while. But no, it was less than love. Less than love but sweeter than self.'

'I could play some blues,' she said. 'Or crack a bottle of gin?'

Sam smiled. 'Because of some woman?' he said. He turned to catch the irony behind Marie's eyes. 'You know what I'd like?' he said. '*Almost Blue*, the Elvis Costello album. The Nashville one. You got it?'

Marie turned to a rack of CDs. 'It's here somewhere.'

'And Brie,' said Sam. 'Some kind of crispbread. And a really big bottle of diet Coke.'

'You came to the right place. I've got all that. Even a small gâteau. But you realize, living like this, it's only a substitute?'

'Oh, yeah,' said Sam. 'I'm really clear about that.'

'What's it like living with Celia?'

'It's good,' said Sam, cutting a thin slice of Brie and placing it on rye, reaching for the red pepper. 'She doesn't fuss. Lets me get on with my life. As a temporary arrangement I couldn't think of anything better.'

'And in the long run?'

'I need somewhere on my own. Geordie's staying with Janet, and they need somewhere with more room. If we could find a house maybe we could split it between us.'

'A house,' said Marie. 'Any possibilities?'

'Well, yeah. Celia has a friend. Dora? Can't remember her second name. She's got a place out near the University. It's rented at the moment, but the people there are moving out, some time in the summer. Big enough to split, a couple of rooms for me and the rest for Geordie and Janet. Sounds like it could work out.'

Marie watched him for a time without speaking. Then she shook her head and said, 'Your movements have all the speed and precision of youth but none of the enthusiasm.'

Sam smiled wryly. 'The "wow" effect.'

'You don't want to talk about Jeanie?'

'Not tonight. Maybe sometime. I'll call you if it gets urgent.'

'You can't make a joke of everything, Sam.'

'I'll call you. It's a promise.' He put the last of the rye in his mouth. 'Did you get anywhere with the kids?'

'Kids?'

'The investigation.'

'It's looking promising,' said Marie. 'I talked with the boy Geordie met outside the gym. Tony, well, you have to call him Tone. If you call him Tony he throws a wobbler. I met a few more of them, the ones who hung around the gym, swapping drugs. They all knew Doc, and a couple of them spent time with Franco. I think Tone will end up making a statement, and maybe one of the others. And there's a homeless kid in the town, Pete, says he was taken to Franco's house when he was eleven years old. He was living in a children's home and over a two-year period he reckons he was driven to Franco's for parties about once a month.'

'By a member of staff?'

'The Deputy Headmaster.'

'Jesus.'

'That's not all,' said Marie. 'He says he wasn't the only one. He knows others who were shipped to different places. Doc used to arrange sex parties. Often they'd last through the night. The kids would be driven back to the home at first light. They'd be falling asleep on their desks.'

'And Mama?'

'Franco's mother. She was involved too. I'm going slowly on this one, Sam. I want to make absolutely certain we nail them.'

'Take as long as you like,' he said. 'I wanna see them stopped as much as you do.'

They listened to *Almost Blue* for a few minutes. Marie poured a large glass of diet Coke for Sam and handed it to him.

He sipped an inch off the top, watched her inhale some gâteau. 'What about you?' he said.

Marie chuckled. 'I knew you were gonna say that. I've been fine, Sam. Especially since I got involved with these kids. I haven't been bingeing. That Brie you're eating, I only bought a quarter of it, and I haven't looked at a Mars Bar since around three o'clock. I'm absolutely in control of what gets inside of me.'

'And after you wrap up the investigation? When Doc and Mama go to prison, and the kids all disappear into their own lives. What happens then?'

'I don't know,' she said. 'I'll deal with it when the time comes. I'll talk it over with you. I've got other friends, too. Geordie and Celia. I'll talk to my therapist. I'm building up a kind of protective presence. For the first time in my life I'm not afraid of the future. Whatever happens, I think I'll cope with it.'

Yeah, she's right, Sam thought as he walked back to Celia's house. She's sorting herself out, and she'll come through. She'll cope with whatever life throws at her. Maybe even end up being happy.

Maybe Sam Turner would sort himself out, too. Fate had taken all of his material possessions. All he had left to work with was himself. So maybe he should do that. People had been telling Sam all his life that he was an over-achiever. Someone who went for the limit as a substitute for the lack of a personal relationship.

Sam knew it was true. In the whole world, in all of his experience, the only one who had been able to slow him down was Donna. Since her death his life had been a marathon.

There'd been personal relationships. Too many to count. Too many to remember. All the women came and went . . .

They went because Sam remained an over-achiever within the relationship. He dominated. He was the strong man. Whatever the relationship lacked, he would supply it. No one knew better than him that that did not make someone love you. They might respect you for it, they might resent you for it. They might be in awe of you; but they wouldn't love you.

People love you for a cocktail of personal strengths and vulnerabilities. People don't love an archetype or a stereotype. They love a human being, a bag of contradictions, someone they can never find because that someone is forever changing and metamorphosing into someone else. 'Yeah, that's it,' he said to himself, and he made a mental note to remember that the next time he met a woman.

Then he forgot it again.